PRAISE FOR CAELA CARTER'S OTHER BOOKS

Fifty-Four Things Wrong with Gwendolyn Rogers

A JLG Selection

A Kids' Indie Next List Pick

"A moving, authentically told story. A compassionate
portrait of what a diagnosis can offer."
—*Publishers Weekly*, starred review

"Recommended to everyone, but particularly for those drawn to
Kathryn Erskine's *Mockingbird* and Ann M. Martin's *Rain Reign*."
—ALA *Booklist*, starred review

"A novel worth adding to middle grade collections. This book
will resonate with neurodivergent and neurotypical kids alike."
—*School Library Journal*

"It's been a few years since Gantos's *Joey Pigza Swallowed
the Key*, so it's good to see a fresh new take on a kid with
processing issues and a much-deserved reason for hope."
—*Bulletin of the Center for Children's Books*

"An important heart-level look inside a girl that
so many other kids will surely relate to."
—Sally J. Pla, award-winning author of *The Someday Birds*

"Urges us to make space in our hearts—and in our world—for
all the forms of neurodiversity we don't yet understand."
—Alyson Gerber, author of *Taking Up Space*, *Focused*, and *Braced*

"Carter doesn't flinch from presenting the complicated reality
that goes hand-in-hand with the issues Gwendolyn is facing."
—Cammie McGovern, author of *Just My Luck* and *Chester and Gus*

"Captures the impossible experience of going through school
feeling like you're a squirrel being told you should be a tree."
—Margaret Dilloway, author of *Summer of a Thousand Pies*

"An up-close, inside look at one girl's extraordinary
brain, and the patience and perseverance she
has to understand exactly how she fits."
—Lindsey Stoddard, author of *Right as Rain* and *Brave Like That*

"I cheered on Gwendolyn Rogers during her honest and
brave struggle with all that's 'wrong' with her."
—Elizabeth Eulberg, author of *The Best Worst Summer*

How to Be a Girl in the World

"Heartbreaking and ultimately empowering."
—Anne Ursu, National Book Award nominated author of *Breadcrumbs*,
The Real Boy, and *The Troubled Girls of Dragomir Academy*

"This book is more than special—it is vital."
—Corey Ann Haydu, author of *Eventown* and *The Someday Suitcase*

"Powerful."
—*School Library Journal*, starred review

"A realistic coming-of-age story of empowerment."
—ALA *Booklist*

"This ambitious novel covers significant, rarely explored ground.
This is sure to ignite mother-daughter book club debates."
—*Kirkus Reviews*

One Speck of Truth

"A compelling portrait of family and all its flaws,
and the freeing power of the truth."
—*Publishers Weekly*

"An absorbing tale that illustrates that knowing one's
ancestry can be an avenue to self-discovery."
—*Kirkus Reviews*

"A touching story about the importance of
understanding as well as having family."
—*Bulletin of the Center for Children's Books*

"Well-written, emotionally evocative."
—*School Library Journal*

"Readers will eagerly read to the last page."
—ALA *Booklist*

Forever, or a Long, Long Time

ALA Notable selection

Kirkus Reviews Best Book of the Year selection

New York Public Library Top Ten Book for Kids pick

NCTE Charlotte Huck Honor Book

"This stunning portrayal of the circuitous path of trauma and healing teems with compassion, empathy, and the triumph of resilience."
—ALA *Booklist*, starred review

"Carter delicately draws readers into the lives of a group of people overcoming obstacles as they learn how to become a family."
—*School Library Journal*, starred review

"Gently weaves the heartache and confusion of abandonment with the struggle for love and acceptance."
—*Kirkus Reviews*, starred review

"Carter's layered narrative doesn't shy from pain as it testifies to resilience and the expansive power of love."
—*Publishers Weekly*

My Life with the Liars

"Absorbing from page to page."
—Rita Williams-Garcia, Newbery Honor author

"A searing story . . ."
—*Kirkus Reviews*

"Carter takes readers on a journey in this thought-provoking and highly discussible novel."
—*School Library Journal*

ALSO BY CAELA CARTER

the WORLD DIVIDED BY PIPER

CAELA CARTER

Quill Tree Books
An Imprint of HarperCollinsPublishers

To Linda,
my fellow everything-nerd,
whose overexcitabilities always complement mine.

{ 1 }

There's a bruise blooming on my thigh. I imagine it getting darker and purpler under my metaphorical math notebook as I scribble in it, adding something that I learned from a podcast this morning. When my hand presses against the notebook's spine, the bruise calls out to me, ringing with pain and relief.

Mom must notice that I'm pressing extra hard because she reaches across her chair and into my lap to pull my hand away from my notebook and my bruise.

"Does it hurt, Piper?" she asks.

"No," I say. It's not exactly a lie. The pain centers of my brain are probably lighting up every time I press the spot where the nurse just injected the medicine, but *hurt* is too simple a word for this feeling. The pain is minuscule compared to what it's preventing.

I hunch over to write again, but Mom puts her hand on mine, stopping my pencil.

Mom says that she loves that I'm gifted because she loves me just the way I am, but sometimes I wonder how much she means it because she's always stopping me from working on my biggest project, my life's work: metaphorical math. On the other hand, she does support all the time and energy I put into my gifted and talented after school program.

"Put the notebook away," she says. "Dr. Grand will be here soon."

"But I just need—"

"Don't talk back, Piper. Be nice." Mom's words pop out short and fast, like staples, sealing my mouth closed.

I want to argue. I want to tell her that my metaphorical math notebook is the best way for me to distract myself from the fact that Dr. JerkFace is now almost half an hour late to our appointment. And I want to say that she's been on her phone the whole time, which is even more rude than writing in a notebook. But I can't.

I have to be nice.

I put my notebook away.

"Why are we in here, anyway?" I ask.

We're in Dr. Grand's office. Like his office-office. I'm not sitting on one of those weird beds with the crinkly paper that you see in every doctor's office. Instead, I'm sitting next to my mom in a bucket chair, both of us facing Dr. Grand's empty desk. He's my pediatric endocrinologist, which is a fancy word for *hormone doctor for kids*. Normal kids don't need to worry about hormones, but I'm not—

Wait. Mom says *normal* isn't a nice word.

(She also says normal doesn't exist. But that part's wrong. Normal does exist. It may be true that no person is normal in every single way, but there's still a lot of normals leftover in a lot of people. Even I, the precocious Piper Franklin, am normal sometimes. Like, I have normal blood pressure.)

But I'm not going to use the word *normal* even if it does exist. Mom is strict about niceness, so I'm careful to only use nice words. I'm systematic about it. I organize my brain into two columns. Not literally, of course, but I read online that a metaphor can help someone learn a new concept, so I made up a metaphor to keep my words nice. The column on the left side of my brain is labeled *Can't Say That*. The right one is labeled *Can Say That*. It's a lot shorter than the left one. If a word from the left side pops toward my mouth and I really want to say it, I cross it out, metaphorically of course, and choose a right-side word instead.

Like this.

~~Normal~~ Regular kids only need a pediatrician, but I also need Dr. Grand. I see him every three months. By literal math, four times a year. By metaphorical math, constantly.

Dr. Grand is the worstbest doctor of all time. He's the best because he fixed everything. Before I met him, I had a condition called precocious puberty. In other words, my body turned on the puberty system way too early. I was six, but

3

my bones were ten and my hormones were teenage, and my body was about to stop growing. At six, I looked like I was eleven. Now I am eleven, and I still look like I'm eleven. That's because of Dr. Grand.

But Dr. Grand is the worst, too, because even though he's a genius, he's also a jerk.

Usually, when I come to these visits, I barely have to see his face. He just pops his head in and gives me a thumbs-up or an "all good" while one of his nurses administers my shot. But today, once the shot was over, we were sent to wait in his office.

Mom swivels around in her chair while answering my question. "Well, it's been a year since the last time we had a consultation with Dr. Grand."

I look up, alarmed. "That long?"

A year ago, Dr. Grand said that because I was ten, it would be OK if I stopped the shots and let my body go into puberty. But I didn't want to, and Mom was "particularly overwhelmed at this time" (her words). She was pregnant and throwing up every day, and worried about how I'd feel when the baby was born and Calvin, my stepdad, became someone's real dad. So, when I said I didn't feel like I was ready for a period, the whole conversation disappeared like magic.

But I don't want to go through puberty now any more than I did a year ago. The shots hurt, but puberty would hurt worse. And TBH, Mom doesn't seem any less overwhelmed, either.

Mom throws her phone into her purse and turns back to the door. "I swear this man is always late."

"Is he going to say my treatment is over? Do I have to start puberty?" I ask.

There's a tremble in my voice, but Mom must not hear it. She answers like it's no big deal. "I don't know, but it doesn't matter."

"It doesn't matter?"

"It's time to be done with these shots either way."

~~No! No way.~~

~~Over my dead body.~~

"Wait, what?" That's what I say out loud.

Of course, at this exact moment, Dr. Grand opens the door and mumbles a hello.

My heart is hammering in my chest, and my hands are sweating. If we stop the shots, that means puberty. Boobs. Crushes. Periods. I don't know if I'll ever be ready for all that, but I know I'm not now. Being a kid is hard, but being a woman is harder. I see that every day when I watch my mom try to just . . . live. If I go through puberty at eleven, I'll be a kid in a woman's body. I'll be two hard things at the same time.

No. No way. Not happening.

Dr. Grand sits heavily behind his desk without looking at us. He's tall and white with pale skin and short gray hair, and he's always frowning. He opens a file folder and starts up his computer. He clicks a pen against the palm of his right hand as he reads. Eventually he says, "I'm happy." As if we asked.

"Oh?" Mom says.

"Look." He nods at his computer even though it's facing

him, and we can't see it. "She's grown again."

He never says my name. He calls me *she* and then looks right from his computer to my mom, like I'm not even there. That's part of what makes Dr. Grand a jerkface.

"She's almost a foot taller since we started treatment at age seven."

Dr. Grand is always talking about this part. And it is a good thing. Precocious puberty would have meant I stopped growing way too young.

"She'll be about ten inches taller as an adult because of this treatment, Mrs. Franklin. It's remarkable, really," Dr. Grand says.

Reason #2 he's a jerk: he never calls my mom by the right name.

"*Ms.* Franklin," Mom corrects him.

When my mom divorced my dad, a long time ago, she kept his last name so that we would still match. When she married Calvin, I didn't want to be the only Franklin in a family of Bogles, so Mom said that instead of taking Calvin's name, she'd take mine. That meant she kept her last name Franklin but dropped the *Mrs.* part. That made me feel special and important and close to Mom, and, actually, it still does. Now, Eloise lives with us, and her last name is also Franklin, and Mom and Calvin named the baby Gladys Franklin-Bogle, so it's actually Calvin who's the only Bogle in a family of Franklins. But he promises he doesn't mind.

A lot of decision-making went into our last names, so it's

important to Mom that people get them right. Dr. Grand never, ever does.

"Excuse me, Dr. Grand?" I say.

"Hm?" He doesn't look up.

"Maybe you can call my mom Dr. Franklin. Maybe that's easier to remember? Since you're both doctors?"

"Piper!" Mom hisses.

"What?" She *is* a doctor. I thought that was a good solution.

"Just . . . just . . . be nice!" Mom says.

I lower my eyebrows. I thought I was being nice.

"Well, as I was saying." Dr. Grand speaks in this huge up-and-down way like we're off track and wasting his time. "She's grown another half-inch in the past year . . ." His gaze stays on my chart. "Of course, her weight is . . . also growing." He chuckles, sounding like a superhero villain. "Her BMI is still too high."

Reason #3 that Dr. Grand is a jerk: whenever we come here, he finds a new way to call me fat. And that's silly. Even if my dot is above the shaded "normal" section on Dr. Grand's BMI chart, the size of my body is not a problem. I can run to El Jardín Muerto and back several times a day. I can do a cartwheel and a ten-second handstand. If I'm able to enjoy being in this body, who cares how tall or fat it is? Besides, when I was first diagnosed with precocious puberty, Calvin gifted me a bunch of subscriptions to medical journals, and now I know that BMI is, as the *Princeton University Medical Journal* puts it, an "outdated and inaccurate metric of a person's health."

"Our treatment helps kids grow but not slim down," Dr. Grand continues. "You should see if you can encourage a more healthy lifestyle."

"Piper's lifestyle is perfectly healthy," Mom says. My heart floods with warmth for her.

Dr. Grand may think that the excessive estrogen from my fat cells is what caused my precocious puberty, but I know better. I know exactly what caused it, even if I can never tell anyone. I've looked up every possibility, every hypothesis, for why precocious puberty occurs in particular girls. There are a few theories, but only one of them is relevant to my life: precocious puberty is overrepresented in girls who live with a man to whom they are not biologically related.

In other words: it was Calvin.

It's true, but it's a left-brain column fact. We can never talk about it.

And Mom must know he's what caused it. You don't need medical journals to learn about this theory. You can just google it.

"Look," Dr. Grand says.

He flips open a file folder on his desk, then turns it so that Mom and I can see. It's my growth chart, divided into three separate graphs: height, weight, and BMI. The height curve advances in a typical slope where it's tracing what happened when I was one and two and three all the way to six. Then it shoots up and levels off prematurely until it gets to seven, when I started treatment with Dr. Grand. The curve is sharp where it's tracking how I grew when I was eight and nine. The curve goes up, but not as sharply, once it reaches ten and eleven.

"According to her file, a year ago you requested to continue treatment because of disruptions at home and Piper's immaturity?"

"Immaturity?" I say. Is it immature to not want a period? Every woman I know hates her period, no matter how old she is.

"Disruptions at home?" Mom says. "No, I was having a baby."

"Exactly," Dr. Grand says, as if we're agreeing with him. "And how do we feel about it now, Mrs. Franklin?"

"Ms.," Mom says.

~~Doctor.~~

It's silent for a full minute as Mom waits for Dr. Grand to correct himself. He doesn't.

"Well, things have calmed down at home," Mom says.

What? No, they have not.

"And Piper is a year older and more mature."

And I still don't want to go through puberty.

"So, I think it's time. Right, Piper?"

I swallow hard. How could she spring this on me here? Now?

"Um, no," I say.

Mom's eyes go wide, like she's the one who's shocked. "What?" she says. "Why?"

Dr. Grand evil-chuckles again. "Most kids are excited to be done with needles. You must be raising some sort of masochist, Mrs. Franklin."

"Ms." Mom corrects him, but he definitely doesn't hear her this time because I'm way louder when I scream, "I am not a masochist!"

Mom's hand lands on my knee and squeezes, telling me to be nice. To be quiet.

"Oh," Dr. Grand says. "I wasn't insulting you. That word means—"

"I know what it means."

Squeeze.

But I can't stop the words from coming. "A masochist is an individual who enjoys self-torture."

"Well—"

"And calling me that *is* insulting."

"I only meant—"

Squeeze.

"And it's not true." Mom is squeezing so hard by now, she might leave a bruise on my other thigh.

But isn't it obvious that choosing to get my period for days and days every single month would be more masochistic than choosing one seconds-long shot every three months?

"Of course she knows the word. We all know Piper's gifted," Mom says, almost sarcastically.

I turn and stare out the window.

After way too long, I mumble, "Sorry."

It works. Mom's face softens. It's always nice to apologize to adults, I guess, even when the adult is the one who should owe you an apology.

"What's going on?" Mom asks. "You don't want to stop the shots?"

"No," I say.

"Why?" Mom asks.

I open my mouth to answer but it takes a long time for words to come. I guess I've always thought this was obvious. "Because puberty should be avoided at all costs."

"What?" Mom smiles, but I think it's to cover up the way I'm embarrassing her. "No, honey. Puberty is natural and normal."

~~Wrong.~~ "Puberty is painful and uncomfortable," I say.

"Piper . . ." Mom lowers her eyebrows like she's trying to read my face, then turns back to Dr. Grand. "If we stopped the shots now, when would her puberty start again?"

"You'd expect to see breast buds within a few weeks of her first missed dose, sometimes sooner. So about three to four months from now."

I sit on my hands to stop them from flying to my chest. I had breast buds before, when I was only six. They hurt. They were so embarrassing. They disappeared after two months of Dr. Grand's treatment. Why does she want me to go through that all over again?

"Menstruation is less predictable," Dr. Grand continues. "Puberty is lengthening in the general population, as well as starting earlier. But children who have been through blockers tend to have a shorter duration between the start and completion of puberty. Even if it's fast, at ten or eleven, most girls are ready to handle a period, so—"

"Not me," I whisper.

The medical journals say the average age for starting a period is twelve-and-a-half, and that it's still considered normal if a kid doesn't start a period until fifteen. I shouldn't be forced into this for years.

Mom is staring at me, confused. Like she thought I'd be excited for cramps and tampons or something.

Dr. Grand folds the file on his desk. Then he says something shocking. "Mrs—Ms. Franklin, as the parent, the decision is up to you, of course. But there aren't many risks to continuing Piper's treatment. The medication is expensive, but you happen to have uniquely comprehensive insurance coverage. And it's perfectly safe. I have many patients who continue the shots for years and don't even start until age eleven."

"Right!" I say, remembering that I also know kids who are older than me and still take this same kind of medicine. I know at least one.

"But those kids are trans, right?" Mom says.

So what?

Dr. Grand looks up at her, one eyebrow raised. "I have some transgender patients, yes. And their parents are just as worried about ensuring that any medical treatment their children receive is safe. In fact, technically, puberty blockers are approved for precocious puberty and used off-label for gender-affirming care. I often tell parents that if these drugs are safe for children with precocious puberty, they're safe for their trans or nonbinary kids as well. But the opposite is true, too. If it's safe for an eleven-year-old child in need of gender-affirming care, it's also safe for Piper."

Mom's cheeks turn a little pink. "Of course," she says. "I didn't mean . . . I'm a big supporter of—"

"Whenever you choose to stop the treatment, it will reverse itself. She'll go through puberty. There's no long-term difference in waiting six months or a year or even longer."

I let out a breath. Maybe Dr. JerkFace is more best than worst today.

Mom clears her throat. "Doctor, these shots have saved Piper's childhood. I'll always be grateful for that. And they've also spared several of her friends from a painful puberty experience with the wrong hormones. I want any kid who needs them for any reason to have access to them. I only meant that Piper doesn't need them anymore. She's not trans. She was taking them to give her body more time to grow. To get a childhood. And . . . and . . . now she has the privilege of stopping them. Of going through puberty with her peers."

"But I don't want to," I say, quietly.

"Why?" Mom says.

I open my mouth, but I can't find the words to explain. I can't say *Because Dr. Grand won't call you "Dr. Franklin."* Or *Because Eloise has to go to school even when her cramps are so bad, she can barely get out of bed.* Those examples are tiny, so they would sound stupid. But they're a part of something bigger that I don't have words for. Somehow little things like that are connected to me and my medicine, but I don't have the word for the bigger thing that the little examples are a part of

"Honey?" Mom prompts.

I swallow. "I . . . I don't want to . . . grow up."

Mom scrunches her face. "You love growing up."

I shake my head. "No, I don't."

"Sure, you do! You love learning everything about the world. You're reading medical journals, for Pete's sake. You're stealing my advanced calculus textbooks."

"But that's the fun part."

"The rest can be fun, too," Mom insists.

"No," I say. "No, it's . . . learning is fun and . . . and being smarter is fun . . . but . . . but my body . . . it's better if . . ."

Where are the words? This is so embarrassing! It's like I'm not even me anymore. Piper Franklin—gifted and talented, precocious in both mind and body—should be able to explain anything.

"What?" Mom asks again.

"If I start puberty . . . I'm scared . . . I don't want to—"

Then the words hit me. They slam into me. Clear and true and loud inside my brain. I know exactly why I don't want to go through puberty.

But I can never say it out loud.

"Listen," Dr. Grand says, in a tone that's definitely meant to convey *I've had enough of this kid.* "You don't need to figure it out right now. Go home. Talk it over with your husband. Just make a decision by Piper's next appointment in three months."

Mom looks at me one more time. "You're sure you can't tell me why you want to stay on the medicine, honey?"

The words are so big in my brain, I almost say them before I can metaphorically cross them out.

~~I don't want to turn into you.~~

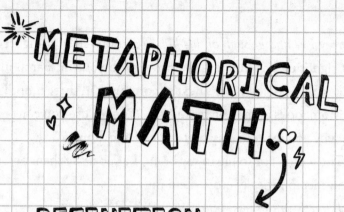

METAPHORICAL MATH

DEFINITION

Math tries to explain the world in terms that are totally *rational* and completely *logical*.

Different **disciplines** within mathematics try to explain slices of the world in ways that are also totally *rational* and *logical*.

EXAMPLES

Arithmetic logically and rationally explains the relationships between integers.

E.g.: $1 + 2 = 3$

Geometry logically and rationally explains shapes and measurements.

E.g.: $a^2 + b^2 = c^2$

Calculus logically and rationally explains the laws of physics.

E.g.: gravity

Problem: According to my medical journals, human emotions are "considered inherently illogical and irrational." But what if that's only because no math has ever tried to explain them? What if I can find the equations to make emotions and behavior totally logical and rational?

Idea: What if math could be used to create the greatest metaphor of all time? What if math can explain humanity to itself?

That's why I'll call it METAPHORICAL MATH!

{ 2 }

A few minutes later, we're back in the car. I'm trying to text my friends, but I can't concentrate because Mom keeps mumbling frustrated sentences under her breath.

"What did you say?" It's boring to sit in someone else's feelings without being given the context for them.

"We're going to be late."

I tilt my head.

Mom is a professor who teaches things like Advanced Theoretical Calculus and Complex Numbers, but she's not very good at practical math, like time. Or temperature. She fans herself as she breaks at a red light because she's wearing a hooded sweatshirt, even though it's a warm October day and it feels like summer outside.

"It's not even five," I say. "HHH isn't until six fifteen."

HHH is where we're heading next. It stands for Happy and Healthy Humans, which sounds corny, but it's actually awesome. It's a club I started going to last year after a nurse from Dr. Grand's office recommended it to Calvin. It's like a support group for anyone who's having a tough time with puberty. Kids go for lots of reasons. At first, I thought I'd hate it because it came from Dr. Grand, but I actually love it. Plus, HHH is how I met my friend Ivan, who's now one of my favorite people in the world.

HHH meets once a month on a Friday, a Saturday, or a Sunday. Since I see Dr. Grand on a Friday every third month, I always go to HHH right after his appointments. I usually go to the in-between meetings, too, the ones on Saturdays or Sundays, because Mom and Calvin are serious about getting me to this group for reasons I don't understand. But I like HHH, so I'm not complaining.

"We need more time," Mom insists, even though, for once, we have plenty of time. "Ugh. Why is Dr. Grand always so late?"

"Because we—"

"What?" she interrupts, like she's daring me to finish. I guess I was about to say something not nice.

~~Because we were late.~~

It's true, we're always late. Today, it was because when we were trying to leave, Mom had about seven thousand *last-minute-but-very-very-important things* to tell my big sister, Eloise, who's babysitting my baby sister, Gladys, for the first time. That makes today the first time I've been alone with Mom since the baby was born.

And we had to waste it with stupid Dr. Grand.

The next traffic light turns red just as we're about to cross. Mom yells at it: "Seriously?"

"Mom," I say, choosing right-side words, "assuming the traffic conditions follow their typical Friday afternoon patterns, we'll be at HHH before 5:45. Even if it takes forever to park, we'll be early."

"It's useless," Mom says, like she didn't even hear me.

"What's useless?"

Mom turns to look at me. She squints, then turns back around. "Ugh . . . It's not going to work, so I may as well tell you. I tried to move our appointment with Dr. Grand earlier because I was hoping you and I could go to the Tea House before HHH."

The Tea House! My eyes go wide. My heart races. My brain starts calculating.

The Tea House is a combination of a British high-tea restaurant and a dollhouse. The furniture and cups and everything are purposely oversized so that when you're there, you feel like you're at a little kid's tea party and you *are* the doll. Mom and I used to go there every time we had to see Dr. Grand. We'd order a whole pot of tea—jasmine or orange or oolong green decaffeinated or something—and a three-tiered tray of miniature crustless sandwiches and scones with clotted cream. We'd spend hours eating tiny food while sitting in enormous chairs. It would feel like the world stopped and my mom and I got to just . . . be. Alone. Together. Whole.

When was the last time we went there? I start counting backward through Dr. Grand appointments. Three months ago, my sister, Gladys, was only a few weeks old, so Calvin had to take me to Dr. Grand's. Six months ago . . . Calvin took me then because Mom was on bed rest. Nine months ago, Mom took me, but she had morning sickness and was throwing up the whole time. No Tea House. A year ago, Dr. Grand needed to talk to us and that took almost the whole time between the appointment and HHH.

It's been over a year. I didn't realize how much I missed it until right now.

"The Tea House is a block away," I say quickly. "And look! There's an open parking spot. So, if it takes the usual two-point-five minutes to walk one block, that's five minutes both ways between the Tea House and the car, plus the typical thirty-seven minutes to drive to HHH and seventeen to park, that gives us . . . eighteen minutes. Maybe we can go for eighteen minutes?"

I'm already thinking about how I don't like to drink tea quickly. About how the whole point of the Tea House tradition is that we spend time. We luxuriate. I'm trying to convince myself right along with my mom that eighteen minutes and a burnt tongue is better than nothing.

"I wish." Mom sighs. "But I also have to pump."

~~I hate that stupid breast pump.~~

"Oh, OK."

My phone buzzes in my lap. I flip it over, thinking it'll be Ivan, but it's my friend from school, Daisy.

Daisy: Knock knock

Me: Who's there?

I smile. A ridiculous Daisy joke is the perfect thing to distract me from the fact that Mom and I are not going to the Tea House right now because she'd rather stick her boobs in a vacuum cleaner.

Daisy: George or Jack. Whichever one is cuter.

Oh, come on. That's not a joke. Daisy's always trying to trick me into admitting I have a crush on one of the boys in our gifted and talented program, but it's not going to work because I don't. I text back an eye-roll emoji. Daisy is one of my best friends, second only to Tallulah, but these days she wants to talk about boring stuff all the time.

Daisy: You seriously don't like-like anyone, Piper?

Me: Seriously!

I hold my phone to my chest and tell myself that's true. I don't have any crushes. I can't have any crushes. I don't have the hormones for crushes.

And even if I did have a crush, it wouldn't be on George or Jack or anyone Daisy knows.

Me: Give me a real joke.

Daisy: OK, fine. Hold on, I'll think of one.

Before she does, we reach the church in Harlem where HHH is held. Mom finds a metered spot and parallel parks. I reach to open my door.

"Hold on a minute," Mom says. "I have to get my pump."

~~Gross.~~

My phone buzzes. I'm ready for the joke but this time it is Ivan.

Ivan: I see you.

I look up and there he is, standing at my car window, smiling.

I jump out of the car so fast the door almost hits him. I throw my arms around him. He laughs and hugs me back. I haven't seen him since HHH met last May.

"*Piper,*" Mom says, like I'm somehow being inappropriate.

As soon as I turn back to her, my face is burning. The flaps of Mom's bra are hanging out of her shirt and the only thing covering her nipples is the suction-cup thingy attached to her breast pump.

"Mom!" I scream. Because seriously? She's the one being inappropriate. A few months ago, I had no memory of her ever walking around without a shirt on, and now she does it in the street in the middle of Manhattan.

"I told you I had to pump," she says.

Shouldn't you do that someplace else?

Like a bathroom?

"Shut the door."

I slam it and turn back to Ivan.

His eyes are wide. Terrified. "What is that thing?" he whispers.

I shake my head. "It doesn't matter. It's . . . gross."

He smiles his silly smile. It's higher on the left side than it is on the right, and whenever he aims it at you, you feel like you said something absolutely perfect, even if you didn't say anything at all.

"Nice braids," I say.

He tilts his head toward me so I can see how his cornrows curve and crisscross over his scalp. "Thanks. Just got them yesterday. You're taller," he points out.

I smile. "I know."

HHH was on hold for the summer and today is our first day back. Kids come from all over the tristate area, so even though HHH meets in Harlem, it's not weird that I'm from New Jersey. Some kids come because, like me, they're going through precocious puberty. Others because they're trans or nonbinary, so puberty means something different for them. Some come because something bad happened to them at some point, and that makes puberty scarier. It's basically a club for any middle schooler who needs more information than they're going to get in an average health class.

I hate the idea of growing up, but I love HHH. That's mostly because of Ivan, but the other kids are cool, too.

"Come on," he says. "I'll walk you there while your mom . . . finishes. Or whatever." Most kids come to HHH with a parent, but Ivan lives in this neighborhood and the group actually meets at his church, so he sometimes walks by himself.

"Cool," I say. We only go a few steps before Mom comes rushing behind us, her bag falling off her shoulder and her phone pressed to her ear.

"No, Eloise," she's saying. "You have to warm the bottle in hot water on the stove . . . no . . . no not from the freezer! Use the . . . um-hmmm . . ."

I roll my eyes so hard I swear they may fall into the back of my skull. Ivan gives me that uneven smile again and something inside me buzzes.

"Hey," he says. "I'm having a birthday party in two weeks. Can you come?"

Huzzah! I get to see Ivan IRL twice in a month.

"Can I?" I ask my mom.

She hangs up with Eloise, but immediately begins texting. I know she's texting Calvin, even though I have no idea what he's supposed to do about Eloise's babysitting issue from his job. Every time there's a problem with the baby, it turns into three or four or five problems for my mom because she has to report it, like, right away to everyone who could have even a remote chance of caring about nap schedules or bottle temperatures or whatever. It's part of why I never see her anymore.

"Mom?"

"Hm?" she mumbles, still looking at her phone.

We stop to wait for the light to change before we cross the street.

"Can I go?"

"Go where?" Mom says, her thumbs flying over her screen.

"Ivan's birthday party."

"It's two weeks from today," Ivan adds.

"Um," Mom's eyes are still on her phone. I'm not sure if she heard us.

I look at Ivan. He shrugs.

"Mom?"

Mom looks up for a split second. "Hm?" She looks back down. "Oh, Piper, I don't think so. I don't see how we'd get you back to Manhattan when it's not even a Dr. Grand day."

Once she says that, little stars explode into my vision. If I lose the shots, will Mom and Calvin stop bringing me to New York for HHH? Will I lose Ivan, too?

"Maybe Eloise can drive me," I say, suddenly desperate.

Mom finally pockets her phone and raises her eyebrow in a half-silly way. "You think she's ready to drive to Manhattan?" It's a good point: my big sister just got her driver's license after failing the driving test . . . twice.

"Um . . . we can take the train. Or I can! By myself."

Mom looks at me, and even though her eyes don't technically move, I can tell she's stopping herself from rolling them. "Honey, you're only eleven."

I open my mouth, and then cross out the words because they're back talk, which makes them not nice.

~~You're the one who just told me it's time to grow up.~~

The light changes and Ivan steps into the street. "Oh well," he says.

Mom tugs gently on my ponytail. "Sorry, kiddo. Maybe next time. You ready?"

We go into the church. Mom stays upstairs in the pews where the parents hang out and drink coffee during our meeting. I don't know why she bothers. She's just going to text Calvin and call Eloise the whole time.

I follow Ivan down the back steps to the basement where Dr. Knapp is setting up a circle of folding chairs. Dr. Knapp is a doctor the way my mom is: not medically. I asked her *What makes you a doctor?* the first time I met her, and it made Mom squeeze my shoulder in a way that was supposed to let me know that it's not a nice question. But Dr. Knapp didn't mind. She told me she's a doctor of social work.

"Hi, Ivan. Hi, Piper," she greets us today, standing up after unfolding a chair. Dr. Knapp is white with super curly gray hair and pointy glasses that make her look like the most awesome librarian ever.

The rest of our group of friends rushes over from their folding chairs for hugs and high fives. There's Emma, who's thirteen and always says the most daring things when we have sharing circle. And there's Lydia, Emma's cousin, who is quiet and thoughtful. Javi is the fashion expert who sews their own clothes. And Brice is our friend, too, even though he says some thoughtless things sometimes. I'm happy to see they're all back this year.

Other kids we know give us waves or say *hey.* Plus, there are new kids this year who look at us with wide eyes, nervous. Their nerves won't last long. This isn't like a regular class or club. It's a place where everything is OK to talk about, where everyone is welcome, and no one ever gets teased.

Once most of the folding chairs are full, Dr. Knapp stands and launches into an introduction about how the group is respectful and everything we say is confidential. Then we play a silly game for an icebreaker.

I've barely settled into the seat next to Ivan when he stands again. "Wish me luck," he whispers. He shoots me a smile and it makes me feel like my heart is glow-in-the-dark or something. Extra *there*. He has a stack of notecards in his hands.

"You're sharing today?" I whisper.

Ivan nods proudly. "Dr. Knapp said I'd be a great introduction for the new kids if I was comfortable sharing my story." Ivan does a spin move and lands pointing at me. "And you *know* I'm always comfortable with that."

I giggle, then settle back into my folding chair to listen to Ivan speak.

Dr. Knapp has asked me if I wanted to share at an HHH meeting before, but I'm not like Ivan. I don't love to tell my story.

Today he stands in the middle of the circle of folding chairs, half of them filled with kids he doesn't even know, and clears his throat.

"So, I'm going to tell you about an important part of my identity," he says, flashing everyone his crooked smile. "And it's not very obvious. In fact, it might be surprising." He takes a deep breath like he's nervous. "But here goes. I'm thirteen."

Everyone laughs.

It's true, though, that Ivan doesn't really look thirteen. He looks eleven, like me. When we met—my first day here last year—he had just gotten his first dose of puberty blockers, which he announced to everyone in HHH by pulling up one leg of his shorts to show off the purple bruise on his thigh.

At the doughnut break that day, I approached him and said, "You get used to the bruises."

He smiled. "You're on blockers, too?"

I nodded.

"Nice!" he said, and high-fived me. "For how long?"

"A while," I said. "Years."

His eyes went wide. "Whoa!" he said. "You're lucky. You didn't even have to start puberty."

I didn't correct him. I just shrugged. I was impressed by how easily Ivan had told me and everyone else about himself, but I wasn't ready to say the words *precocious puberty* out loud yet. I'm still not. Those are two gross-sounding words that sound even grosser smushed together.

Today Ivan says, "Another part of my identity is that I'm a guy. But that part's pretty obvious, finally. Right?"

He holds his hands by his sides to show off the whole picture of him: jeans and a Nike T-shirt, smooth warm brown skin, and kind open eyes. And dimples. Of course.

"One day I'll look like I'm both the right age and the right gender, but I'm choosing gender for now. Thank you, puberty blockers."

He turns and smiles right at me, and a little *zing* goes up my spine.

"I don't really mind looking like a little boy for now, because I didn't get to be a little boy."

I look around. A lot of kids are nodding like they get it. A few whooped when he mentioned blockers. Maybe I'll find some of them at the doughnut break. It's always good to have friends who know what you're going through. Emma, Lydia, Javi, and Brice are all here for different reasons. Ivan's the only kid I know who's on blockers like me.

"Instead, I had to be a little girl," he continues. "Back then, it felt like I wasn't real. Like I was Pinocchio. Ironic, right? Because, like me, Pinocchio is a boy." I chuckle along with Lydia beside me. "But it felt like I wasn't really living. I was parroting life. I was pretending, and I didn't even mean to be. It was like I was being controlled by marionette strings, just like him, except my strings were invisible. But those invisible strings have disappeared. Now I get to be myself. Now I'm in control. Also . . ." He pauses like he might actually be nervous to say the next part, even though Ivan isn't ever nervous to say anything. "Just because I don't look thirteen doesn't mean I can't act thirteen. I mean, I do have a girlfriend now."

With that, Javi and Brice are out of their seats whooping. Emma leans over Lydia to whisper to me. "He does?"

I shrug. "I guess so," I say.

My cheeks are hot for some reason.

Everyone snaps for Ivan, and Dr. Knapp calls for the dough-nut break. My friends all swoop in on him with questions about his girlfriend, but I hang back and watch for a minute.

Pinocchio was a perfect metaphor. If Ivan's parents ever wanted him to stop blockers, he'd be able to tell them that story and they'd let him keep them.

I can't use that metaphor to convince my mom that I need blockers, too, because I'm not trans. But I still need the block-ers just as badly as I did last year.

I wish I could explain why I need them as well as Ivan explains why he does.

{ 3 }

Afew hours later, while I'm helping Calvin prepare a dinner of Mom-can't-stop-pumping-to-cook peanut-butter-and-jelly sandwiches, my BFF, Tallulah, texts me: **Official request for a gathering of the minds.**

I smile. She's texting in our secret code.

Me: Request granted most enthusiastically.

Me: Will we be pursuing the ordinary agenda or is there a new element for review?

Tallulah: Tengo noticias aburridas!

Me: Yay!

Me: I mean, hurrah!

Tallulah: 7:00? El Jardín Muerto?

Me: Just returned from medical professionals in major metropolis. Still in need of provisions. 8:15?

Tallulah: 👍

Tallulah is my BFF because she's like me: not ~~norm~~ . . .

because we're both officially gifted, according to school and the tests and all that stuff. Ms. Gates, who runs TGASP (which stands for Talented and Gifted After School Program), always says that Tallulah and I make the perfect pair because we're both *hyperintelligent,* but we have different *overexcitabilities* (which is just a polite word for *obsessions*). When Tallulah is overexcited, it's contagious and I start to be overexcited about the same thing. For example, Tallulah loves mystery shows and logic puzzles and true crime documentaries and *secret codes.*

Last summer, when we got our first cell phones, we wrote the perfect code to text in. It's super important because our parents read all our texts, and our parents are also smart, so we had to come up with something that would stump them. Tallulah taught me that the most important part of a good secret code is that it has multiple steps, and that it's easy for BFFs to read while being impossible for intruders to decipher. Our code has three steps.

Step one: Use English for literal meaning—
but use formal vocabulary words in order
to exhaust would-be code breakers.

So, when Tallulah says, *Official request for a gathering of the minds,* it means *Let's meet up.*

Step two: Use Spanish to say the
opposite of what you mean.

We chose this one because we both take Spanish in school, and we were both overexcited about communicating in a different language for a while. Since *aburridas* = boring, Tallulah's news is exciting!

Step three: use Latin when it's a
matter of life or death.

(TBH we never use step three because we aren't ever in life or death situations, and if we were, we'd probably call our parents instead of translating the danger into Latin and then sending a message to another seventh grader. But Tallulah says every good code has an alarm signal, and I think it's pretty fun to have a secret 911 with my bestie.)

Me: I restlessly anticipate the moment at which I can possess the information that you long to bestow upon me!

At 8:10, I grab the huge camping flashlight Mom gave me for my last birthday and wave goodbye to Calvin. He thinks I'm just going for a walk with Tallulah. I skip out the back door of our house. According to our parents' rules, Tallulah and I are supposed to stay inside our gated community, which is stupid because it's not technically a community, just a part of town that everyone leaves every day to go into the actual community for work or school. Mom says it is a community because you need a passcode to drive through the gates. I don't know what passcodes have to do with communities. The only two things all the people who live here have in common are A. we live here and B. we know the passcode.

So when I shimmy through the row of hedges that lines the back of our yard and start to climb the chain-link fence behind it, I feel only a little guilty for breaking the rules. Technically, El Jardín Muerto is not *inside the gates* as our parents define them, even though it's a lot closer to our houses than many things our parents do consider *inside the gates*. But what can we do? They never listen to us when we try to tell them that this rule makes no sense. They don't even want to hear about how when they say *gates*, they actually mean *fence*.

I jump off the back of the fence and into another world. Instead of manicured grassy lawns, there's rocky ground, weeds, and spindly trees that grow in the haphazard way things do after deforestation. There's also litter everywhere, which I don't understand. The only other person I've ever seen in this no-man's-land between gated communities is Tallulah, and we never, ever litter.

Sustainability used to be one of my overexcitabilities, so I know a lot about it, even though it's just a regular excitability now.

After a few strides, I reach a hill so steep it looks like a cliff. I step down it slowly, shining the flashlight ahead of me so I can be careful not to turn my ankle on one of the rocks. Then I pick my way through the weeds, broken glass, and cigarette butts at the bottom of the hill until I've wound through multiple bunches of skinny trees and jumped over the little creek that's sometimes full of water and sometimes empty. Finally, my flashlight illuminates the raised hatchback of a red SUV: the welcome flag of El Jardín Muerto. That means "the dead garden," but our garden is anything but dead. We named it that because El Jardín Muerto is ours, and only ours, and who would be interested in a dead garden?

Tallulah is there already, sitting on the roof of a white minivan, a book open in her lap, and one of those headband-flashlight thingies shining from her forehead. Orchids reach out of the moonroof behind her, painting shadows across her lap. The lilies in the open hood beneath her reflect in her glasses.

El Jardín Muerto was Tallulah's and my first project. We were new friends, barely more than neighbors, when Tallulah and I started exploring out here. We found three abandoned cars in a circle at the bottom of a hill of rocky soil. It's not like this is some beautiful forest, but Tallulah and I were enraged to see rotting, not-at-all-biodegradable cars in the middle of one of the only greenspaces nearby. We decided to make up for the cars decomposing here by filling them with oxygen-producing, CO_2-destroying plants. We read books about sustainable gardens and googled and YouTubed gardening experts, and then pooled our allowance at the plant nursery near our school. Now the cars are all filled with soil and bursting with flowers and vegetables. Tomato vines wind up the open doors of the yellow car. Sunflowers reach sky high from the middle of the circle of cars. Flowers spring up where the engines used to be, and watermelon vines tumble out of the trunks and onto the rocky ground. In the back seats we've planted carrots and potatoes and radishes—root vegetables that require less sunlight. In the front seats, we have seeds resting on the windshields on top of damp towels, their shoots about to sprout. El Jardín Muerto is our contribution to the lungs of the Earth.

Plus, it's what turned us from same-age neighbors into best-best friends.

Tallulah looks up from her book when she sees me and waves frantically.

"Piper!" she calls, as if I'm in a big crowd and it'll be difficult for us to spot each other. "Piper, I've been here fifteen minutes. I was so excited, I got here early, and . . . Wait."

I stop walking. "What?" I look up at Tallulah, her headlamp a spotlight on me from the roof of the car.

"You look weird," she says.

Tallulah is almost completely missing her *Can't Say That* column.

"Huh?" I say.

"You're rubbing your leg. It's . . . strange. Are you OK?"

"Oh." I glance down at my hand over my jeans. My thumb is rubbing my bruise in tiny, loving circles. "Yeah, it's just a bruise."

It's not that I don't want Tallulah to know about Dr. Grand and early puberty and everything. I trust Tallulah completely. But ever since I started precocious puberty and Mom started trying to get pregnant, I feel like bodies are all we talk about. Bodies are all almost anyone wants to talk about. I talk about bodies at all those doctor's appointments, and in health class at school, and at HHH. I talk about bodies with Mom: her body adjusting after giving birth, Gladys's body growing. My other friends talk about bodies that are the best at playing sports, or bodies that are the best at looking good in certain kinds of clothes. Or they talk about hydrating lotions or face creams that tingle or sting. Eloise talks about bodies, too: her boyfriend's muscles, her own period, how important it is to wear deodorant at my age.

But Tallulah is different. With her, life is about ideas. Learning. Overexcitabilities. The Academic Decathlon. Tallulah is my ticket out of the World of Bodies and into the World of Brains. That's my happy place.

"Oh no!" she says. "A bruise? It must hurt if you're rubbing it like that."

"No, it—"

"Is that why you went to see the doctor?"

"Um, no, I—"

"Are you OK to climb up?"

"Yeah, I—"

"Because I can come down if you need me to. I don't want you to be uncomfortable when I give you the biggest, most life-changing news you've ever heard."

When Tallulah is excited, she can't stop talking. Ever. She gets in trouble for it at school almost every day. Her parents get frustrated with her. Even Calvin, who's the most patient person on Earth, sometimes looks a little annoyed when Tallulah's at our house and she can't stop herself from overexplaining how to assemble a crib or that the green mush that comes with our sushi isn't authentic wasabi, it's actually green horseradish, because it's almost impossible to get real wasabi outside of Japan. It sometimes exhausts me, too, how she talks and talks without stopping. But I love her anyway.

"But if you can come up, you should because it's warm, so

we can sit outside, and it's October so who knows how much longer it'll be warm? Warm at night is the best, especially for you because there's no sun, so you can't get a sunburn. I never think that much about sunburns unless I'm with you because I've never gotten a sunburn. Although I could, of course. Black people do get sunburns. A lot of white and other non-Black people don't know that but—"

"Tallulah!" I yell.

She finally pauses.

"I'm fine. I'll climb up."

Mom always tells me that interrupting isn't nice, so I try not to, but sometimes Tallulah gets stuck in an endless loop of words, and she looks almost relieved when I interrupt her.

"Yay!" She shoves an index card into the spine of her book and inches over on the roof of the car to make space for me. She uses her fingers to adjust the corners of her glasses, which always leaves them so smudged, I don't know how she sees out of them.

The smell of the lilacs hanging off the car door hits me as soon as I settle in next to her. I close my eyes and breathe in deeply.

"I love it here," I say.

I take in another big breath of lilac, and Tallulah does the same next to me. The smell is so strong, it can even pause her stream of words.

I turn and say, "OK, your *noticias aburridas*." I reach up and turn down the brightness of her headlamp, which she always forgets to do when she looks directly at me.

"You're not going to believe it," she says. "It's the best news of our lives."

"Really?" The excited energy is radiating off her and into me. "Is it about the decathlon?" I whisper.

"Yes!" Tallulah says.

Ever since we met, Tallulah and I have been planning to enter the Children's Academic Decathlon of the State of New Jersey in seventh grade. We've spent years and years helping the older seventh graders in TGASP prepare for it. Now it's our turn.

Teams of two seventh graders from all over the state get to compete. The winning team gets a full scholarship to a six-week academic summer program at the University of North Bend in Indiana, as do the two smartest seventh graders from every other state in the country. Some other smart kids get to go, too, even if they didn't win. Their parents pay the tuition. I've never even asked mine about tuition because I don't need to. We're going to win. Even Ms. Gates thinks we can win, and she's never had any students win before.

"Tell me!"

Tallulah hops to her feet, right on the roof of the car, and holds her hands out beside her like she's just finished some sort of dance and is waiting for applause.

"OK . . . ready?" she says.

"Wait," I say. Because, suddenly, I'm not ready.

Tallulah freezes.

I squint, at first not believing what I'm seeing. Then I hold the flashlight closer to her legs, which are now right next to my eyes. They're covered in tiny hot-pink Band-Aids, at least three per leg. And they're missing something.

"Did you shave your legs?"

"Oh," Tallulah says. She reaches down to lightly rub her thigh. "Yeah. My mom finally let me."

"Finally?"

I use my hand to shade my eyes from the headlamp glare and lean back to look up at her. Other than her legs, she looks the same as always: feet bare except for Nike slides, silver polish chipping on her toenails, long black basketball shorts and a purple tank top, dark brown hair box-braided and then pulled into a ponytail in the middle of her head. Serious eyes staring me down from behind smudged, purple-framed glasses. All per usual, except the bare and sort-of-bleeding legs.

My face gets a little warm the same way it does when Mom decides to breastfeed Gladys in the grocery store, like I'm embarrassed to just be near her hairless legs. My hand goes back to my own leg again, right over the bruise. I'm wearing jeans so I can't feel it, but I know my leg hair is still there and, at this moment, it feels like a security blanket.

"I've been asking her forever," Tallulah is saying.

"You have?"

"Well, since, like, last week." She laughs. "She kept saying how I wouldn't be responsible enough to keep it up, to be diligent about exfoliating before and moisturizing after, blah

blah blah. All that normal stuff she always says. But, anyway, I finally convinced her. Ugh. Leg hair is so embarrassing."

It is?

"Daisy's been shaving her legs for weeks now."

She has?

It's weird Daisy didn't tell me that. But maybe Daisy tried to tell me and I didn't listen, the same way she was trying to tell me about having a crush on either Jack or George earlier, and I didn't listen to that, either.

"Don't worry, Pipes"—Tallulah pats the top of my head like I'm a toddler or something— "I'm sure your mom will let you do it soon."

I nod because that's true. My mom wouldn't even stop me if I wanted to shave my legs right now.

But Tallulah's legs look cold and battered. Who wants that?

"And maybe I'm a little older than you," Tallulah giggles. "Metaphorically, I mean."

I smile up at her because, unlike anyone else, Tallulah understands metaphorical math. My life's work.

Everywhere we go, people tell Tallulah and me that we're so smart, but then there's all this stuff we don't understand about weird things that grown-ups seem to automatically assume, but that are sometimes stupid to us.

So Tallulah gets the point. She understands how I'm trying to discover the math that will explain human emotions and contradictions. You know, the way Sir Isaac Newton invented calculus to explain physics? When I'm old and dead like him,

I'll be known as Ma'am Piper Franklin, the mother of metaphorical math.

"OK, I can't take this anymore!" Tallulah says. "Can I please tell you the news?"

"Yes!" I say.

Tallulah raises her hands toward the darkening sky and yells, "The specialties announcement is coming!"

"What? How could you know about that already?"

Tallulah sits down next to me again. "Ms. Gates called my mom about my behavior in TGASP today," Tallulah says. She puts the word *behavior* in air quotes.

I recall how, this afternoon, Teddy wouldn't stop purposely humming right in Tallulah's ear while she was trying to map out volcanic activity in ancient Asia, so she turned and threw a pencil at him. Teddy didn't get in trouble, but Tallulah did.

"Uh-oh. She called your mom?"

Tallulah's parents, Joy and Edward, aren't like mine. My mom is always concerned that my giftedness could ruin my childhood. Tallulah's mom always worries that her childishness could ruin her gifts. Because Tallulah isn't just smart, she's scattered. It's like there's so many smart parts inside her and they're all competing to show off, so they get in the way of each other, and they get in the way of regular parts of life, like remembering to hand in your homework.

My mom doesn't care if I hand in my homework, like, ever. But also, I'm smart, but not so smart it scrambles me up, so I always do hand in my homework.

"Yeah. Anyway. Ms. Gates called my mom to tell her how awful I am."

"Tallulah," I say, softly.

"What?" Tallulah shoots back.

"You aren't awful. And Ms. Gates knows that."

Tallulah gives me a look like I just said the periodic table is imaginary or climate change isn't being created by humans.

"And so does your mom," I add.

"Well, duh," Tallulah says. "She's my mom. But sometimes with my ADHD . . . I mean, Ms. Gates thinks . . . And I actually am kind of awf—never mind."

"Wait, Tallulah," I murmur. "You're—"

"I was *saying* . . . Ms. Gates told my mom that the official start of the decathlon is this Friday!"

"Really?" I squeal.

All my worries about Tallulah saying she's awful, about her newly bare legs, about my own shots go flying out of my head. This is too exciting.

"Yeah. The committee is zooming into schools to pick the specialties on Friday."

"One week. Seven days," I whisper. That's serious *noticias aburridas*. I have goose bumps.

Tallulah swings her legs off the roof of the car so that her slides slip in and out of the open back window. "A whole week! I'm never going to make it," she says, dramatically.

"I hope there's physics this year. And algebra. Or geometry," I say.

"I hope there's a Shakespeare specialty. Or Chinese history."

"*Chinese* history?" I ask.

Tallulah loves all kinds of history, but her interests change so quickly I can't keep up.

She nods. "Oh! Or volcanoes!"

I raise an eyebrow. "Volcanoes?"

She smiles. "It's my new thing. I spent all Sunday afternoon watching YouTube videos of simulated eruptions. Did you know that the biggest volcano in existence actually isn't even on Earth?"

"What?" I ask. "Where is it?"

"Mars!" Tallulah says, gleefully.

"Wow," I say. I can already see it happening. Volcanic contagion. I'm going to be obsessed with volcanoes before you know it.

Tallulah makes everything interesting.

"We should work on the garden, huh? Because soon it's going to be all studying, all the time, and even El Jardín Muerto will be a distraction."

"True," I say.

"I think some of the baby seeds are ready for soil," Tallulah says. "And the bulbs should go in the hood of the blue car, right? Plant in fall, bloom in spring."

"You do the bulbs; I'll do the seeds?"

"Perfect."

I smile at her. We're back to being the same metaphorical age. A team. I don't need her leg hair after all.

TIME AND E = MC²

metaphorically, time doesn't move at the standardized rate calculated by this equation. Instead, time drags when you're bored, but it **FLIES WHEN YOU'RE HAVING FUN.**

Observation:

I'm at the pool with Daisy and Caroline and Josie playing marco Polo. We arrive at 1:00 p.m. ① and we are told we need to leave by 5:00 p.m. ⑤. After what feels like one hour, Daisy's mom tells us to get out of the pool. In this problem,

$$5 - 1 = 4 \text{ BUT } 5 - 1 \wedge 1$$

(Note: $\wedge$ denotes "feels like" in metaphorical math)

→

Equation:

$$T \wedge t \div n$$

where T = experienced time

t = actual time

and n = a real number between 0 and 10 according to a human's level of fun

Proof:

If time at the pool is fun to the level 4, and if we were at the pool for 4 hours, then

$$T \wedge t \div 4 \, ,$$

therefore $T \wedge 1$ hour

If going to the doctor with mom and the baby is fun to the level .025, and I was at the doctor 1 hour

$$T \wedge t \div 0.025 = 40 \, ,$$

therefore $T \wedge 40$ hours

This proof explains why four hours at the pool with friends feels shorter than one insanely boring hour at a baby doctor.

QED**

(P.S. El Jardín with Tallulah: $t = \frac{1}{10}$

So that's why 1 hour with Tallulah in El Jardín yesterday only felt like 6 minutes!)

**This is Latin for "it is demonstrated." mom's textbooks use it, so I should too!

{ 4 }

The next day, I'm lying on my bed on my stomach, enjoying the way it doesn't hurt my chest. My orange notebook is open beside me, a page full of cross outs and revisions turned up toward the ceiling. My chin is resting on the huge textbook I'm reading. *Theories of Complex Equations.* It's one of my mom's. I have Mozart playing in my headphones. I'm totally captivated by math and patterns and rhythms. I'm happy.

Then there's a knock on my door.

I glance at the other side of the room. The empty side. I wish it were Eloise knocking, even though that makes no sense because no one knocks on their own bedroom door. And it's a Saturday. She probably won't be home until Monday.

Eloise didn't used to live with us. She used to live with her mom, who I barely know. We're sisters because we have the same dad, but he peaced out of both our lives right after I was born. Our moms became friendly after our dad left, and we all hung out sometimes. Then, about five years ago, something happened to Eloise's mom—I don't know what because Mom says it's private. But Eloise started sleeping over most weekends, then sometimes for whole weeks, and eventually she moved into my bedroom. I know that the something that happened was a bad something, so I wasn't supposed to be happy about it. But I can't help but be happy any time Eloise is around.

Whatever it was must have gotten better though, because lately Eloise has been spending more and more time with her mom. Or she's at school. Or at her job. Or volunteering at the dog shelter. She still technically lives with us, but she's so busy it seems like she barely lives anywhere these days. It's different now because she's seventeen, which is almost an adult, so Mom says she can choose to live with us or with her mom or go between both houses.

Mom says we should be happy for Eloise because she's closer to her mom again. But I know Mom misses Eloise the way I do. Mom treats Eloise like she's her second daughter. Or third daughter, now, I guess. Or first daughter because she's the oldest?

Anyway . . . I think the person Eloise is actually getting close to isn't her mom, but her boyfriend, Bobby. He lives near her mom, and, in my opinion, that's the real reason she never sleeps here on weekends. She's too busy having fun with him to drive all the way back to this side of town after a date. And

I don't have to be happy about that.

Right?

Knock, knock. Again.

I roll over and pull my headphones off one ear. "Come in."

The door swings open. "Whatcha doing, Sweet Pi?" Calvin says.

I sit up, cross my legs, and shove Mom's math book under my pillow. I'm supposed to ask before taking her textbooks, but when I went to find her today, she was feeding Gladys, so I didn't.

"Nothing," I say, shrugging.

Calvin leans on my doorframe. He slides his bottom jaw back and forth like he always does when he's thinking, his rust-colored beard rearranging on his face. He wrinkles his nose to push his brown glasses higher. Mom and Gladys appear beside him.

"Can we come in, honey?" Mom asks.

I don't answer, but suddenly they're all in my room. Four people live in this house with me, and the only one I actually want to talk to right now is the only one who isn't here.

I wiggle closer to my pillow trying to block their view in case a corner of the book is sticking out or something. Mom always tells me that when I take her books without asking it's stealing, not borrowing, because she's not a library. But she sort of is a library because I always return them. She's only caught one-fourteenth of my supposed "stealing" incidents. In metaphorical math, that's a very insignificant number.

Mom shifts Gladys to one shoulder and uses the heel of her hand to rub her eyes. She has dark rings around them.

"I'd like to have a chat."

I know she wants to talk about the puberty stuff from Dr. Grand's office, but that's not what I want to talk about.

"OK. Guess what?" I jump to my knees. "Tallulah told me that Ms. Gates told her that the decathlon is—"

"No, no," Mom interrupts me. "About the shots."

"Oh." I fall onto my butt. A corner of the textbook pokes into my back.

Mom crosses the room and tries to sit on the edge of my bed, but the minute her body even leans toward me, Gladys starts fussing and she stands up again.

"I need you to . . . explain . . ." Mom says. She trails off. She's looking at Gladys, shifting her around.

"Piper, Mom said something about you trying to avoid puberty?" Calvin says, finally.

"Yes, thank you," Mom says, as if Calvin is some big help and not two of the four ears that don't belong in this room for this conversation.

I look from Mom to the back of Gladys's head to Calvin and his shifting red beard. I nod.

If only I could find a way to explain why I need the shots that's as clear as Ivan's Pinocchio metaphor.

"But, honey," Mom says, swaying in front of me so Gladys cries a little more quietly. "Puberty is OK now. It's natural."

But it's not. Natural puberty was going to happen to me at

seven years old. When we stopped it, we made it unnatural. It won't ever be natural. That's impossible.

I open my mouth to try to explain, but the same thing happens. No words appear.

Mom sits, Gladys screams, and she stands back up. She looks so tired. I want to change that, to be the easy one, but I can't hurry into puberty because Mom is tired.

"You don't even like Dr. Grand," Mom says.

"It's not about him."

"What is it about, honey? I'm listening." She says it like she means it, but her face is so focused on Gladys, I don't see how she can be listening.

I try to explain anyway. "I want the shots because . . . you know . . . all the . . . the stuff." I fail.

Mom's eyes narrow. "What stuff?"

"Baaaahhhh! Aaaaah!" Gladys screams. Even when she's happy, she's still interrupting.

"Like . . . you know. Like the stuff with you," I manage.

Mom and Calvin both look surprised. They take a half step away from me in their shock.

"Me?" Mom says. "Stuff with me?"

"Yeah . . . like . . . what happens to you."

"What happens to *me*?" Mom points to herself. "Me?"

I stare. I have to do better than this.

Gladys screams.

Mom is still pointing to herself.

"Ugh. Like how Dr. Grand is always calling you *Mrs.*"

"What?" Mom laughs. "That sounds like a reason to *stop* seeing him."

She looks at Calvin who smiles at her like this is a joke. My face is starting to heat up.

"But lots of people call you the wrong thing." I'm shouting now, but not because I'm angry. It's just that Gladys is so loud.

"And?" Mom yells back. It's like she's purposely trying to not understand me.

"And . . . and then they act like *you're* annoying for caring about your own name."

"Piper. What does that have to do with you and puberty?"

I knew it. I knew she wouldn't see the link. I need more examples.

I stand. "Plus . . . like . . . remember how you're always saying that at those math professor conferences the air conditioning is so high, and all the women are freezing, but the men get to wear suits, so they don't even notice?"

"What?" Mom says. But I know she must remember. She says that all the time.

"Or . . . OK. What about all those books you read Gladys?"

"What books?" Calvin asks. There's an edge of a chuckle in his voice that makes me want to hit something.

"Like *Soar Far, Race Car* and *Win the Game, Airplane.*" I move my hands around ridiculously as I say those stupid titles.

"What about them?" Mom says.

"How come all the trucks and cars and boats and planes use he/him pronouns?" This time they just stare. "And did you know that Eloise says that at her dog shelter almost no one comes in looking to rescue a girl dog?"

"Piper!" Mom yells. This time she actually yells. "Stop trying to distract me."

"I'm not," I shout over Gladys. "I'm answering you. Also, there's *never* been a woman president."

I stomp my foot on the word *never*.

Gladys screams and cries like this fact upsets her the way it should.

Mom shouts over her. "I don't care about any of that!"

"You don't?" I cry. "There's never been a woman president and you don't even care?"

"Of course she does," Calvin says, trying a reasonable voice. He's always way too reasonable in these moments, like he doesn't understand the value of a good fight.

Mom shoots him a look. "At this moment, I don't, actually," she says. "At this moment, I care about you, Piper. And none of this has anything to do with you."

~~Are you nuts?~~

It has everything to do with me.

Or it would. It will. It will when I'm in a body like Mom's and Eloise's and Kamala Harris's. It will when I have to grow into what they are.

I sit back on my bed.

"Piper," Mom says softly. "Just tell me the truth."

I snap my mouth shut and stare at her. That was the truth.

Gladys writhes and screams between us.

"Listen, honey, you're eleven and—"

"Only chronologically," I say.

"Oh, this again," Mom sighs. She hates metaphorical math. Every time she reminds me how much she hates it, it's like a pin in the balloon of my heart.

I pull my pillow onto my lap and sink my elbows into it, trying to give myself a hug.

"Piper!" Mom yells suddenly.

I jump.

"What is that?" she demands. She lunges behind me, and then I remember her textbook. I exposed it when I moved the pillow. She reaches for it, screaming baby and all. *"Complex Equations.* Again? Seriously?"

I shrink away from her.

"Anna," Calvin says, quietly. "I think she was just reading a math book."

"Yeah! Why do you even care?" I yell. "It's not like *you* need your books."

"I will soon. I'm going back to work," Mom says through clenched teeth.

"I would have returned it way before then."

"OK, OK," Calvin says. He speaks in the annoyingly slow and patient way he often does with Tallulah. "Piper . . . there's nothing wrong with you being interested in math, but—"

"Actually, there is something wrong with it, Cal!" Mom yells.

"There is?" Calvin asks with that half step of surprise again, and I'm glad because I have the same question.

"She should be spending her time doing something normal."

"Normal?" I ask. How come she gets to use that word?

"You know what I mean," Mom yells in Calvin's direction, even though she's answering me, and I'm clearly the one she's mad at. "She should be acting like a kid. Having fun. Not holing up in her room with math books."

My jaw drops. I fall back onto the bed, muscles loose again. This is the thing about my mom. As soon as she's making me the most angry, she says something that reminds me of how easily she loves me. I'd rather have a mom who's mad at me for studying too much than one who forces me to study all the time.

"I'm going outside to hang out with Tallulah in a little while, Mom," I say.

"Oh. Good," she says, nodding.

I'm still sort of angry, but my mouth is twitching into a half smile. My family is confusing. Mom is both impossible to understand and really good at loving me. Calvin is both compassionate and annoying. Eloise is perfect but almost never here.

Gladys is only one thing: *loud*.

"And, honey," Mom says, putting a soft hand on my shoulder, "if you had asked to borrow the book because you want to relax with some complex math equations or whatever . . ." Now Calvin and Mom and I are all giggling because even I know that it's funny to find math textbooks relaxing. (And yet they are so relaxing.) "I'd say yes. But you need to ask."

"OK." I don't say that I didn't want to ask because she was feeding Gladys, and I don't like to be right next to her when she's doing that.

"And if you ever *do* borrow my books *without* asking," Mom says with a little twinkle in her eye, "and it happens to be one of the very uncommon times that I catch you doing such a thing . . . maybe you can find a way to defend yourself without reminding me about how I don't get to work right now because I'm stuck at home with a screaming baby twenty-four seven?"

"Huh?" I say. "Oh." I tilt my head at her. "OK."

She doesn't *want* to be stuck at home with a screaming baby twenty-four seven? That has never occurred to me.

Gladys wails louder.

"Honey, I need you to understand that you can't not be eleven. Numbers aren't metaphorical."

It feels like she slapped me.

I open her textbook and point to a small, italicized *i*. "What's that?"

Mom breathes in sharp. "That's an imaginary number, but—"

"If numbers can be imaginary, they can be metaphorical. It's just that no one has figured metaphorical numbers out yet."

Calvin is laughing out loud now, a big, round belly laugh. I don't know if that means he's on my side or Mom's. Mom looks at him with a face that's so different from the one she just used for me. When she was looking at me, her face was saying, *Please stop making my life impossible.* To Calvin, her face is saying, *You're also difficult, but it makes me happy because I love you a lot.*

She takes a deep breath. "OK, Piper. Fine. Just give me a reason, all right? Just one good reason that you need to stay on the shots. Not nonsense about dogs and books and presidents. Please."

"I . . . I have a million reasons."

And you just called them all nonsense.

Mom sighs and puts her arm around me. Gladys settles down once she's wedged between us. "Honey," she says. "I mean . . . give me the reason from your heart."

I stare at her. My brain wants to keep giving her all kinds of reasons—reasons from math, history, biology, literature. My brain has reasons for not wanting to be a full-grown woman from every possible subject, every possible Academic Decathlon specialty.

But my heart has no words. It just wants to scream.

Gladys does it for me. She screams so loudly, she's suddenly puking all down Mom's back and Mom is saying, "For Pete's sake!" and running out the room. "Cal!" Her voice ricochets down the hallway. "I need wipes. And burp cloths. And please fill her bath."

Calvin hesitates. "You know we love you more than life, right, Sweet Pi?"

I nod. I do know that.

Then he leaves, and I realize Mom took *Complex Equations* with her, so I have nothing to distract myself from how sad and desperate I am.

I need those shots. If Mom needs a reason, and she can't help me figure out the real one, I'll have to find others.

I move to my desk and switch on my desk lamp. I pull six colored index cards out of the drawer: red, yellow, green, blue, purple, and orange. I'll give Mom all the reasons. A rainbow of reasons. Then she'll have to let me stay on the shots.

I start with red, Ivan's favorite color. *If Ivan's on the shots and he's thirteen, I should be allowed to stay on them at least that long.* After I write it, I pin it words-down to the corkboard above my desk.

I shuffle to yellow. Yellow is the color of the inside of a daisy, so I write, *None of my friends has a period. If I go off the shots, I'll still be the only girl I know with a period. I'll still be first. And isn't that what we were trying to avoid?* I pin that one down, too.

Green is the color of the puke Gladys just splattered all over Mom's sweater, so on the green card I write, *Besides, puberty and periods are about having babies one day and I NEVER EVER EVER want to have a baby.*

On the blue card I write, *And Dr. Grand said the shots are totally safe!* because the needles from Dr. Grand's office are always blue.

Purple is Tallulah's favorite color, so on the next card I write, *This is my decathlon year. I can't be distracted by things like periods and hormones.* Now I have a row of five colored rectangles pinned to my corkboard, each hiding one reason that I should stay on the shots.

I reach for the orange card. My favorite color. I want to write my heart's reason on it. But my heart's reason is all mixed up. It's all these tiny things that are connected somehow, even if I can't say how.

I need a metaphor.

Ivan said he was being controlled by invisible marionette strings, like Pinocchio. But the tiny things I notice—Dr. Grand and abandoned girl dogs and male presidents—are super visible. They're happening around me all the time, attracting my eyeballs like something gross you can't help but stare at. And whatever they are, whatever it is that connects them all into one thing, it isn't controlling my mom's movements like in Ivan's metaphor. It's more like she's tied up. Restricted.

It's like every example I see is one link in a chain that weighs on every adult woman I know, but there are only words for the little pieces of the chain, not for the whole thing.

Hey, that's it. It's the Wordless Chain! That's why I don't want to stop the shots.

I did it. I have a metaphor.

For a second, I'm thrilled. For a second I feel accomplished. I pick up my pencil and I write it out on the orange card. The real reason. My heart's reason.

I need the shots because of the Wordless Chain.

Then I stare at it, deflating. What good is a reason if it's wordless?

I hear the door creak behind me.

And there she is, standing in the bedroom doorway. My big sister. "Eloise!" I don't think I've seen her since last week except when I roll over in the middle of the night and find her sleeping in the twin bed across from mine.

Being near her always makes me feel the same way I do when I smell lilacs.

Her thick black hair is pulled back in a low ponytail with a purple headband outlining the top of her head. She's wearing skinny jeans that stretch over her hips and butt, and a black T-shirt that's cut low in the front. A necklace with a silver tree on it hangs below her collarbone.

"Iper!" She greets me with the name she made up for me when I was a baby and she was, like, six. She barely ever saw me then, but when she did, she'd always leave the first *P* off my name. Even once her speech improved, she never stopped calling me Iper. I still love it.

"Hi," I yelp.

I'm so excited to see her, my heart is jumping rope. Maybe we'll pop popcorn and watch Netflix on her computer. Maybe we'll go together to walk dogs from her shelter. Maybe we'll do something else, something new. For some reason, I feel like I need to swallow my excitement, though. Like it's in the *Can't Say That* column or something. Even though being excited to see someone is definitely nice.

Eloise sits on the side of my bed. I want to collapse into her, to put my head in her lap, to sleep with her in my bed the way we did when she was twelve and I was six, and she first moved in with Mom and Calvin and me. She and I would sleep all tangled together because that seemed like the only way to make up for all the lost time. Then . . . simultaneous puberty. Regular for her, precocious for me. Now I have to settle for her balancing on the edge of my mattress.

She bumps her shoulder against mine.

"Want to watch a movie?" I ask, my words plowing out of me like I'm Tallulah. "I've been waiting for you to watch this documentary about dogs who saved—"

Eloise sits up straighter, so our shoulders aren't touching anymore. The movie is not going to happen.

"Where's Bobby today?" I ask. A guess.

Eloise fidgets with her silver tree. "He's picking me up at 12:30."

I glance at the clock. It's 12:20.

One doctor appointment with Mom.

Ten minutes with Eloise.

That's it.

"How was Dr. JerkFace yesterday?" She's the only one who knows my nickname for him.

"He called me fat again," I say.

"What?" Eloise says. "Don't listen to that."

"Don't worry." I smile. "I never do."

Eloise stands up and does a spin on our gold carpet, followed by about six steps of salsa. She wiggles her curvy hips and waves her thick arms, showing off every bit of her. "I mean, maybe you are fat. But who cares? Fat isn't bad. It should be like saying you're tall or have long hair. But I'm guessing he didn't say it like that?"

I laugh. "Nope."

Eloise spins. "Well, Dr. JerkFace may be smart, but I know two things he doesn't. One, I'm fatter than you. And two"— she spins once more, then leans back on the bed like she's just dipped herself—"I'm beautiful."

She giggles and so do I. She really is beautiful.

She yanks me up, and the next thing I know I'm salsa-ing with her, spinning under her arms, wiggling my hips the way she does. If this is the post-puberty version of sleeping curled up, I'll take it.

We collapse back onto my bed together. "If Dr. Grand is such a jerk . . . and he is . . . why do you want to keep seeing him?"

Oh. Mom must have talked to her on her way in.

I shrug.

"It's . . . I'm . . . I'm a kid."

A kid who doesn't have to think about being a girl unless I'm looking for the correct bathroom door. A kid who doesn't have to worry about . . . whatever links all those things I see. A kid who has better things to think about.

Eloise nods. "When I first got my period, I definitely still felt like a kid."

My eyebrows go up. It sounds like she might understand. "How old were you?"

"Twelve."

"And you were upset? You didn't want it, either?" I ask.

She shakes her head, laughing. "I wasn't so wise. At first, I was happy about it."

"And then?" I ask.

She groans and falls backward on the bed, covering her face with my pillow. "And then . . . cramps." She laughs, and it almost sounds like that secret code, so I do, too. But I can't decode this one. Maybe it's something I'll understand after puberty.

"But . . . you're not thinking about *my* period when you say you don't want to go through puberty, right?"

I lower my eyebrows and shrug. Of course I am.

"Oh, Ipey. Yours probably won't be like mine. Most of my friends have periods that aren't a big deal."

"I guess. But—"

"And the period isn't the point, sis. It's just one part. The rest of growing up—that's the fun stuff!"

"It is?" I ask, surprised.

Eloise beams. "Do you know how fun my life is right now?"

"No," I say. It doesn't look fun. It looks complicated and busy and confusing. And periodically predictably painful.

Her phone buzzes. She flips it over and I see Bobby's name on her screen.

"Listen, Iper," she says, not looking up. "Every woman you know has gotten a period. And they're all fine."

"No, they aren't," I whisper.

I don't think she hears me, though. She's looking at her phone.

"I gotta go," she says, standing. "You'll be OK. I promise."

Then she leaves, and for the first time ever it seems like she doesn't know what she's talking about because she said I'd be OK, but I'm not OK with her leaving at all.

It's only 12:28.

{ 5 }

It's finally Friday afternoon. I'm huddled with the other seventh graders in TGASP—Mark, George, Daisy, Caroline, Nora, Eric, Josie, Jack, Teddy, Kelly, and Tallulah. We've pulled our chairs to the front of the room in a semicircle around Ms. Gates's SMART Board where our destiny is about to be announced. Tallulah's left arm presses against my right, like I'm keeping her tethered to the earth. I feel like I might float away, too. The others used to tease us about how excited we were for this moment, but now they're leaning close to the screen, breathless right along with us.

The non-seventh graders in TGASP are gathered around laptops in the back half of the classroom. Ms. Gates gave them a free day, so they get to do whatever they want, which means they're playing *Everything Bee*, an online trivia game we all love. I hear some of them cheering about how, since Tallulah and I won't be playing, a different team will get to win for once. I couldn't care less. All I care about in this moment is the decathlon.

The screen glows blue and we all manage to lean in even closer, holding a collective breath.

"Give us five minutes," a voice says. "We're running a little behind."

We let out that breath and, metaphorically, time morphs to a new equation and drags. Five minutes never seemed so long.

"Hey, knock knock," Daisy says. She's sitting on my left side, Tallulah on my right. George is on Daisy's other side.

I turn to her and smile. "Who's there?"

"Disguise."

"Disguise who?"

Daisy points her two thumbs at herself like she's telling a *this guy* joke.

"Disguise excited to be your teammate."

"Huh?" George and I both say.

"You don't get it?" Daisy chirps. "Because *disguise* sounds like *this guy is*? It's a combo. Two corny jokes in one."

I got the joke part. I didn't get the real part.

"Wait . . ." George says with the same nervousness I feel. "I thought we—"

But then Daisy hushes him because the screen brightens and a face appears saying, "Welcome, seventh graders, to the annual Children's Academic Decathlon of the State of New Jersey!"

Daisy can't think we're going to be teammates. Everyone should know Tallulah's my choice. I always partner with Tallulah, and Daisy always partners with George.

On-screen, the panelist pauses as if for applause, and my classmates cheer even though he can't hear us. After a second I join in the cheering. Daisy was joking. She had to be. And I need to focus on this moment that's finally here.

Ms. Gates is standing behind her podium next to the SMART Board, smiling at us like we're the most precious things she's ever seen. "This is one of my favorite days of the year," she says.

On the screen, the six adults who make up the Academic Decathlon panel sit at a long table on a sort of stage, each behind a small microphone stand. The New Jersey state flag is pinned to the curtain behind them. It looks so official. So important. I have goose bumps.

The first panelist leans toward her microphone. "Your preliminary entries are due this Monday. After that you can rearrange teammates, but no new individuals can enter. Final entries are due the following Monday."

Any two seventh graders from any school in the state can enter the decathlon as a team. Over the course of the school year, competitors have to be ready to answer questions about nine different subjects. In the Academic Decathlon, we call them the nine *academic specialties*. They're chosen at random every year during the Opening Ceremony—a.k.a. today.

After today, we fill out entry forms with our chosen

partners. You don't have to know which teammate will compete in which specialty to do the entry forms. In fact, that can change constantly as the competition goes on. But Ms. Gates says it's best not to fill out the entry form until we know how we're going to split specialties so that we don't end up in a last-minute panic with a specialty no one has studied for.

There are four different events, four levels of competition, and it works like a tournament with the winning team of one level advancing to the next. First, the school level is in late December. There, we compete against the other seventh graders in our school in two of the nine academic specialties. The tricky part is that we won't know which two until that very day, so we have to prepare for all of them. The team that wins at the school level goes on to counties in January, where the panelists will pick three of the remaining specialties. The county champions compete in regionals, North Jersey and South Jersey, where there are two more specialties. And the winning teams from each region—just four kids total—get to compete in finals.

Of course, the *dec-* in *decathlon* means *ten* so there's a tenth specialty, but it's not like the others. It's always last. After the last two academic specialties are completed in finals, there's what's called the *creative specialty*. Instead of answering questions in the last round of competition, the finalists present creative pieces.

It feels like we're all holding our breaths again as the panelist on the screen goes over the rules and procedures we've had memorized since like third grade. They show us a graphic.

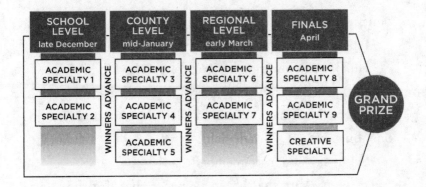

SCHOOL LEVEL late December		COUNTY LEVEL mid-January		REGIONAL LEVEL early March		FINALS April	
ACADEMIC SPECIALTY 1	WINNERS ADVANCE	ACADEMIC SPECIALTY 3	WINNERS ADVANCE	ACADEMIC SPECIALTY 6	WINNERS ADVANCE	ACADEMIC SPECIALTY 8	GRAND PRIZE
ACADEMIC SPECIALTY 2		ACADEMIC SPECIALTY 4		ACADEMIC SPECIALTY 7		ACADEMIC SPECIALTY 9	
		ACADEMIC SPECIALTY 5				CREATIVE SPECIALTY	

Daisy leans closer to me again and whispers, "OK, so strategy: you take any sciences."

I press my arm into Tallulah's, a silent message that she has nothing to worry about. That I'm her partner no matter what.

"I'll take any art or music, obviously," Daisy says. "And in school, I take Japanese and you take Spanish, so that's perfect if any lang—"

"Daisy," I say. I have to stop her.

"Wait," she says. She glances at Tallulah, then back at me. "Wait. No."

I'm biting the inside of my cheek. Mom would tell me I have to be nice about this but there's no nice way to say *I don't want to be your teammate.*

"You're partnering with *her*? Seriously?"

As if Tallulah doesn't have a name. As if Tallulah smells bad.

It's hard to find a way to be nice when someone is being so not nice, but Mom says it's important, even then.

"I thought you'd team up with George," I say.

Tallulah is definitely, without a doubt, one hundred percent the smartest kid in TGASP. But George, Daisy, and I are all a pretty close match for second smartest.

"Piper," Daisy whines. "You promised."

"Huh?" I say, lowering my eyebrows. "No, I didn't."

"Yes, you did. When we were in fourth grade. You said you'd work with me and not Tallulah this one time, for this one thing."

"Oh," I say. "I don't remember that."

I'm pretty sure that never happened, but if it did, I was probably just trying to be nice.

On my other side, Tallulah is silent, but her arm gets more and more solid against my shoulder. Almost like she's trying to support me.

"I'll let you choose whichever specialties you want," Daisy says, a note of pleading in her voice.

"I'm sorry, Daisy," I whisper.

She huffs and turns back to the screen. "I can't believe this," she mutters.

Then, we're awkward and silent as the panelist explains the rest of the rules and procedures we already know. I still get goose bumps when she talks about the grand prize.

The winners get to go to college. For the whole summer.

It just has to be me and Tallulah.

"Now," the panelist says, "we'll use the traditional hopper to determine this year's specialties."

She pauses and our classroom erupts into another round of applause. I cheer but I can't clap. My hands are pressed together too tightly. I'm so nervous. And Daisy is trying to set me on fire with her eyeballs or something. I don't want to think about that. I don't want to think about anything except the next nine words that will be said on that screen, the next nine words that will determine my efforts and my thoughts and my dreams for the next six months.

The camera pans to the left and focuses on an old-fashioned, round, cage-looking thing. It's full of what looks like multi-colored Ping-Pong balls, each with one word printed on it in black ink, and there's a crank to the side that you can use to spin it. I know from watching this ceremony the last two years that the panelist will crank the hopper until it spins the balls around in a rainbow hurricane and then *whoosh* one of them will slide out. The word printed on that ball becomes one of the specialties. Tallulah's and my fate rests in that hopper.

"Are you ready?" the panelist asks.

We're screaming and clapping so loudly it's shaking the classroom windows.

A different panelist stands and walks to the hopper. He cranks the handle so that the balls click-clack through the spinning cage. Tallulah holds her breath beside me. I can almost hear her thoughts out loud: *Volcanoes. Shakespeare. Something about spies. Chinese history.* I add my own prayer to the G&T gods: *Physics. Algebra. Geometry. Plants.*

The first ball slides out and the judge looks into the camera. "The first specialty will be . . . botany."

"Yes!" I say.

Tallulah claps next to me. Teddy fist-pumps the air. Daisy

is saying "I *am* botany. Get it? *Daisy?*" A lot of people know a lot about plants.

The hopper rolls again.

The panelist pulls out a yellow ball and turns it over. "Two. African American poetry."

Daisy says a quiet "Yes."

I look at Tallulah and smile. She's got that one.

"Three. Music theory."

That's Tallulah, again. In my head I start a tally.

African American poetry—Tallulah

Music theory—Tallulah

Botany—Either

"Four. Earth sciences."

Mine. Finally!

I turn to high-five Tallulah, but she's jumping out of her chair so hard she knocks it over. "That's where the volcanoes will be!"

Oh, yeah. She wants that one, too.

"Tallulah," Ms. Gates says, flatly.

She fixes her chair and sits back down.

"Five. Geometric patterns."

"Perfect, Pipes," Tallulah whispers.

Botany—Either

African American Poetry—Tallulah

Music Theory—Tallulah

Earth science—also Tallulah?

Geometric patterns—Me

"Number six. Chinese dynasties."

"Yes!" Tallulah screams.

I don't know how we're ever going to split this up. Tallulah wants everything.

"Seven. Culinary arts."

Tallulah looks at me. I shrug. I don't know much about cooking. But I know this one has to be mine. Tallulah already has too many, especially since we know she'll take the creative specialty.

"Eight. Female and nonbinary athletes."

Tallulah yelps. "Hello, WNBA." Then she turns to me. "But actually, maybe that one should be yours, Piper. I don't know anything about sports except the WNBA."

But I know even less.

I should have predicted this would happen. Tallulah has too many overexcitabilities. I'm going to be stuck with jocks and recipes.

This is not how today is supposed to feel.

There's only one left. Please be something in the sciences. Please.

"Nine. Endocrinology."

My jaw drops. Around me, my classmates look at each other wide-eyed. Jack whispers, "What even *is* that?"

No one answers him.

In this entire room of geniuses, I'm the only kid who knows the word.

And I know more than that. I know all about the hormonal systems from the thyroid to the pituitary to the gonads. I know about stress hormones and sleep hormones and reproductive hormones. Thanks to Calvin and his gifted medical journals, I know everything about this stupid subject.

But I hate it.

Endocrinology ruins everything. And now it's showing up here. At TGASP. With Tallulah. In this place that's supposed to be solidly in the World of Brains.

Tallulah is staring at me, confused. Even she doesn't know endocrinology.

The last thing I want to do is spend my school year preparing for the Academic Decathlon by reading even more about hormones and how they're going to resume messing up my body. I want to say, *What's that word? Never heard of it. Endo-crypt-coin or something?*

But I can't. This is the decathlon. Our dream.

"Don't worry," I whisper. "I got it."

Tallulah raises her eyebrows as if to ask how I know the word, but we don't have time to discuss before a new panelist stands up and carries a much smaller hopper full of white balls over to the judge who has been choosing all the subjects so far. He takes it and spins it a few times.

I'm barely listening by now. I'm trying to get my head around how different this year will be from the way I imagined it. Instead of equations and experiments, it'll be full of penalties, prosciutto, and progesterone.

"And the final, creative, specialty is," the man at the hopper says, "self-expression."

One of the panelists at the table stands up with her mic. "This is very exciting," she says. "Creative self-expression is the most open-ended of all the tenth-round specialties. We'll send a specific rubric soon, but simply, it means you'll need to find a creative way to invite the judges into your internal world. The substance and method of your expression of self is up to you."

Well, at least that's perfect. Tallulah spends so much time expressing herself it's almost like it's an overexcitability.

The panelist continues, "The school level will take place the last day before the school break in December. Remember, submission forms are due Monday. And kids?"

She pauses and looks right at the camera. There's still a buzzing excitement in the classroom, even though I'm not a part of it anymore. I watch as Tallulah and Daisy and George and Kelly all lean so close to the screen they could fall right out of their seats.

"Good luck."

The screen goes blank.

The room is silent for a moment, then erupts into chatter.

"Piper," Tallulah whispers. "We can do this."

I suck up my disappointment so she can't see it on my face, smile, and nod at her. She's right. We can, and we have to.

The next morning, Saturday, I'm sitting at my desk. I've been sitting in the same position for so long my butt is sore. Nine piles of color-coded index cards sit next to my computer, which is open to the Academic Decathlon website. I'm reading information they posted about each specialty. I'm supposed to be writing down my "ideal split." Tallulah's words. She said we should each take time to split the subjects five and five, the way we would if we could have everything we wanted.

TBH, I don't know what the point is when Tallulah wants almost every subject.

I've outlined what I have so far on a piece of loose-leaf.

PIPER	TALLULAH	TBD
*Geometric Patterns	*Afr. Am. Poetry	*Botany
	*Music Theory	*Earth Science
*Endocrinology	*Chinese Dynasties	*Female and Nonbinary Athletes
	*Self-Expression	*Culinary Arts

I'm not supposed to have a TBD column. But I'm stuck. I want to give myself both sciences, but that would be selfish because I know Tallulah wants them both, too. The right thing is probably to split them up, but that doesn't feel good to me because Tallulah is excited about everything in her column, and I'm only excited about one thing in mine.

I'm hoping that taking notes on the information on the website will inspire me to make a better chart.

But I can't concentrate. I usually work quickly. At least, I do at school. And at TGASP. But today, no matter what I do, no matter how loud the white noise is in my headphones, no matter how tightly I put them against my ears, I can hear Gladys screaming or crying or squealing or giggling in the living room, all the way down the hall.

I used to study in the living room, so that I could be close to Mom and Calvin all the time. It used to be that quiet in our house.

It takes two hours to finish notes on botany. I move on to culinary arts, which I manage to take notes on in about fifteen minutes. *Huh.* I pull off my headphones.

It's quiet!

Gladys must be napping. I have to get as much done as possible in the next twenty-to-forty-five minutes before she's up and loud again.

I turn my phone over to send Tallulah a quick text.

Me: The Lilliputian Homosapien has commenced her morning siesta. My concentrative aptitude art, therefore, temporarily increased tenfold. Shall we reconvene in our customary locality after the midday provisions?

Me: Me encanta esta casa ruidosa

Meaning: *I love this noisy house.* Code meaning: *I hate this noisy house.*

Tallulah doesn't text back right away, so I turn my headphones on and continue reading.

> Competitors should be familiar with
> the history of women's sports and with
> women's contemporary athletic programs—
> professional, collegiate, and amateur—in
> every country, paying particular attention to
> Olympic medal winners from all countries
> in all sports in both Summer and Winter
> Olympics, the history of women at the

Olympics, all professional women's leagues in
all countries, intercountry athletic events such
as marathons, triathlons, and . . .

I look up thinking this is going to be a ton of studying for
whoever takes this subject.

"Hey."

I jump a metaphorical forty feet. Calvin is standing over me.

"Sorry," he says. "Didn't mean to scare you. I tried to knock
and then I cracked the door and called your name. Those must
be some strong headphones."

~~Not strong enough to drown out your demon baby.~~

"Come down to the kitchen. We can have a chat while
Gladys is napping."

~~What? No way!~~

"Mom is making you a study snack, too."

She's going to steal my only chance to concentrate.

"OK?" Calvin finishes.

I glance at my index cards. It feels like they're begging for
me. *Fill us out, Piper. Refuse to go, Piper. Just sit down and do
what you want to do for once, Piper.*

I stand. "OK."

I follow Calvin down the hallway of our ranch-style house
to the kitchen where Mom is rolling a ball of cookie dough in
a bowl of cinnamon sugar. My back gets a little straighter. I
feel the beginnings of a smile pinch my cheeks.

"Snickerdoodles?" I ask.

This is not what I thought Calvin meant by a study snack.

Mom nods from across the kitchen island. "Wash your hands and grab an apron."

Outside, a sudden peal of thunder makes all three of us freeze and look at each other with faces that say *please tell me that doesn't wake the baby*. When it's still quiet a minute later, I join my mom in dipping a spoon into her homemade cookie dough, rolling it into a ball, and then covering it in cinnamon sugar. I start to feel cozy. It's warm inside the kitchen. Calvin is humming as he pours three glasses of milk. Rain is beating on the windows. Mom's shoulder is so close to mine I sometimes brush against it when I reach for more dough.

I only miss studying the tiniest bit. Wait! Maybe this *is* studying.

"Mom," I say. It's been so long since this was part of our usual routine, I almost forgot how much my mom loves to bake. "You can help us, right? With the culinary arts part of the Academic Decathlon?"

Mom beams. She already knows all the specialties because she asked about them as soon as I got home yesterday. "I'd love to," she says. "I'll help with the geometric patterns, too."

Calvin appears across the island from us, a warm smile on his face. "Maybe we should let you each keep your love affair with math separate," he says, chuckling.

Mom and I are laughing, too. Calvin is good at this: taking what used to be a fight and finding the perfect love-filled moment to turn it into a joke instead. Jokes have a way of making a fight really, really over. That's why, in metaphorical math, good jokes are worth B. (That's a really big number.)

"We don't have to talk about math," Mom says. "But, with Gladys napping, this is a good time to finish the conversation about Dr. Grand's shots."

~~No.~~

~~No, it isn't.~~

~~It's a terrible time.~~

"OK," I say.

She puts her finger lightly on my chin and tilts my head back so I'm looking at her.

She's gazing right into my eyes. She's touching my chin and standing close and there's no baby between us. It's been forever since we've had one single moment this connected, and that used to be my whole life.

"You still feel that you'd like to avoid puberty, as you put it?" Mom asks.

"Yes," I say.

"Do you have a reason for me, honey?"

The rainbow of reasons appears inside my brain. I wish didn't need them. I wish Mom would listen to the real things that are making me uncomfortable and help me understand why it feels like they're connected to puberty, even if she thinks they aren't.

But I nod.

"Go ahead. Tell me. I'm listening," she says.

"I . . . I need the shots because . . ."

What are my reasons again?

Oh yeah: Ivan still takes them and he's older than me (red index card), none of my friends has a period yet (yellow card), I don't want to ever have a baby anyway (green card), the shots are safe (blue card), puberty would distract me from preparing for the decathlon (purple card) and the Wordless Chain (orange card). They seemed brilliant when I wrote them, but now they feel pretty pathetic.

I choose blue.

"Remember what Dr. Grand said? The shots are safe."

Mom doesn't contradict me right away. She doesn't call me ridiculous or say I'm trying to distract her. Instead, she stares at me extra long, then sighs. She moves her hand to the back of my head and pulls me into her. Mom isn't curvy like me and Eloise, so her hugs are always full of bones and angles, but they still feel like home. For a second, I relax against her. Maybe that's all it took. Maybe I don't need the rest of the rainbow.

"That's not right," Mom whispers.

"What?" I ask, leaning back to look at her. "Yes, it is. He did say that."

"What I mean is, that's not a reason to take medicine."

I yank the rest of the way out of her hug. "He said kids older than me take it. He said it was perfectly safe."

"He also said the shots aren't necessary," Mom says.

~~So what?~~

~~He doesn't know anything.~~

He's not in my body.

"Piper, it would be safe for you to take a Tylenol right now, but you aren't, right? It would be safe to ice your leg anytime you want, but you don't do that unless you've hurt it."

I freeze. She's right.

"I want to know why you think you need this medicine, not hear an argument against my reasons. I feel like there's something you aren't telling me, and if that's—"

"I did tell you."

The words slip out. Arguing words. Left-side words. I'm certain I'm going to get reprimanded for not being nice, but instead Mom eats them up like she was hungry for them.

"What did you tell me? Can you try again?"

Maybe.

Maybe I can try again.

Maybe, if you listen like this, and don't call me ridiculous.

She puts a finger on my chin again. She stares at me, imploringly. Her eyebrows vibrate on her skull, waiting for my words. "I can see it, Piper. I can see there's something, just beyond your eyes. . . ."

I feel the words starting to form on my tongue. If I can explain the links to her and she actually sees the whole chain . . . if she sees it . . . well, Mom's really smart. Maybe she'll know a word for it. Maybe Mom can make the Wordless Chain not so wordless. Maybe Mom can make it go away.

"When . . . when I see things like that . . . like what I was talking about last time . . . like the dogs at Eloise's shelter or like when Dr. Grand calls you Mrs. . . ." She doesn't cut me off. So far so good. "It makes me—"

But then we hear "Uh-uh-uh" crackle over the monitor. Gladys.

Most of my mom doesn't move. She's still standing only five inches from me. She's still holding my chin. Her face is still angled like she's looking at me. But her eyes dart toward the bedroom, just the tiniest bit, and I know it. I've lost her.

"I'll go," Calvin says, quickly.

Mom's still looking at me, but she shakes her head. "Hold on. She'll need to nurse, and I don't want to pump. Just . . . one minute. Piper?" she prompts.

I try again. I really do. I open my mouth— Then Gladys is crying hard.

"Anna. I'll get her," Calvin says.

"She'll be OK for a minute, Cal!" Mom yells.

But don't need a minute. I need a lifetime.

And Gladys is hungry. Gladys is a baby. Gladys has needs that are easy for everyone to understand. Even me, and I don't like her that much.

So I say the sentence that does only take a minute: "I just want the shots."

Disappointment slackens Mom's whole face. "Piper—"

Gladys cries louder. My mom squeezes her eyes shut, then opens them and says, "This isn't over" just like yesterday, and runs away to get her new baby. My chin is cold where her finger was.

Calvin moves around the island to put the sheet of cookies into the oven. "Listen, Sweet Pi. If you want to stop having this conversation with us, you'll have to talk to someone else."

The answer comes to me at once. A sudden flash. Like I'm on the stage at the Academic Decathlon and the panelists just asked a question I didn't think I knew the answer to and then *poof*, there's the answer, right here in my brain.

"Eloise."

Calvin shuts the oven and turns to look at me. "You'll talk to Eloise? For real?"

I nod.

He moves his jaw back and forth. "Well, I think we meant an adult. But Eloise is . . ." he trails off.

"She's good at helping me find the words for things that are hard to say. And . . ."

And I miss her.

And I know if you tell her that she's the only one I'll talk to, she'll be here. Fast.

"And I'll talk to her."

"OK, then," Calvin says. "It's a start at least."

"Thanks," I say.

We're quiet for a moment and then he does another good Calvin thing and ends the conversation by changing the subject.

"So," he says. "Culinary arts. Geometric patterns. What else?"

A little voice in the back of my head tells me that I should be going down the hallway to study these things instead of talking to Calvin about them. But I also know that in about five minutes the whole kitchen is going to smell like vanilla and cinnamon, and I don't always get anyone's attention like this anymore, so before I know it, I'm talking and talking about everything I already know about botany and how I'm afraid Tallulah will take most of the subjects I want.

Mom and Gladys come into the kitchen, Mom rubbing Gladys's bald head where it rests on her shoulder.

Part of me wants to reach out. To ask to hold her. Or to ask Calvin to hold her so that Mom can hug me again.

"Isn't this a nice scene?" Mom says.

I see it from above. A family gathered in a kitchen during a rainstorm. A baby on the mom's shoulder while the dad and the kid chat over a bowl of waiting-to-be rolled out cookie dough.

But that's not right. Calvin's not my dad. And Gladys is once again where I want to be.

"I have to study," I say.

I walk past Mom and Gladys and out of the kitchen. The warm vanilla and cinnamon smell is just starting.

{ 6 }

As soon as I get back to my room, Tallulah texts.

Tallulah: Hace sol. Debería ir a tu casa?

In Spanish, that means, *It's sunny. Should I come to your place?* But in code that means, *It's raining. Should you come to my place?*

Me: Indubitably

We can't study in the garden when it's raining, and it's not like my house is an option.

The kitchen is empty when I walk through to grab my rain boots and umbrella. The snickerdoodles are cooling on the counter. I send a quick text to tell Mom and Calvin about where I'm going, and take a step toward the cookies, but then I change my mind. They don't even smell good anymore.

I arrive at Tallulah's house soaked and freezing, but I feel better the minute I step inside. Her mom wraps me in a big towel and Tallulah runs off to grab me some dry clothes. A few minutes later, we're sitting together on her plush gold carpet wearing fuzzy sweatpants and long-sleeved T-shirts, listening to the rain pound on the windows as we each set up our computers and notes. Everything feels the way it's supposed to.

"Look!" Tallulah says. She spins her laptop toward me to show me her new screensaver: an aerial view photo of the University of North Bend in Indiana. "I've been waiting my whole life for this summer."

It unspools before me: six straight weeks of living in a college dorm, taking challenging classes, meeting other gifted kids, sleeping on a top bunk with Tallulah underneath me, staying up late reading and studying until my eyes hurt. And doing all that, every single bit of it, in quiet. I wanted to go to this program long before I knew how loud and inconvenient baby sisters are. But now I don't just want to go. I *need* to go.

"OK, let's see what we got," Tallulah says, rummaging through a notebook, then discarding it for a handful of scrap paper a foot away.

While I have neatly stacked color-coded index cards spread out all around my area of the rug, the rest of the floor is littered with Tallulah's lopsided piles of half filled-in notebooks and scribbled-upon textbooks, each stuffed with various bookmark alternatives: ribbons, pencils, pen caps, scraps of paper, tissues, what looks like an old shoelace. Her computer buzzes on her lap as she grabs notebook after notebook, opens it, moves around the various off-label bookmarks, and then discards it for the next one.

"I have it somewhere," she says. She stands and walks right on top of her notebooks and loose scraps of paper to get to her desk.

"Mine's here," I say.

I glance down at my loose-leaf. I'm a little embarrassed. I know I did it wrong.

PIPER	TALLULAH	TBD
*Geometric Patterns	*Afr. Am. Poetry	*Botany
	*Music Theory	*Earth Science
*Endocrinology	*Chinese Dynasties	*Female and Nonbinary Athletes
	*Self-Expression	*Culinary Arts

"Aha!" Tallulah says.

I don't know how she ever manages to study with how much time she spends looking for the things she has to study.

Tallulah sits across from me, holding a tiny piece of scrap paper, so small it doesn't even cover the palm of her hand.

"Let's trade on three, OK?"

"OK."

"And remember, no getting upset. If we disagree, we'll talk it out. No hard feelings allowed." She's doing that excited talking thing where her words come too fast for me to answer, so I just nod. "Like, maybe, say you took music theory even though you'd know I'd want that one and—"

I'm shaking my head.

"I know you're not going to take music theory." She chuckles. "I've been playing the violin since I was a baby, practically, and you don't even read music."

I nod.

"It's just an example. . . . Let's remember what Ms. Gates said about splitting specialties: it's better to be careful than to be fast. For the rest of the decathlon, we have to be both, but right now we should be slow and careful, not get upset, listen to each other. Because we're going to be a team for a whole school year, and it won't be fun if we're mad."

I have a feeling I'm about to be mad.

"And roommates for a whole summer!" I chirp.

Tallulah squeals. "Ready?" she says, flattening her scrap paper against her chest.

I nod. "Ready."

"One. Two. Three!"

I thrust my loose-leaf toward her and take her tiny scrap paper. It's so small, her writing is minuscule and almost impossible to read. I hold it close to my face and squint.

Tallulah: botany, music theory, Chinese dynasties, earth sciences, culinary arts
Piper: geometric patterns, endocrinology, female and nonbinary athletes, self-expression, Afr. Am. poetry

My eyes go wide.

This isn't right. She's taking both sciences? She wants me

to take self-expression? And poetry? Tallulah reads poetry for fun. Any poetry I know is because Tallulah has recited it to me.

I'm searching for right-side words when she blurts, "Nope. No. You're doing self-expression."

I put Tallulah's tiny paper down and grab my loose-leaf out of her hands. "You're the creative one. You need to do it. And you love poetry."

"I don't love self-expression," Tallulah says. "Whatever that is."

"Yes, you do! You're always talking."

As soon as I say it, I realize I shouldn't have.

Her shoulders slump and her face falls. "Just because I can't stop talking doesn't mean that I love it."

"You know what I meant," I say, softly. I nudge her foot with mine. We're both wearing her fuzzy purple socks. I feel worse for hurting her feelings when she's made my feet so comfy. Even if her scrap of paper did hurt my feelings, too. "I love all your talking."

"You and no one else," she says.

"What? Tallulah that's not—"

"Besides, what would I even express?"

"Yourself!" I hear the desperation lacing the edge of my voice.

Tallulah took all the things she loved and then assigned me the leftovers. If I'm going to deal with that, we at least have to win. And there's no way we win if I'm in the creative specialty.

"I love words but only if other people write them," Tallulah is arguing. "I read poetry; I don't write poetry. I study music; I don't compose. I watch basketball; I don't play. You at least have something to say. You at least have original work."

"Original work? What?" I'm losing the battle to control my voice, my volume, my brain columns. We're supposed to be careful not to get mad, but it feels like we're fighting.

Tallulah looks at me like I've lost my marbles. "Metaphorical math."

I raise my eyebrows. "Huh?"

Tallulah is suddenly standing, her hands flying everywhere, her feet going back and forth on the gold carpet as she talks.

"Wait . . . you didn't even think of that, Piper? It's perfect."

"What's perfect?"

"You! You have a totally new way to talk about the human condition. You have a totally new mathematical system. No one's ever done that in the history of the world."

"Well, Sir Isaac Newton—"

"That's my point," Tallulah says. "If you're similar to Sir Isaac Newton in any way, we need to show that part of you to the judges. Metaphorical math—your life's work—could be why we win."

It's not as though that thought doesn't thrill me. It sends a quick set of goose bumps down my spine, but they disappear after a nanosecond.

Anything that could be why we win, could also be why we lose. And my mom—the only professional mathematician we actually know—hates metaphorical math. What if the judges also say that metaphorical numbers can't exist? What if they also think it's nonsense? What if they laugh at me?

I'd lose the competition and my life's work all at once.

"You know you have to do this," Tallulah says. "Nothing is more important than the decathlon."

Except metaphorical math.

I shake my head. "It's not . . . ready. I'm not finished."

"Duh, Ma'am Piper Franklin. It's your life's work and you're only eleven. Just use what you do have."

~~No.~~

I don't say anything. After a silent minute, she grabs my loose-leaf back from me and shakes it out.

"OK, whatever. Let's talk about the rest. You really only want geometric patterns and endocrinology?"

I bite my lip. "I want geometric patterns."

But not endocrinology.

Tallulah nods. "Right. And if you're neutral on all of these"—she points to the TBD column—"we only have two differences. We only need to figure out self-expression and poetry."

I raise my eyebrows. I didn't mean I was *neutral* on all those subjects when I put them under the TBD column. But I did it wrong, and Ms. Gates wants this all worked out by Monday, so it's probably too late now.

"OK," I say. "Let's talk about poetry."

"Piper?" Tallulah says. "You look sad."

I shrug.

"Wait, did I make you sad?" she asks.

That's an impossible question. Yes, I'm sad. Yes, she made me sad. But telling her that isn't nice.

"You can't sit there saying *OK* while being sad. We have to get this right. We're going to be working on it for, like, all of seventh grade. You can't just . . . be sad. For all of seventh grade."

"I'm . . . never mind." I don't have any right-side words.

"No." Tallulah leans closer to me, and I know she's about to make the same kind of convincing argument, this time about how I have to take poetry. Instead, she says, "Stop it."

I glance up, surprised. "Stop what?"

"Stop this . . . this thing you always do," she waves her arms around like I'm supposed to understand what she means.

I stare.

"This niceness thing or whatever."

"What? Don't be nice?"

Tallulah dives back to sitting, accidentally knocking around notebooks so that a pen cap and a few scrap papers go flying. "No. We don't have time."

"Being nice is a waste of time?"

"Yes. Or no. I don't know if it's a waste of time, but it is stupid."

"Being nice is stupid?" Now I'm shocked.

"No, of course not. Just . . . blah! I mean . . . it's me. Tallulah. Your best friend. So, just be *honest*." Tallulah holds up my chart. "Is this actually how you want to split the subjects?"

My face is hot. I shake my head.

"I knew it!" Tallulah says triumphantly. She pushes my loose-leaf back at me. "Do it over."

"What?"

"Fill in a new chart. Take everything you want."

I stare at her. "But you said you also want earth—"

"Stop!" She interrupts. "Don't worry about what I want. Just take everything you want and then give me the rest."

"Really?"

Tallulah breathes out audibly like I'm frustrating her, but I don't mean to. I really don't understand. "I know your mom tells you to be nice all the time or whatever, and I'm not saying not to listen to your mom. I'm not saying *be rude* or *be mean*. I'm not saying be niceness's opposite, whatever it is. I'm just saying, whenever I hear Anna say that stuff, I try to figure out what she means, and I never can. It's like that word—*nice*—doesn't have a real meaning."

"It doesn't," I say. I think I mean for it to be a question, but it comes out like a statement. My brain is rushing, sprinting to keep up with Tallulah, but I think she's right. I think part of what's so hard about being nice is that it sounds simple, but it's actually confusing.

Tallulah nods. "And maybe sometimes you work so hard on figuring out how to be nice, we can't get anything else done."

"Whoa," I whisper. I've never, ever thought about it like that.

"Plus," Tallulah says. "You're with me. We're best friends. We trust each other. We shouldn't have to think about being nice to each other. We should just know that we'll never be mean. I trust you enough to drop the nice stuff when I'm with you. Is that OK?"

"Yeah," I say. "Of course, it is."

Tallulah's smiling. I'm smiling, too. Maybe this isn't a fight.

"So just . . . just do it over. And instead of being nice, be selfish. Be honest."

I nod.

I make a new chart, and before even touching Tallulah's column, I fill in everything I want. I give her the leftovers.

It looks very different.

PIPER	TALLULAH
Botany	Afr. Am. Poetry
Geometric Patterns	Music Theory
Earth Sciences	Endocrinology
Culinary Arts	Self-Expression
Female and Nonbinary Athletes	Chinese Dynasties

"Yes!" Tallulah says, when I hand the paper back to her.

"You . . . you're OK with this?" I ask. It's the way I'd be most happy, but it's not even what I think we should do because it's not the way we're most likely to win.

She laughs. "No. But now that I understand what you want, we can figure it out."

"But—"

"But what?"

But I have to be nice all the time. Even with you.

Those are the rules.

I shrug. "But I know about endocrinology, and you don't."

Tallulah laughs. "Well, yeah. You're still going to have to take that one. Why do you know so much about it anyway?"

I swallow.

Honest. Selfish.

I can't be both right now because I selfishly don't want to say the honest thing.

"I don't *love* endocrinology. I'm not interested in it. I know about it, like, by accident."

"You aren't interested?" Tallulah asks in disbelief.

I shake my head.

"Really? Wow. When I googled the word last night, I ended up reading about it for hours. I used to think that hormones were just about like periods and boobs and stuff, but actually they're about everything. Like there's a hormone secreted by the adrenal glands . . . you know, the ones right by your kidneys?"

I nod. Of course, I know.

"Anyway, there's this one hormone that floods your body when it senses sunlight. And that's why it's easier to wake up in the morning, no matter how much sleep you got. After I learned about that, I slept with my shades open last night, and, sure enough, I woke up gradually and naturally right with the sun thanks to . . . what's that one called again?"

"Cortisol," I say.

"Jeez," she says. "And you know this by accident?"

I nod. My cheeks are hot. I feel a little ashamed for some weird reason.

"I don't think I've ever known anything by accident. But it makes sense. Gladys."

"What?" I say, surprised.

"When your mom was pregnant and you had to go to all of those appointments with her, you must have learned a lot about endocrinology because there are a lot of hormones involved in pregnancy. Right?"

"Oh, yeah. Exactly," I say.

I don't say: Also, I have my own endocrinologist.

"OK, you definitely need to take that one, sorry."

"I know," I say.

She grabs a notebook from the floor and rips a piece of paper out. It tears in the middle, but she starts writing on it anyway, leaning on one of my blue index cards for support, even though it doesn't give her nearly enough actual support and her pencil goes right through to the carpet on the third word.

"So, here's what we agree on," she says, and holds up her new chart in her teeny-tiny writing.

Piper: Geometric patterns, endocrinology
Tallulah: Music theory, Chinese dynasties

I nod.

"But I want both of mine," she says. "So this looks even, but it's not."

I almost do a double take. The thing my brain has been whining about just came out of Tallulah's mouth.

"Why don't you want poetry?" I ask.

Tallulah sighs and puts down her pencil. "I wish it was just poetry. But it's African American poetry."

I lower my eyebrows.

"Doesn't . . . isn't African American the same as . . . I mean . . . aren't *you* African American?"

"Yes, exactly," she says. "I mean, I prefer Black. But yes. Both terms work for me."

I wait but she doesn't say anything else, so I have to ask. "Exactly?"

"OK, I'll try to explain. But . . . you're white. You might not get it," Tallulah says.

Before I can help it, my eyebrows jump, and my cheeks are hot. I'm not used to being called *white* like that even though Tallulah calls herself *Black* all the time. It feels uncomfortable, even though I know it shouldn't. And being uncomfortable when I know I shouldn't be makes me even more uncomfortable.

I just say, "OK."

Tallulah looks out the window. "Do you know how many Black kids were in finals last year?"

I nod. "None."

I remember watching the live stream of finals on Tallulah's iPad. It was four white boys. I remember thinking about how they were all boys, but it's kind of messed up that this is the first time I'm thinking about how they were also all white.

"Right. And do you know how many Black kids were in regionals? Ours, I mean. North regionals. I know there were a lot more in south regionals."

"Um, not a lot?" I say.

"Five," Tallulah says. "Five out of, like, two hundred kids."

"Oh," I say.

I can see how that isn't fair, but I don't understand how that relates to her studying poetry. It's like Tallulah can see a link I don't. It's like I'm Mom in the conversation we just had about the Wordless Chain. I decide to say to Tallulah what I wish Mom had said to me.

"I feel a little ignorant . . . I can see how that's unfair but . . . how does it connect to you and the poetry specialty?"

"Because . . . Look. Yes. I know about poetry. And it would be no big deal to compete at it in level one. But imagine if it doesn't get called until we're at counties or regionals. And what if we're in a big auditorium, and I'm the only Black kid there?"

I do imagine it. The picture immediately invades my head, making me cold all over.

"But, Tallulah," I say, softly. "That might happen . . . no matter which specialty."

"I know that!" she says. "I'm the only Black girl in TGASP every day."

"Right."

My cheeks burn as my memory skims through all the faces of the kids in TGASP. Out of thirty kids, three are Black: Jack, Tallulah, and one fifth-grade boy. There are other kids of color: Caroline is Korean, Josie is Puerto Rican, and George is Chinese and Mexican. But most of the club is white. Most of our school is white.

"I'm the only Black kid a lot of the time in this town. I'm used to that part. But if I'm the only Black kid in the room and then I get called up to compete in African American poetry . . . What if I don't know something? What if I freeze? What if there's one question I can't answer, and everyone is looking at me, and then some white kid gets it right? If that happens . . . if we lose in that way . . . I'm not just letting you down. I'm letting down my entire race. Or at least, that's how it feels to me. There's already pressure to represent Black kids well basically everywhere I go, but if I'm the only Black kid answering questions about African American poetry on a huge stage like that . . . I know I just said nothing's more important than the decathlon but . . ."

"But some things are," I finish.

She nods. I pat her shoulder.

I'm feeling weirdly good. Important. I'm feeling some new level of closeness with Tallulah that I didn't even realize was possible. We've talked about race before, of course, because Tallulah and I talk about everything, but we talk about it, like, because of history or the news. Not . . . personally. Tallulah trusted me to listen and do my best to understand something that we both know I'll never totally understand. I never knew Tallulah felt pressure like that, pressure to represent a huge group of people, everywhere she goes. I've never had to think about it. Now I'll never be able to *not* think about it. I've never felt pressure like that, but Tallulah shared it with me anyway. She was honest with me, even when I couldn't give her the honest reason why I didn't want to do endocrinology. "OK," I say. "I'll study poetry. It's interesting anyway."

Tallulah breathes out with relief. "I'll help you," she says.

She writes poetry next to my name on her paper.

"Wait, but now you have two things you don't want. That's not good," she says.

A light bulb flashes in my brain.

"It's OK! I'll just also take the two things I really want. And you can still have Chinese dynasties and music theory."

"Really?" Tallulah asks. "You mean this feels OK if you get the two other sciences?"

"Sure," I say.

She starts to fill them in. My section looks way better.

Piper: geometric patterns, endocrinology, poetry, earth sciences, botany

"Wow," Tallulah says, as fills in the subjects next to her name. "I can't believe we're almost done with—wait. No. No, Piper, you need to do self-expression."

"I can't. I already have five."

"I'll take botany. We know an equal amount about plants."

"No," I say.

"I'll take endocrinology, then."

"No!" That's just bonkers. I mean, we have to win.

"Why can't you just talk about metaphorical math, Piper? It's perfect."

I pause. "You said to be honest, right?"

"Yes," Tallulah says.

"Because I don't know how to say this nicely."

"Who cares," she says.

"I'm not doing the creative one. You need to do it."

Tallulah looks down at the paper in her hands, then looks back up at me. It looks like she may cry behind her smudged glasses.

"Oh my god," I say. "What's wrong?"

She blinks a lot so that the tears don't fall. "I'm sorry, Piper. I'm sorry but . . . I can't. I don't . . . I don't know how and . . . we'll lose."

I'm so surprised she feels this way, my jaw drops.

"That's exactly how I feel," I say. "If I do it, we'll lose. And I can't talk about metaphorical math because I don't think it would win, and if it didn't . . . I can't lose the decathlon and metaphorical math at the same time."

"Yeah," she says. "OK. That's your thing that's more important than winning."

"Right."

We freeze, and for a second, it feels like our dream is dying.

"All right," Tallulah says, wiping her eyes and sniffling. She wiggles her whole body for half a second, like she's literally shaking it off. "I have an idea. Technically, we don't need to know all of this in order to fill out the entry form, right? Ms. Gates told us to divide up the specialties, but it's not like the decathlon requires it."

"Yeah?" I say.

"So, what if we do this?"

She hands me a new piece of scrap paper.

Piper: geometric patterns, endocrinology, earth sciences, poetry, botany, self-expression
Tallulah: music theory, culinary arts, female and nonbinary athletes, Chinese dynasties, botany, self-expression

"We'll both prepare for self-expression, we'll present it to Ms. Gates, and we'll let her tell us who should take it. The other person will do botany."

"Oh," I say, nodding slowly. "Yeah. That's a good idea."

Ms. Gates will choose Tallulah. I know that. Even if Tallulah doesn't love talking, she's a lot better at it than I am.

"Agreed?" Tallulah says, holding out a hand.

"Agreed," I say, shaking. We both giggle.

"We're done!" Tallulah leaps up.

My feelings have been so up and down today I almost can't

find them anymore, but when Tallulah pulls me onto her bed and starts jumping, excitement rushes back through me. This time it's real and pure. This time it finally feels like it's supposed to.

"Piper," Tallulah says. "Now the fun part starts."

"What's the fun part?" I ask, spinning to face her.

She belly flops onto her bed, rolls to her side, reaches down to grab her computer, and then rolls back onto the bed.

"Now," she says. "We study."

And that's what we do, in her cozy, dry bedroom, for the rest of the day.

METAPHORICAL MATH

THE GOLDEN RATIO

THE GOLDEN RATIO is a geometrical equation
that makes things pleasing to the eye. It's somehow
responsible for things like the curve of a snail shell
and the Greek pyramids.

✦ EQUATION FOR THE GOLDEN RATIO ✦

$$\varphi = \frac{(1 + \sqrt{5})}{2}$$

(NOTE TO MA'AM PIPER FRANKLIN: add an
explanation of how to understand this equation
once you learn about it in college or whenever you
figure it out. What even makes it a ratio instead of
just an equation? Add that once you know it, too.)

In **REGULAR MATH**, basically, the Golden Ratio is
the ultimate harmonious relationship between two
LINES.

In **METAPHORICAL MATH**: The Golden Ratio can be found between two PEOPLE when

A. their differences make them closer instead of tearing them apart;

B. disagreements make each person like themselves MORE instead of feeling shame; and

C. the addition of others makes them closer rather than threatening their bond.

THAT is a metaphorical Golden Ratio!

Examples:

1. mom and Calvin
2. me and Tallulah

{ 7 }

Tallulah and I spend so long sprawled out on her carpet in silent concentration that when her mom knocks on the door, I'm shocked to see that it's dark outside. It's a lot easier to lose yourself to an afternoon of studying when you're in a quiet house.

"Dinner in five," her mom says. "Piper, I checked with your parents, and they say you're welcome to join us. Your mom will pick you up after."

"Great," I say. "Thank you, Joy."

"Of course." Then Joy shakes her head. "Really, Tallulah. This room," she says from the doorway.

"I have to study, Mom," Tallulah says. "I don't have time to clean."

Her mom bends over and gathers a few balled-up pieces of paper, then turns toward the trash can. "Don't you think it may be a little easier to study in a clean room?"

"What?" Tallulah looks at me with her eyebrows high over her purple frames. Like her mom just said something ridiculous.

I don't want to laugh because I don't want to make either of them feel bad. Deep down I agree with her mom. It's way easier to study in a clean room. But that's for me, not Tallulah. Tallulah wouldn't even know if it's easier to study in a clean room. I doubt she's ever even tried it.

I roll onto my back and check my phone. I have two missed text messages.

Joy puts another paper in the trash and Tallulah says, "Mom! I need that one."

"Oh," her mom says, bending down and retrieving the teeny scrap where Tallulah has taken notes on something. "Sorry. I'll get out of your way. Keep studying."

When she closes the door, I read my texts. The first is from Ivan. It's a screenshot of his birthday party invite. It's on Saturday at a laser tag place in Manhattan. My heart squeezes a little extra tight for a few beats when I think about missing it.

Ivan: Just in case your mom changes her mind . . .

I text back. **I wish!**

If it weren't for stupid Gladys, I bet I could go. Mom and Calvin would drive me and wander around Manhattan for the afternoon while I went to the party. Somehow one little baby took me from two available parents to zero.

Ivan texts a gif of a cartoon duck crying.

Ivan: Too bad

Ivan: Was hoping you'd vouch for me to the rest of the HHH-ers.

Me: Vouch for you?

Ivan: You know, tell them my gf is real. Haha.

My heart skips. I'm the only HHH friend he invited? That means I'm officially his best HHH friend, and he's mine. We're getting closer. I want to go to his party. I want him to be an actual friend, not just an HHH friend.

Me: I'll try to talk to my mom again.

I won't though. I know it's useless. But at least that shows I want to be real friends, too.

My other missed text is from Daisy. It's a picture of a million books and note cards all lined up perfectly. Proof that she also spent all day studying.

Daisy: It's not too late! We can still be partners.

I don't answer her. I can't. There's nothing nice to say. I look around Tallulah's room with all its messes and piles and creatively discovered bookmarks and I smile. There's nowhere I'd rather be.

"Girls, dinner!"

Suddenly, I'm starving. My hand is cramping from taking so many notes, and my arms are aching from propping me up in front of my computer for hours. The idea that my mom is going to pick me up and walk me home from Tallulah's sounds so deliciously normal. I'm happy.

But thirty minutes later, once my stomach is warm and full

of pizza, the doorbell rings and it's not Mom. It's Calvin, with a plate of snickerdoodles.

Joy and Edward ask him to come in for a minute, and he sits at the table with us. We listen to the adults talk while we dunk cookies in big glasses of milk.

The disappointment fades a little. This is still almost deliciously normal. Without Gladys screaming and Mom constantly rushing around mumbling about sleep schedules and diaper changes, there's room in my brain. Even Tallulah is quiet in a way she only gets after hours and hours of deep study.

Calvin makes a joke I don't understand, Tallulah's mom and dad laugh, and my insides grow even warmer.

After a few cookies, we leave. It's not raining anymore, and there's never any traffic here at night, so we stroll down the middle of the wet road, side by side. Calvin is whistling.

"Is Eloise home?" I ask him.

He stops whistling. "No. She's staying with her mom tonight. But she said she'll be by soon."

I bite the inside of my lips to stop my loneliness from leaking out my eyes. *She'll be by soon.* It sounds like she's coming for a visit, like she doesn't even live with me anymore.

I know what it's like to miss your mom. I know I should be happy for Eloise. But I thought once Calvin talked to her, she'd come to me right away.

When we get home, I go to my room, unload my backpack, and check off everything I got done today. I have notes on every subject. I've requested a bunch of books from the library.

I have articles on Paul Laurence Dunbar and Maya Angelou and tectonic plate activity bookmarked on my phone. These specialties are what should be on my mind. Ms. Gates said winning takes dedication, creative problem-solving, and strategizing. It takes finding ways to keep all the information at the front of your brain, even as it fills up with more and more.

But I can only focus on today's biggest revelation: when I stopped trying to be nice, things got easier. If I ever get to talk to Eloise, I need do it Tallulah's way: honesty over niceness.

I pull out a new orange index card. I need to find words for the Wordless Chain. Eloise isn't going to understand the metaphor.

Put down the best, most honest words even if they're not perfect, I tell myself.

Disjointed images flood my mind again: the way, when my mom was pregnant, people touched her stomach without asking; the way, one day, some men outside Dr. Grand's office whistled at a woman on the sidewalk who was not even looking at them, who was just listening to her headphones; the way the lines for the ladies rooms in public places are always so much longer, but I once glanced inside an empty men's room, and I swear it was bigger.

I still don't write anything down. I'm trying not to care if my words aren't nice, but I can't make the pencil move. After a lifetime of trying to be nice, it's impossible to be honest right now, even when I only want to shape my feelings into words and letters.

I put on my headphones and play my favorite song. This calls for a pop girl anthem. I switch my pencil to a pen, committing these words to this index card forever. I close my eyes and tell my hand to take over. The words are bad. Awful. But they zip out of my hand and onto the orange card.

I don't want to look like you, Mom.

My eyes fly open, and I stare down at the card. It's messier than anything I've ever written. The letters are too big and some of them overlap. Mean and messy: two things I never knew I could be, even in private.

But I'm not actually being mean. The way I feel this isn't mean. These words are only mean once they get outside my head.

I flip the card so the blank side is face up, and I pin it next to the yellow one on the board. Then I take down the blue card and throw it away. Mom was right. The shots are safe. But that's not a reason to be on them. It's just an argument trying to prove Mom wrong. I have five actual reasons. That has to be enough.

I change into pajamas and crawl into bed. Before Gladys was born, Mom used to come and kiss me goodnight, but now she keeps forgetting because Gladys is always awake. I usually go find her, but tonight, I'm exhausted. My brain feels almost mushy. My bed feels so comfy.

And even though the words aren't bad inside my head, and they didn't come from a bad place, I can't face Mom after writing such not-nice words about her.

★ ★ ★

The next day, Eloise still isn't here. I'm trying to study, but I keep pausing to compose texts to her and then deleting them:

Hey, let me know if you come home.

Hey, I know we're supposed to talk soon, so come find me if you're around.

Hey, did you forget about me?

After about two hours, I give myself a study break to work on some metaphorical math, and when even that fails to hold my attention, I spread myself across my bed and watch gardening videos on YouTube. Finally, Eloise opens the bedroom door.

"Iper!" she says. She holds out her arms for a hug, but I don't go to her. I jump up off the bed and start ripping down my reason cards. I have to show them to her—all of them—before I lose my nerve.

"What's going on?"

I thrust the rainbow pile at her.

"What's this?" she asks.

I'm so nervous, I can't look her in the face. "My reasons."

"Reasons?" She takes the cards but doesn't flip them over. "For what?"

"Didn't Calvin tell you?" I ask. Suddenly my face is hot. I've been waiting to talk to her, and she didn't even know?

"He mentioned that you want to talk to me, but . . ."

Eloise trails off as she starts to read.

"Oh," she says after a few minutes. "This is about Dr. Grand?"

"Yeah," I say.

She shuffles from purple (*puberty would distract me from the decathlon*) to yellow (*none of my friends has her period yet*) to green (*I never want to have a baby anyway*).

"You want me to help you convince Anna to keep your treatment going?" Eloise asks.

"Um, yeah?"

Orange is next. The mean one. I feel like running and diving onto my bed, burying my head under my covers. Instead, I walk. I slouch onto my pillow. I try to make my body say *no big deal.*

My nerves keep me talking. "Or maybe I just want to see if you get it. If you can help me explain—"

I stop. Eloise is laughing. The orange card is in her hand, and she's laughing.

Laughing!

"I'm sorry, Ipey." She sits on the edge of my bed. "I just . . . I can see why you're finding it so hard to talk to your mom about this."

She turns the orange card so that the mean words and I face each other again.

My face is on fire.

She scoots away from me, so far that she has to flex her legs to stay on the edge of my bed. "So, you don't want to look like your mom? That's why you want to keep seeing Dr. Grand?"

"Well . . . yeah," I say.

"But she's so pretty," Eloise says.

"Oh," I say. "No. I mean, yes. She is pretty. That's not what I—"

"And I hate to tell you this, little sis, but you look like Anna already. You have the same high forehead and brown eyes and red-brown hair."

"Yeah, but . . . that's just shapes and colors."

"So . . . shapes and colors are OK?"

"Of course." I love looking like Mom in those ways.

Eloise tilts her head. "I don't get it."

"Like . . . I'm OK with looking like I match my mom. Like I'm her kid. I just don't want to look *like* her. . . ."

"OK, um . . . I'm trying to understand," Eloise says. "Is there anyone else you don't want to look like?"

~~Yes.~~

I don't say it, but Eloise must be able to read the answer on my face.

"Who else?"

~~You.~~

"It's not like that," I say. "It's not about *pretty*. It's . . . I'm just not . . . ready."

"Not ready for what?"

"To be . . . to have . . . for a body that looks like . . ."

~~Hers.~~

~~Yours.~~

"That."

"Oh!" Eloise says, like a light bulb has just switched on. "But you know puberty won't make you look exactly like her, right? I mean, even if you do eventually, you won't right away."

"I know," I say.

"Your mom is, like, forty or something. I know that they say puberty is the process of your body becoming an adult body, but a twelve-year-old adult body is a lot different than a forty-year-old adult body."

There shouldn't even be a twelve-year-old adult body.

I bite my lip to keep myself from crying again. She still doesn't get it. It's not about how my mom's body looks. It's about how people look *at* my mom's body: like she's less than . . . not as much . . . nothing. People look at Eloise the same way, and she's only seventeen.

"Have you seen the pictures of your mom in her twenties? She was beautiful then, too, but in a, you know, young way. If you do take after her, that's a good thing. Believe me."

I hug my pillow.

"It's not an insult to my mom. It's . . . no one understands. I don't think you do, either."

Eloise looks at me in a way that makes me think maybe she actually does get it. What she says is completely different, but still important. "It must be lonely, sometimes, to be so smart."

I lower my eyebrows. I didn't realize this had anything to do with being smart.

Eloise shifts to the last card, the red one.

"Wait. Iper," she says. "You can't say this." She points to my words. *If Ivan's on the shots and he's thirteen, I should be allowed to stay on them at least that long.*

116

"Huh? Why?"

I didn't say anything even kind of mean about Ivan.

"It sounds like you're jealous of him," Eloise says.

I lower my eyebrows. "I guess I am?"

"But Ivan needs the shots because he's trans," Eloise says.

"Who cares?" I burst.

"Piper!" Eloise says. My full name. She only uses that when it's serious.

"What?" I say. "I don't mean who cares that he's trans. I know all about being trans."

"No, you don't," Eloise says. "I know you're an ally, but you can't know all about being trans unless you *are* trans."

"OK, fine," I say, because Eloise almost never lectures me like this, and a lecture is the last thing I need. "But even though I'm not trans, I still need the shots, just like Ivan does."

"No," Eloise says. Her head is shaking back and forth, so fast. "No, no, no."

"I do need them. I really thought you'd be the one who believed me."

"I'm not saying you don't. I only mean it's different." She tries to say more but she keeps getting stuck after two words. "You should— Ivan isn't— Trans kids— It's not—" Finally she throws all my rainbow reasons in the air like confetti and says, "Never mind! I'll be right back."

Then she storms toward the door.

"Where are you going?"

"To talk to your mom," Eloise calls over her shoulder.

"Wait," I cry. "What are you going to say?"

She turns back around to face me. "That you need to stay on the shots, obviously," she says. It was very not obvious.

"Oh," I say, my heart slowing and my face cooling. "Now?"

"I have to leave for the dog shelter soon so, yeah. Now."

My heart falls. I'm glad I got to talk to Eloise, but if that was all the time we had, I wish I got to spend it a different way.

"Do you want to come with me?" she adds.

"To your job?" I squeal. Eloise has taken me there before, but it's been months.

She laughs. "To my—*ahem*—extremely important volunteer position of walking dogs and picking up their poop."

"Yes!" I say, not even bothering to laugh.

Eloise leaves. I post my index cards back on the corkboard, and then tiptoe after her. I stop in the kitchen to grab a glass because I've tried this old trick and it really does work. It's physics. I bring it to Mom and Calvin's bedroom door. Both of them and both my sisters are on the other side. I press the glass to the door and put my ear against it to listen. The words are clear.

"She's worried about being distracted," Eloise is saying. "You know how important the decathlon is to her."

Interesting. She's going with the purple card.

There's a *smack* sound, which I know means Mom just brought her hand to her forehead. "Why didn't I think of that?" she says.

"Of course," Calvin says slowly.

Good choice, Eloise.

They're quiet for a minute. Even Gladys doesn't make a peep. It's like they're all thinking about how much they messed up by not realizing what was going on with me. It makes me feel like I'm the star of my own life, and I almost walk away at that moment.

"Now I know how to talk to her," Mom says. "Seriously, honey, come here. Thank you."

There's a rustling sound like they're hugging.

"I think she's right, you know?" Eloise says. "Puberty is distracting. And she's been looking forward to this Academic Decathlon stuff for a long time."

"Years," Mom says with a chuckle.

"Forever," Calvin adds.

"I don't know what we'd do without you," Mom says. "Piper and me."

"And me," Calvin says.

And even though I'm on the other side of the door from all of them, I still feel warm and happy. Because Mom and Calvin and Eloise and I are a family, and I'm the one and only connecting link. They wouldn't have each other if they didn't have me. I'm right in the middle of all that love, even from the other side of the door.

"And . . . one more thing," Eloise says.

"Yes?" Mom says.

Gladys starts to fuss.

"I think Piper needs to see Ivan."

Wait, what?

"Eloise, if this is Piper's way of angling to go to that birthday party, please just tell me," Mom says.

"What party?" Eloise says. "I don't even know about a party."

"Really?" Mom sounds doubtful.

"I didn't. But if Ivan's having a party, Piper has to go."

Why is she saying this? Does this have to do with the red card? Does she think Ivan's birthday party will somehow make me un-jealous of him?

"It's all the way in Manhattan," Mom says. "This Friday."

"OK. I'll . . . I'll take her," Eloise says. "I'll take her myself."

There's total silence on the other side of the door, then Mom says, "You think it's that important?"

"Anna," Eloise says. "I really do."

Mom sighs.

"Then we'll figure it out," Calvin says. "Right?"

"Right," Mom says. "If it's that important, we'll get her to that birthday party."

I'm so shocked I almost drop the glass.

I tiptoe back into the kitchen to return it before I get caught. My smile is so big my cheeks ache.

I get to keep my shots. I get to spend today with Eloise. *And* I get to go to Ivan's birthday party.

I run back to my room to text him.

My sister is a genius.

{ 8 }

The following Friday, I'm on my way to Ivan's birthday party. Even better, I'm sitting next to my sister. In the end, Mom said no way to Eloise taking me to Manhattan by herself, so Calvin volunteered. But Eloise still wanted to go to the city. She and Bobby are going to wander around Central Park during the birthday party and post gooey videos to TikTok or whatever else teenagers do. But for now, I have my sister all to myself because the train was crowded, and we had to split up to find seats. Calvin and Bobby are a few rows behind us.

Eloise bumps her shoulder against mine. "Excited for your first teenage party?"

"Oh. Right," I say. I've been thinking about Ivan's birthday, but not about the fact that most of his friends will also be older than me. Not just chronologically older. They'll be bone-age older. Metaphorically older.

"It'll be good for you," Eloise says, laughing. "Maybe after seeing Ivan's friends, you won't be so worried puberty is going to morph you into looking like a forty-five-year-old."

So that's why she wanted me to go?

"Why can't I just go to the birthday party to have fun?" I ask.

"Oh. Of course, you can," Eloise says. "But. OK. Look, Piper. You can't be jealous of Ivan."

I face her, quick. I didn't expect her to say that.

"I can't be jealous of him? Like at all?"

She shakes her head.

"Why?" I ask.

"It's messed up, Ipey. Your red card is messed up."

Guess I'm messed up.

I'm jealous of Ivan for a million reasons, not just because of the shots. I'm jealous of how comfortable he is talking about himself, how easily he makes friends, how he gets to live in New York City and take the subway around without needing adults to drive him everywhere.

"This medicine," Eloise says, slowly. "It's a good thing because it means he doesn't have to . . . to look like someone he's not. And because you needed it when you were younger."

I still do.

"But it's different for you. You can stop whenever you want."

And OK, yeah. Even if it's messed up, I'm jealous of Ivan for this, too. For the fact that he doesn't have to constantly have these conversations just to keep the medicine that's saving us both. I get that it's saving him. No one seems to get that it's saving me, too.

Eloise continues, "Plus, when you do stop puberty blockers, whenever that is, it'll be a lot simpler for you than it will be for him."

"Simple?" I challenge. Does she forget how two weeks ago she was taking both Tylenol and Advil just to get through day one of her period?

"Yes, simple. For Ivan, the medicine hit this big pause button and—"

"And that's exactly what I want," I say.

"No," Eloise shakes her head. "I know you think you aren't ready to give up the shots yet and that's OK, but . . . but look at me, Ipey."

She gestures to her whole body, which is the body of someone unknowingly wrapped in the Wordless Chain. A body I don't want to have.

"Look at my life! It's so exciting. I have a job, and I have a driver's license, and, Iper, I have a whole awesome boyfriend who's crazy about me. My life is so . . . so . . ."

Busy?

Exhausting?

Painful?

"Happy! I want that for you one day, Iper. And even though I don't know him, I want that for Ivan, too. And yes, he *can* have this kind of life, but it'll be a lot less complicated for you to move on to the next step when you're ready. That's why you can't be jealous of him."

She's wrong. Even if a job and a car and an awesome boy-friend would make me happy—and they wouldn't—I don't want any happy things that come attached to the Wordless Chain.

"You're still jealous?" Eloise asks.

I shrug.

"That's messed up, Ipey."

Now my face is burning. Eloise has never called me *messed up* before. She's never used anything close to a left-side word about me before.

I turn away because I don't have anything nice to say. I thought Eloise was on my side, but no. She has an agenda—the same agenda as my mom. She's just like everyone else. She's trying to trick me into growing up.

My phone buzzes. I turn it over thinking it'll be Ivan or Tallulah, but it's Daisy.

Daisy: Wanna hear a joke?

Me: Sure.

Daisy: Knock knock.

Me: Who's there?

Daisy: Baby Yoda.

I smile. This seems like a normal corny joke from my proud cornball of a second-best friend, and not silly question about crushes.

Me: Baby Yoda who?

Daisy: Baby, Yoda teammate for me!

My heart falls. Another trick. I already have so many things on my mind between my shots and Ivan's party and the decathlon. I get that it's technically Daisy's decathlon, too, but Tallulah and I have been planning and preparing for this for years. It feels like Daisy is intruding. It feels like she's making something complicated that doesn't have to be.

When I don't reply, she texts again.

Daisy: I just really want to work with you. Have you made up your mind?

Yes!

I made it up years ago.

~~There's zero chance of me choosing you.~~

I can't think of a way to let her down nicely. And I especially have to be nice on text message. My mom reads all my texts.

Me: Not yet. Sorry.

Daisy: So, you're saying there's a chance!

She texts me a string of emojis, and I silence my phone and put it in my pocket.

I lean my head on the window and pretend to sleep, wasting thirty precious minutes of big-sister time. I don't want it anymore. I don't want to go to this party at all if it's part of some master scheme.

When we reach Penn Station, we find Bobby and Calvin and regroup. Eloise and Bobby take one subway toward Central Park; Calvin and I take a different one toward Ivan's party uptown. It's at huge arcade kind of place with lots of kids from toddler through teen running in every direction. I have no idea how I'll find Ivan.

"I'm coming in with you," Calvin says at the entrance, as if he's declaring a law. I lower my eyebrows. What else would he do, leave me here alone?

But when we find Ivan playing Skee Ball with a group of kids at the back of the arcade, I realize that I'm definitely the only party guest who has a parent here.

I've never felt so weird about being eleven.

Ivan spots me. "Piper!" he calls. "You made it."

He runs over and gives me a high five.

"Hi," I say.

"Happy birthday, Ivan," Calvin says.

"Oh, yeah. Happy birthday," I say.

It's weird I didn't say it right away, but it's hard to even hear myself think in here. There are so many lights and so many loud noises and so many people running in every direction. And I thought I was here for fun, but apparently now I'm here for a Life Lesson or something.

A man who must be Ivan's dad because he looks exactly like a taller, bigger, broader Ivan with a beard walks up to Calvin, and they shake hands.

"Come on," Ivan says. "I want you to meet everyone."

Ivan's fingers wrap around my wrist, and something magical happens. All the bitterness I felt on the train escapes my body at that exact spot. Who cares if Eloise has some sort of hidden agenda? I'm at a *teenager's* birthday party in *New York City* with a bunch of older kids. I'm the only HHH person even invited.

I'm . . . cool.

For today, I'm cool. And no one can ruin that. Not even Eloise.

Ivan leans into me so his whispered words tickle my ear. "My dad doesn't know I have a girlfriend, so don't tell him, OK?"

"OK," I say. Ivan's wearing something weird. He smells like a mixture of El Jardín Muerto and way too much soap.

He pulls me to the left-most Skee Ball machine where a girl who's several inches taller than both of us is swinging a blond ponytail out of her face and lining up her shot.

It's a little quieter in this Skee Ball corner. Kids who look about the age and size of the blond girl are crowded around three other machines. The boys are wearing basketball jerseys or sports-themed T-shirts. The girls wear high-waisted jeans, crop tops, and makeup. I look down at my gray leggings, orange T-shirt, and knock-off Converse.

Funny how I don't exactly feel cool. I feel young.

"This is Natalie," Ivan says, sounding almost like Mom does when she introduces Gladys to anyone. "My girlfriend."

The blond girl turns around. She's pretty. Her eyes are dark blue, almost purple. Her smile is wide, revealing clear, barely there braces. Freckles sprinkle across her forehead. She's not wearing as much makeup as some of the other girls, but she looks older than me. Than us. Me and Ivan.

"Oh, is this Pipe?" she asks.

"Pip*erl*" Ivan corrects her. Her face turns pink, and she giggles. He pinches her side.

Something deep inside me pinches as well. My side, right above my left hip, starts to tingle. Like it wants Ivan to pinch it. Or like, it could want Ivan to pinch it. Like one day, not too far away, it will want Ivan to pinch it.

Blech!

"You're Ivan's friend from that H group, right?" Natalie says. She looks at me so closely it's like she wants to know everything there is to know about me. She's like Eloise that way.

"Yeah," I say.

She leans in even closer like she's going to say something sneaky, but in a playful way that Ivan can easily overhear. "What's he like in there?"

"Nat!" Ivan says, bumping her shoulder. "I told you about con—"

"I know, I know," Natalie says with a dramatic eye roll. She puts her hands on her hips then moves them around like she's using pom-poms as she says, "C! O! N! F! I! D! E! N! T! I! A! L! I! T! Y! What's that spell? Confidentiality!"

Ivan is laughing. I wish I could make him laugh like that.

"Exactly," he says. Then he turns to me. "Everyone's always telling Natalie that she should be a cheerleader, so she pretends to be one in the worst moments."

"You aren't?" I ask her. She looks like a cheerleader.

"No," Natalie says, tossing her hair in performative pettiness. "I have my own personal cheerleaders."

Huh?

Ivan is laughing again. "Nat!"

It's like they have their own language that's at once secret and welcoming. As soon as an inside joke appears, they open the door and let me in to it, too.

"I'm on the basketball team," Natalie says.

"Oh!" I say, laughing along with them.

Ivan squeezes her hip again. Mine tingles again.

"I might be short, but it's true," Natalie singsongs.

Ivan looks at me, fast. For a second it's awkward. If Natalie is short, Ivan and I are tiny.

The awkwardness ends when a perky voice suddenly calls, "OK, gather up, friends of Ivan." A woman with a sleek brown ponytail and light brown skin appears in the middle of the Skee Ball crowd. "I need you all to cheer his name!"

Ivan's friends turn around to look at him. Because he's standing next to me, it feels like there's suddenly a bunch of thirteen-year-olds looking at me. A few mumble his name.

"Come on, now," the perky lady says. "Louder! This is your chance to embarrass him. That's what birthdays are for, right?"

Now his friends scream his name. I join in. Ivan puts his hands up to cover his embarrassed smile and we all scream louder. I haven't had fun like this in forever.

"OK, Birthday Boy," the lady says in an overly babyish tone that makes us laugh again. "You and your friends should follow me for laser tag."

Natalie comes up beside me and says, "You're on my team,

Pipe. I know that's not your name but it's what I'm going to call you. Come on!"

I pretty much forget everything Eloise said about me being *messed up* until the party is over and Ivan's dad invites Calvin and me to their apartment for supper. Calvin stays in the kitchen, but I go to Ivan's bedroom with a few of his other best friends—Natalie, Richie, Curt, and Cheryl. The other kids drape themselves on his desk chair and across the navy sheets and gray comforter of his unmade bed. Ivan sits backward in a folding chair. Natalie scoots over to make room for me on the bed.

This should feel awesome because I'm with Ivan and his *other* best friends. As in, I'm one of his best friends, too, now. And that does feel awesome.

But I also feel weird. I don't usually sit on my friend's beds, unless they're Tallulah-level close. Of course, that's only because life, and bedrooms, and furniture, is different in the suburbs.

I sit on the side of his bed Eloise-style: gingerly, my thighs flexed to keep me from falling.

Natalie and I watch the other kids set up consoles and video game controllers.

Ivan stands to shout playfully at Richie, who's several inches taller, his shoulders broader, his voice deeper. Next to them, Curt raises a hand to grab a wire from a top shelf, and I see armpit hair poke out the sleeve of his T-shirt. Cheryl smacks

Richie in the chest and a sliver of bra strap peeks out from under her sweater. Richie strokes his chin like he's got a beard, and, I realize, he might. Or he might soon.

Ivan's friends are growing up. They look thirteen. But Ivan looks . . . like me. Well, not really because I'm a girl and he's a boy, and because I have auburn hair in a messy bun and he has cornrows, and because I'm white and he's Black.

But he looks eleven, like me. No one would ever guess he's their age and not mine.

The medicine hit Ivan's pause button. It's almost like when I was six: he's chronologically thirteen, intellectually thirteen, but his bone age is eleven. It doesn't match.

But unlike me, Ivan has no options. He doesn't have the choice to stop the medicine and have his body grow like the bodies of the boys around him. His next step is going to involve more doctors, more medicine. This is what Eloise wanted me to notice.

Beside me, Natalie groans. "I hate video games. So boring."

I chuckle, grateful for the distraction. "Me too."

I wonder what she does like. Maybe part of her also wants to hide from all the screens and hormones and dive into quadratic equations.

She flips onto her stomach and leans over the end of Ivan's bed, then pulls something out from under it. "Shh," she says. "Don't tell those hooligans, but Ivan always has a secret stash."

My heart speeds toward panic because I'm at a teenager's birthday party, and I don't know what kind of stash she's talking about. But when she shows it to me, I laugh. It's Twizzlers.

She sneaks one to me while the others are plugging in wires and controllers. We pass the candy back and forth, breaking off pieces and sneaking bites, making a game of it. Natalie bumps her shoulder against mine and, for a second, I want to be her. I want to be able to have this kind of fun all the time. I want to be like them all. I want to able to joke and shout "Bro!" at my friends. I want someone to pinch my side and for my body to respond the way a body would after puberty.

Maybe I do want to stop the shots. Maybe Eloise's plan worked.

But as soon as I think it, the thought shatters like a crystal glass hitting a marble floor.

"Bro! Why do you always have to choose the girl avatar?" Curt yells.

What's wrong with a girl avatar?

I look at the TV. On the side Ivan is controlling, a computer-generated man in a black suit is walking down a hallway like he's searching for something.

On Richie's side, the avatar is a woman, and she's not wearing a black suit. She's wearing skintight purple pants that show off a large, round butt. I've read enough medical journals to know that this body is, what some would call, *anatomically impossible*. No one's waist could be that small while her butt could be that big.

Richie whoops. "Because she's *hot!*"

My face burns as boys scream and laugh.

The avatar wears a crop top that reveals a skinny, yellow waist. We're looking at her from behind, so she has no face, no personality. She's a stack of shapes.

"Plus, I can make her do this." Richie presses buttons on his controller so that she bends over and stands up, bends over and stands up.

The boys all whoop. Even Cheryl laughs. I hold my breath and wait. I know Ivan. Ivan goes to HHH. Ivan knows this is wrong. Ivan is going to stop them.

But when I look at him, Ivan is bent over, laughing so hard he might cry.

My stomach tries to crawl from my abdomen to somewhere else in my body. My hip. My throat. Out my eye socket.

I glance at Natalie.

She rolls her eyes. "Boys."

I squeeze mine shut.

I can't be like her after all. I'll never be able to roll my eyes and shrug at these things. The things that make me feel that deep sting that says *People like you are the butt of the joke.*

Is part of being a woman pretending you don't care about all the unfair things you see? I can't do that. I can't go through puberty. I won't.

I never want to be the same thing as that avatar.

On the train home, there's plenty of space, so we're all four sitting together. It's one of those trains where the seats can flip in different directions so four people can face each other. We're playing Uno. My heart is still buzzing from how fun it was to go to Ivan's birthday party. My face is still burning from how awful it was to watch him laugh at that avatar.

I win the first round anyway.

Calvin throws his cards down on his seat in a fake show of bad sportsmanship. "That's it. I'm out of here!" he declares, then he marches to the train's bathroom.

Eloise scoops up all the Uno cards and starts shuffling.

"How was the party, Piper?" she asks. I can tell she's trying to be casual. She's trying not to sound like some adult saying *Did you learn anything?* But she used my full name, so she's not succeeding.

TBH, I did learn something. I learned that no one will ever understand me.

I shrug. "It was fun."

Her hands pause their shuffling. She raises one eyebrow at me. "Fun? That's it?"

"Yeah," I say.

I look at Bobby. I wish I could tell Eloise how it felt to watch that avatar squat, to hear all the laughter, to know that my mom and my sister and everyone wants me to turn into something like her. But I can't say that in front of Bobby.

He probably laughs at girl avatars, too. Maybe Eloise even shrugs at them.

"It's OK, Ipey. We can talk. Bobby knows all about the shots."

That definitely makes this day worse, not better.

"Fine. I won't be jealous of Ivan anymore," I say. "But it doesn't change anything."

Eloise lowers her eyebrows. "It doesn't change what?"

"I still don't want to look like—"

~~you~~.

"I still need the shots, OK?" I finish.

"Oh, Ipey, I know that."

I was all ready to start yelling at her, but my mouth snaps shut.

Eloise reaches across the seats toward me. "I'm sorry. I wasn't trying to convince you that you don't want the blockers. When it comes to the medicine, I'm completely on your side."

Some of the heat dissolves out of my face. "You are?"

"Of course," she says.

Does Eloise understand now? Does she see the Wordless Chain? Does she have the words to make Mom see it, too?

"What's your reason? Why do you think I need them?" I ask.

"It's your body," she says. "It should be your choice."

"Oh. Right. True."

Eloise starts to distribute Uno cards. "You OK?"

"Huh?" I say. "Yeah. Of course."

She tilts her head. "You sure? It looks like something's on your mind."

Something is on my mind, so close to my mind that the memory of it is still ringing in my ears: *Because she's hot . . . I can make her do this . . .* so much laughing . . . Ivan laughing.

I glance at Bobby again. Maybe I need to say this in front of him, even if I don't want to.

"Something happened today," I say.

Eloise drops her cards. "What happened?"

"I saw something that bothered me."

"Something bad? Something dangerous?" Eloise is speaking too fast now. She's gone into Protective Sister Mode.

"No." I shake my head.

"Something violent?"

Bobby puts a hand on her shoulder and says softly, "Babe, she's going to tell you."

It's like those words snap her back into her body. Her eyes refocus on me, ready to listen.

Except now it feels silly. Who cares about a bunch of stupid boys laughing at a fake butt when there are dangerous and violent somethings happening out there?

"This might sound silly," I say. "But when we were at Ivan's place after the party, his friends were playing video games . . ."

"Um hmm," Eloise says. Bobby is nodding at me, too.

"And one of them was using an avatar of a woman . . ."

"Um hmm," Eloise says again, while trying to hide a smile.

She was worried something bad had happened to me, but what actually happened isn't bad. It's silly. She's relieved that it happened. It's that silly.

It's too late to stop, so I finish telling them.

"Oh, bummer," Eloise says. She shakes out her long hair and picks up her cards. "Yeah. Boys can be such doofuses."

Exactly like Natalie.

She continues shuffling. Like this conversation is over. Like *boys can be such doofuses* is all there is to say. The Wordless Chain rattles louder and louder in my brain, and still Eloise doesn't notice.

Bobby gently touches Eloise's shoulder. He says, "No, babe."

Eloise looks at him with her Signature Bobby Look, the one she wears in all the photos of them doing ridiculous things like tie-dyeing socks or baking forty-seven-ingredient cookies.

"Oh, I don't mean all boys. I didn't mean you."

But he doesn't give her his own Signature Eloise Look. He looks serious. "I know, El. But, no, boys don't get to just be doofuses."

He turns to me, his blue eyes still, steady, and serious, and says, "Piper, you're right."

"I . . . I am?" I manage, surprised.

He nods. "Your friend shouldn't have laughed."

My jaw drops. "I . . . really? You . . . you wouldn't have laughed?"

"No way," Bobby says. "That wasn't funny. It was wrong."

We're all frozen for a moment, until Eloise throws both her arms around Bobby and coos, "I love you. I love you so much."

He laughs. "I love you, too, babe."

Then they start dealing cards like it's over.

The bathroom door slides back open, and Calvin calls, "Rematch! Rematch!"

So that's it. That's the end.

But in between turns, I glance at my sister's boyfriend. He goes back to being quiet and smiley. He gives Eloise that gooey Signature Look. He beats me on the final hand in the second game.

Is it possible that *Bobby* sees the Wordless Chain?

{ 9 }

On Saturday morning, my phone buzzes, waking me up. I glance across the room, but Eloise is already gone, probably at the dog shelter. I hold the phone up and read the text with sleepy eyes.

Daisy: Knock knock.

But I don't feel like another *knock-knock* joke. Corny jokes have been this fun thing between Daisy and me since we got phones last year, but now she's using them to manipulate me, ruining it. When I don't reply, she switches to normal texting.

Daisy: We'd be really great partners!

Daisy: LMK!

I thought I already let her know, back in TGASP last Friday. Why does she keep asking me to hurt her feelings all over again?

My fingers hover over the keyboard, trying to find the right way to answer. Could I write my own knock-knock joke to let her down easily?

Before I can type anything, my phone buzzes again.

Ivan: Hi! Did you have fun yesterday? What did you think of my gf?

This is even worse. How can he text me like nothing happened?

Both of them text again, almost simultaneously, before I reply to either. They use different strings of gifs and emojis. I groan and roll onto my stomach, burying my head in my pillow.

~~I don't want to talk to either of you.~~

I need to go somewhere where none of this matters. I need to get my hands dirty. I'm supposed to study with Tallulah later, but it's only seven thirty. There's finally a little fog on our bedroom window, indicating a chill in the air, so I pile on a long-sleeved T-shirt and an extra sweatshirt, and I wear big, warm socks under my rain boots. It's not raining but they protect my feet from the frost and the dew. Before I leave my room, I pull the red card off my corkboard and throw it away. I'm not jealous of Ivan anymore. I'm mad at him now.

Thanks a lot, Eloise.

I leave a note in the kitchen, then I go outside and hop the fence.

The air tastes fresh, like newness, like beginnings. I weave through the spindly trees, jump over the stream, and breathe in a big, greedy gulp of air. I'm alone in El Jardín Muerto. Where bodies don't matter. Where brains don't even matter. Where the world reduces to only two things: Piper and plants.

I start by weeding the root vegetables in the back seat of the red SUV. Then I move on to the bulbs under the hood of the yellow car. I rotate the soil on top of them so that when it rains tonight, they'll get more nourishment. Even though it's chilly, I didn't put on gloves. I love the feeling of cold dirt under my fingernails. It makes me feel present, alive, calm.

I wander to the circle of sunflowers in the middle of the cars. I know they'll be gone for winter soon, but for now they still stretch their yellow petals upward, smiling as if their best friend is hanging off the clouds. I kneel to weed around their roots, and I find it's all freshly weeded. I guess Tallulah has been alone here recently, too.

As soon as I have the thought, I hear her voice. "Hey, Piper," she yells. Although I've been enjoying my alone time with the garden, my heart leaps with happiness at the sight of her. She has an overloaded bag on her shoulders and a huge smile on her face as she shimmies down the hill and appears on the other side of the creek. "It's you and me all day, study buddy. You ready?"

I jump to my feet. "I was born ready."

We laugh as Tallulah and her huge bag join me in the middle of the cars.

The rest of Saturday morning, we sit in the back seat of the yellow car to brainstorm our creative self-expression presentations, mostly complaining that we'd rather be studying anything else, but by lunchtime, the complaining has died down. Sunday afternoon, we work in Tallulah's room, side by side and silent, like this is any other project. Ivan sends a few more texts, but I ignore them. I don't know how to tell him that he hurt my feelings without hurting his feelings. And I don't know how to be friends with someone who acted like that. I text Daisy back and just say *Let's talk Monday.* Tallulah is focused, and I need to be, too. We're preparing like we want to win, which is weird, because we actually want Ms. Gates to choose the other person.

By TGASP on Monday, though, I almost do want to win. I'm excited to share my project with Ms. Gates. I decided to talk about one metaphorical math concept, without discussing my entire life's work. I walk into the classroom on Monday with my tenth-round notecards in hand.

TGASP is an academic club, not a class, which means everyone here wants to be here. Ms. Gates doesn't assign specific work. Instead, she helps us understand how to pursue our overexcitabilities. She teaches us how to learn what we want to learn. And she teaches us about, as she says, "living life to its fullest as a gifted person." She says she's an outlet for the outliers.

Most days, everyone comes into TGASP quietly, even Tallulah, because we're eager to get back to whatever we're working on. The room has SMART Boards on both the front and back walls. The back is set up like a regular classroom, with rows of desks and chairs. Ms. Gates calls the front of the room her "café," but it looks more like a living room: there are couches with throw blankets that we're allowed to snuggle under when we read. We can even take our shoes off. The overhead lights turn on only in the back of the room. The front is lit by reading lamps on end tables. A plush green rug fills the middle where Josie and Kelly always spread out on their stomachs to study. Ms. Gates says this is the time in our week when we get to "follow the whispers of our brains right to the edges of the universe." Even the Academic Decathlon is technically optional, although everyone opts in.

Today I sit on one of the sofas and pull out the creative self-expression notes I worked on this weekend.

Daisy plops down on the couch next to me, *The Encyclopedia of Plant Life* in her hand. "So, can we be partners yet?"

"Daisy, I . . . I'm still . . ."

~~I don't want to deal with you today.~~

I'm nervous enough to show Ms. Gates my self-expression without Daisy making everything unnecessarily complicated.

Tallulah flies into the classroom, crashing right into Ms. Gates at her podium.

"I don't know how you stand her," Daisy says, rolling her eyes.

There's nothing nice to say to that so I don't say anything. I shrug and shuffle my notes.

Tallulah starts following Ms. Gates around the room, motor-talking.

"She's, like, a baby," Daisy says. "You'd obviously rather work with me."

~~Wrong.~~

~~Especially now.~~

~~I don't want to be anywhere near you when you're this mean.~~

I don't answer. It's weird how there's no nice way to tell someone they aren't being nice.

"I mean, why would you even want to be on her team?"

Now I look up, perplexed.

Because we'll win.

"I know, I know. She's smart, and you want to win," Daisy says, like that's a bad thing.

"Tallulah is really smart," I say, glad to finally have words from the right column.

"But so are you," Daisy says. "So am I."

I shake my head. "Not like Tallulah."

It's true, and I'm confused when it seems like I'm the only one who understands this. Metaphorically, Tallulah is smart to the nth power, while most of the rest of us are only smart to the power of seven. Even Ms. Gates is smart only to the power of twelve. Tallulah is the smartest person here. People act like that's a conundrum because she's also the person who gets in the most trouble. But it's not. Tallulah has trouble *because* she's so smart. To me, that's obvious even if Daisy and the rest of our friends can't see it. (Maybe that makes me smart to the power of 7.25 or something.)

I don't love Tallulah because she's smart or because of all the trouble she gets in. It's more that I love her, so I love all the trouble-y parts that come with her.

But smart to the *n*th power . . . that's why I want to be her partner.

"Ugh, come on," Daisy says. "You don't actually want to work with her."

"Daisy," I say, then I stop. Because I can already hear Mom's voice in my head. Even the way I said her name wasn't nice.

"She's smart, but I mean, she's—"

"Stop." I say before Daisy can get even more mean. More right-side words come to me. Finally. "Tallulah never says mean things about you."

Daisy looks down at her book like she's going to open it, but then breathes deeply and looks back at me. "You're right. And I don't actually think all those mean things about Tallulah. I like Tallulah. I just . . . I'm only trying to convince you to be my partner. I mean, don't you think we could win? You and me?"

~~No.~~

"Daisy . . . I . . ."

"We could!" Daisy says. "I mean, we work so well together. We're both really smart. We know about different things and . . . and . . . and you're my best friend in TGASP."

"Daisy, I—"

She sighs to interrupt me. "I know. You're going to choose Tallulah. Like always."

I don't know what else to say. It doesn't feel like I'm choosing Tallulah for the decathlon. It feels like destiny.

"Were you ever even considering me?" Daisy demands.

I open my mouth, then close it, not sure whether to choose nice or honest.

"You should have just told me that instead of leading me on all weekend."

Is that what I was doing? "I . . . I'm sorry. I just couldn't think of a nice way to say it."

"To say what? That you think Tallulah's smarter than me?"

I shrug.

"You're wrong. I can win. I'm smart enough," Daisy says.

"I know," I say. It sounds flat, though. I don't really believe it.

Daisy looks like she can't decide between yelling at me or crying.

Suddenly, someone else is in front of us. George. "Are we partners now?" he asks Daisy, impatiently.

"No!" Teddy yells from across the room. "Piper, choose Daisy so I can work with George."

My face is on fire. I didn't realize how many people spent the weekend waiting for me to repeat a decision I had already made.

"I'm working with Tallulah," I tell Teddy, firmly.

"Fine!" Daisy stands and grabs George's wrist, tugging him toward the back of the classroom without even answering him. She looks right at me. "You and Tallulah act like you're the only possible winners," she hisses. "Like you should get to go to counties just because you want to. But we all want to. Right, George?"

"Um, I guess," he says. He looks like he's begging me to find a way to end this conversation. I wish I could.

I stare at Daisy, dumbfounded.

She forces a laugh. "You know what, Piper? You think you're so nice. But then all you think about is winning. That's not nice. That's . . . that's full of yourself. Stuck-up. Selfish."

I gape at her. Is that true? Is it not nice to want to win?

In my silence, we hear Tallulah talking to Ms. Gates. "I timed myself last night and my creative self-expression is less than ten minutes already."

Daisy and George freeze.

"Wait," Daisy says slowly. Her smile turns crooked. "Is she talking about the tenth round?"

Ms. Gates and Tallulah don't notice us eavesdropping as Tallulah keeps whining. "So, we're only asking for a little bit of your time. Less than ten minutes each."

I'm thinking about how, actually, I'm not confident my presentation is under ten minutes and even if I were, that's twenty minutes, which isn't an insignificant amount of our ninety-minute after school program to suddenly demand from Ms. Gates at the last second. Maybe this isn't such a great plan.

"Tallulah, my concern is—"

But Daisy starts talking before I can listen in on why Ms. Gates doesn't like our idea for a creative round-off.

"OMG. You're more stuck-up than I realized," Daisy says, gleefully.

"I . . . what?" I raise a hand to try to cool my burning cheek.

"You're thinking about the end when we aren't even at the beginning."

"No," I say. "No we—"

"Yes. We haven't even gotten to the first question and you're already so sure you're better than everyone here."

I close my mouth.

~~Yes.~~

Yes, we're going to beat everyone in this room. Yes, we're already thinking about the final round. Yes, I want Tallulah to be my partner. And yes, that's because we can win.

~~I guess I'm selfish.~~

My face is flushed with either anger or shame. Maybe both.

Daisy yanks George again, still laughing. "You and Tallulah are going down."

I watch her sit at the desk next to her partner. If Tallulah and I didn't exist, Daisy and George would win the first level. They're definitely the second-best team in this room. I know we'll beat them . . . but I'm starting to feel like a bad person for knowing that.

I look down at my notes, but Ms. Gates says, "Piper, please come here for a minute."

Daisy says *"Oooh!"* like I'm in trouble. This is making me sad. Are we not friends anymore?

I join Tallulah by Ms. Gates's desk. She's eerily quiet now.

"Tallulah has brought it to my attention that the pair of you are preoccupied by the question of who will take on the final specialty?"

I nod.

Ms. Gates shakes her head. "This is disheartening. You've squandered an entire weekend."

"But—" Tallulah tries to interrupt. Ms. Gates holds out a finger to stop her.

"Now. If you both want to compete in the creative round, we'll—"

"No!" Tallulah interrupts again, then immediately shuts her mouth. I wait for either the interrupter or the interrupted to continue. No one does.

"Neither of us want it," I say.

Ms. Gates's eyebrows pinch. "What? But . . . why?"

Ms. Gates rarely says anything that doesn't include at least one word that's at least three syllables. We must have really surprised her.

Tallulah rushes to answer. "We didn't know how to split up the specialties, and we thought we had a good plan to—"

"No," Ms. Gates interrupts. "*Why?* Why after years of preparation, why with all of your enthusiasm, why between the two of you with all your brilliance . . . *why* does neither want that final spotlight?"

Tallulah shrugs, which is weird. She almost never shrugs. I shrug beside her.

"Is this a crisis of confidence?" Ms. Gates asks.

We're silent.

"Or is it your zeal and fervor about the nine academic specialties?"

"Yeah," Tallulah says. "That."

I squeeze my lips together. That's a lie. This *is* a crisis of confidence.

I glance at Daisy, bent over the encyclopedia on her desk, taking notes. How can I be stuck-up *and* have a crisis of confidence?

"I suppose that's reassuring," Ms. Gates says. "If the two most talented students I've ever met were suffering from insecurity, that would be . . . well . . . heartbreaking. And I firmly hold that triumphing in this decathlon requires one to be well-assured of her own talents."

My stomach feels like I'm on a roller coaster.

Tallulah thrusts what looks like a rolled-up poster board toward Ms. Gates. "Can you choose a self-expression now, please? Then, it's done."

"No," Ms. Gates says. "I'm afraid your plan is foolhardy. You cannot rush to complete a creative endeavor in one November weekend and expect to be victorious in April. In fact, your focus should be exclusively the nine specialties on which you must be experts in a matter of weeks. The first level requires diligent preparation."

Tallulah presses her shoulder to mine. I look at my shoes.

Ms. Gates sighs. "All right. Here's an alternate plan: If botany is called in the early rounds, whoever has studied most recently or feels most prepared should step forward. If botany still has not been called after counties, in February, you should each begin to prepare a creative piece and I will consider and choose one at that point. In February. And not before. Although my guess is that, by then, either fate or your own good judgment will make the decision, and my involvement will not be necessary."

"OK," we both say. We turn toward the couches.

"And girls?" Ms. Gates says.

We turn back around.

"Either of you has the capacity to win that tenth round. Of that, I am certain."

Tallulah takes a shaky breath. I shudder beside her.

If you say so, Ms. Gates. If you say so.

{ 10 }

The rest of the week is great. I study. I throw myself into isosceles triangles, the works of Zora Neale Hurston, and the functions of the pituitary gland. No matter where we are—school lunch, TGASP, El Jardín Muerto, Tallulah's bedroom—you can find Tallulah and me bent over books, scribbling, typing up notes, barely talking. It doesn't matter that we're working on different subjects. It's motivating to be near each other. We're in this together.

Friday afternoon, I'm halfway out the back door in our kitchen, on my way to join Tallulah in the garden when Mom stops me.

"Wait, Piper. You can't go out now," she says to my back.

I turn. She's sitting at the kitchen table with Gladys and her laptop.

Mom must be exhausted because she's triple-tasking: one

hand typing, one hand holding a baby, and one boob feeding said baby. And now she's talking to me. Quadruple-tasking.

"And close that door," she snaps. "It's freezing."

It's not my fault she chose to sit in the middle of the kitchen, right by the back door, and take off half her shirt.

I close the door. "I'm meeting Tallulah to study," I say.

"Not today," she says. Her eyes on her computer. It's like she doesn't realize what she's saying. Like it's no big deal.

"What? Why?"

"You've been studying all week."

~~So?~~

"I have to study today, too," I say.

Mom waves her hand around her face in some sort of body language I don't understand.

"We have to talk about . . . you know," she says. "It."

She means the shots. "Can we talk tomorrow on the way to HHH?"

"I'm not taking you to HHH," Mom says.

"What? No. Please, Mom," I beg the top of her head as she types. "You have to take me."

I have to see Ivan. I still haven't figured out how to reply to his texts. I have to see him in person. I have to remember all the good things about him so that I can try to forget that awful laughing.

"Sit down," Mom says, still not looking up. "I just need to finish one thing, and you'll have my full attention."

I don't know how she manages to type one set of words

153

while saying another. And I don't know why she's always promising me her attention when I want it the least.

"But I have to study," I say, not sitting. "And I really need to go to HHH tomorrow. Like more than usual."

She looks up so fast, Gladys loses her grip and starts wailing, but still Mom's eyes stay on me. "Why, honey? Is something wrong?"

"No . . . I just . . . I have to see Ivan."

She lowers her eyebrows. "Is he OK?"

"Oh, yeah," I say. "It's not like that."

I'm not OK.

"Are you two in a tiff?"

I pause.

"Not exactly."

She looks away to refasten Gladys. She doesn't look back.

"Well, I didn't mean you aren't going. Calvin's taking you. Does that help?"

"Oh," I say, relieved. "Yeah."

I'm pretty sure this is the part where I'm supposed to be getting her full attention, but Mom doesn't look away from the top of Gladys's head. Something from Mom's computer dings. Her eyes go right from Gladys to the screen without even a pit stop on me.

"Anyway, I asked you to put this afternoon aside so that—"

"You asked me what?"

She looks at me for a half second before her computer dings again.

Mom curses. I jump.

"Sorry," Mom says in my general direction. "I have two weeks before I go back to work, and yet the emails won't stop. They want me to . . ." Mom gets too distracted to finish her sentence.

My heart stops inside my rib cage.

"You're going back to work in two weeks?"

"Yeah. I told you, didn't I? I go back next Friday."

But that's the first day of the decathlon.

I don't say it. I tell myself I don't have to. I tell myself Mom will be there even if she's working that day. She'd never miss my debut as an Academic Decathlon-er.

I think.

"I knew you were going back, but I didn't realize it was so soon."

"Oh. But . . ." Gladys pulls away and Mom switches her into her typing hand so that she can reclip her bra strap. She squints at me. "I told you this, right? I told you to set this afternoon aside?" She straps herself and Gladys into a baby carrier.

~~No!~~

~~You never tell me anything anymore!~~

~~You never remember anything!~~

"I don't think so," I whisper.

"I could have sworn . . ."

Mom is still multitasking. Now she has two hands on her computer but she's bouncing in her chair because Gladys has started fussing in the baby carrier on her chest. Work gets her hands, Gladys gets her body, I get her words. I used to get all the parts of her at once.

"Honey," Mom says. She's finally looking at me, so when she pats the chair beside her, I sit. "I think maybe you're studying too much."

"What?" I say, shocked. "That's what you want to talk about?"

"I want to talk to you about everything, Piper." Mom looks hurt, which feels unfair. "And yet anytime I try, all you want to do is study."

That's because you only talk about puberty.

Maybe she isn't going to come to my decathlon. Maybe this conversation is about building up some fake philosophy to explain away how she's going to miss the first of the four most important days in my life.

"I wish you were more like Tallulah's mom!" I burst. "She never wants her to stop studying."

Mom raises one eyebrow. "I know you didn't mean that."

Of course, I don't mean it.

I don't want Tallulah's mom.

All I want is you.

I huff.

"I mean it when I say I want to talk about everything," Mom continues. "But I do particularly need to know what's so scary about puberty, Piper. Can you dig deep and try to tell me?"

I've done that twice and it's gotten us nowhere. Instead, I

dig deep and say something else. Something definitely from the left column of my brain.

"You're wrong, Mom."

"I'm sorry?"

"You think my whole life is about studying? You're wrong. You know what my whole life actually is about?"

Mom sighs. "Enlighten me."

"Puberty. My whole life is about puberty."

"Honey," Mom says softly. "Once we stop the shots, once we let puberty happen, that part of your life will be over. It's not eternal. But you have to start it in order for it to end."

I'm shaking my head. "No," I say. "Nope. No, no, no. I'm not going to fall for another one of the ways you try to trick me into growing up."

"OK, hold on," Mom says, standing slowly while talking loudly, which seems like patting your head and rubbing your stomach: hard to do at once. "I'm not tricking you. I don't need to *trick* you, OK? I don't even need to *care* how you feel about this treatment ending. I'm your parent, and—"

"And it's not your body! It's mine."

"Yes. It's your body, but I'm legally responsible for it. I have to make the best decision for you, not based on what you think right now, but based on who you will be as a grown-up."

I huff and stand to match her.

"No matter how much you may want to believe that magical math or whatever can freeze time, Piper, it can't. You don't get to fill your brain with facts and never grow up. That's not how life works. And I can't even consider your feelings in this decision right now because you won't tell me why you're scared to—"

"I need to win the decathlon. I can't do that if I'm all hormonal. Eloise already told you!"

"Oh, Piper. That's just more pitter-patter."

"Pitter-patter?"

"Being prepubescent is not a decathlon requirement, OK? You can win without the treatments. You can win on your period."

No, I can't.

"And you may not win anyway."

I gasp, like she slapped me.

Gladys starts crying. Mom says, "Great. You woke her up."

It's so short, my breath catches. My hands ball at my sides. My mom has yelled at me before, but she's never talked to me like that. Sarcastically.

She curses, loudly. I look up and see that Gladys has puked all down the front of her black sweater.

"I'm leaving," I say, broken.

"No, honey. Wait," Mom says. "Calvin!"

Her fingers wrap around my wrist to keep me here as Calvin removes a crying and disgusting Gladys from my mom.

She pulls on my wrist until I look at her. "I'm sorry. You don't deserve to be spoken to that way."

I glare. My mom is finally focusing on me, and I have to be face-to-face with four hundred liters of baby vomit.

"I messed this all up," Mom says. "I'm . . . I have too much going on. And I'm trying so hard not to let it affect you, but I'm failing."

I still don't say anything.

Mom sits back in her seat and pushes her computer away. She nods at the chair next to her. It's like she doesn't even realize she's wearing regurgitated breast milk. I don't sit.

"OK, honey," she says when she sees I'm still standing. "How about a compromise? How about if I walk with you to Tallulah's? Maybe you can tell me about all these feelings on the way there."

That doesn't work for a million reasons. First, it would take way longer than the seven-point-five-minute walk to Tallulah's to tell my mom about the Wordless Chain. Second, if I ever thought I could tell her about it, I know I can't now. Not after watching her quadruple-task and melt down over being so busy. She's more tied up in the links of that chain than ever. Most importantly, I'm not actually going to Tallulah's. I'm going to El Jardín Muerto, which Mom can't know. And finally . . .

I tilt my head at her.

"What?"

"Um, maybe you should change first?"

Mom looks down at the white crusty stains all over her sweater. I hold my breath for a half second, thinking she's going to yell. But she laughs.

"OK, let's call a spade a spade. We'll try this again when we both have time. And next time I'll remember to let you know in advance."

Her laugh cracks a smile out of me.

"OK," I say.

"Go on, study," Mom says. "Have a nice time."

When I walk outside, the sun is already setting, and I run into Tallulah on her way home from El Jardín.

"I tried to wait for you, but it was getting dark," she says.

"It's OK." I trudge behind her toward her house. When she asks me where I've been, I shrug, and she doesn't push it.

We settle into studying in her bedroom. After a few minutes I start to feel better, working at Tallulah's side, *The Super Earth Encyclopedia* open on my lap.

Then Ivan texts me.

Ivan: See you tmrw? HHH?

That's a weird question. I always go to HHH.

"Who's texting?" Tallulah asks.

"Daisy."

I don't know why I say that. It's not like Tallulah would be upset that I have other friends. But I have two worlds. In one, my brain makes me a star, and Tallulah is my costar. In the other, my body makes me a weirdo, and Ivan is my life raft. If they were ever together it would feel like precocious puberty all over again: being two things at once.

"You don't have to lie," Tallulah says. "You can tell me it's private."

"What do you mean?"

"I know it's not Daisy."

I pull my phone closer to me, even though I'm on the bed and Tallulah is on the floor so there's no way she read Ivan's name on my screen.

"It *is* Daisy," I lie again.

My phone buzzes.

Ivan: Nat & I are hanging at the park after. Wanna come?

A week ago, this question would have given me goose bumps. Now it makes me nauseous. I know Calvin would let me go, but if I have to risk hearing Ivan laugh like that again, I don't want to.

Tallulah interrupts my thoughts. "Daisy isn't talking to you right now. After whatever happened with you guys, she's not talking to either of us."

"I— What?"

I somehow thought Tallulah didn't notice how awful things were between us and Daisy. Why would I think that? Tallulah is the smartest person I know.

"I . . . I'm sorry" I say. "I didn't know you knew about that."

Tallulah shrugs. "It happens all the time."

"What does?" My phone buzzes again. I ignore it.

"People think I don't realize when someone's being mean to me just because I don't react that way you'd expect. You know, like with anger or hurt or something."

I push my buzzing phone away, giving her all my attention. This is another new kind of conversation for us. It's like we're entering a new level on a best friendship video game or something.

The level where she tells me hard things, and I lie about my texts.

"Just so you know," I say. "*I'm* hurt when Daisy is mean to you. I hate it."

"Yeah, I'm hurt, too," Tallulah says. "Just people can't tell because it looks different on me or something."

"It looks different?"

"I mean . . . I see the world uniquely. It's my ADHD or my smartness or something. Like, I notice things that other people don't, and I can't notice the things that most people do. I say and do things that make it harder for me to fit in without realizing that will be the consequence. I think sometimes it takes a little more effort for most kids to get to know me. Except like Teddy or Kelly or Eric."

"Huh?" I say. I was expecting her to say except for me.

"I just mean that they're neurodivergent, too, so they probably get it in a way someone like Daisy just doesn't."

"Oh," I say. "I didn't know that."

Tallulah shrugs. "Why would you?"

Good point.

"So, when Daisy is giving me the silent treatment and I don't even know why, yeah, it hurts. But it's OK you couldn't tell. Most people can't. Because the hurt doesn't come out of me the way it does for you and other normal people."

"Hey!" I say. "I'm not normal people."

"See? Like that."

We're laughing, but something else is going on, too. Something important.

Someone knocks on her door, and we're quiet immediately.

"Are you girls studying?" Joy calls from the hallway.

"Yes," we call back.

She cracks open the door. "It doesn't sound like studying from out here."

"Mom," Tallulah says flatly. "We're always studying. It's literally all we do."

"I'm just saying . . . I know this is your dream, Tally. And what do we say about dreams?"

"They only come true with a lot of hard work," Tallulah parrots. Her mom says this so often, I could parrot it back, too. It's the part of Tallulah's mom I'm sometimes a little jealous of. The part that always wants her to study. That doesn't ever say things like, *You might not win anyway.* Joy wouldn't even say that by accident because she doesn't ever think it.

"You know, Mom," Tallulah says. "Sometimes work is joyful." She raises her eyebrows expectantly.

Joy laughs. "Well, it definitely should be. You got me there, Tally," she says and shuts the door.

Tallulah goes back to her books with a groan, and I guess the new level of friendship conversation is over, so I pick up my phone again.

Ivan: We can get pizza from the place on 116th & candy from the bodega

Ivan: Junk food picnic!

Ivan: You in?

Ivan: I'll ask Lydia, Brice & them too.

My thumbs hover over the keyboard. It sounds so fun, but my memory is still hearing Ivan laugh.

"Hey, Tallulah?" I say. "What does it look like for you?

When you're hurt . . . what do you do that normal people don't?"

"Ask questions," she says.

"Questions?" I ask, surprised.

"Yeah. If I ask the right questions, a different feeling comes to cover up the hurt. Like, sometimes I feel fascinated that someone tried to hurt me because, what is it in human's brains that creates that instinct? Or sometimes I feel, like, whatever, that was pointless and they're ignorant and I don't need to talk to them anymore anyway. Or sometimes I feel something like . . . like . . . pity? Yeah, pity. That's better than hurt, too."

"Wow," I say. I never knew any of that. I decide to try it.

Me: Hey, can I ask a question?

Tallulah continues. "But sometimes nothing works, and I just stay hurt. That happens, too, like with Daisy, and I try to ignore it because being hurt is boring. What do you do?"

I smile. "I don't have strategies like that for being hurt. But I wish I did."

Tallulah pauses, looking at me. Then she smiles back. "I'm sorry. I don't know how to answer because I don't want to call you *normal* again, but the shoe is kinda fitting."

"Hey!" I say. And we're both giggling when my phone buzzes this time.

Ivan: Sure. Ask me anything.

I don't know what to ask, though. I mean, Ivan wasn't trying to hurt me. He wasn't even thinking about me. It takes me so long to figure out how to phrase the question that he's texted **Piper?** two times before I finally get it typed out.

Me: At your birthday party when you laughed at Richie's avatar . . . why was that funny?

His thought bubbles blink for a long time. I watch them patiently, expecting something profound and enlightening.

Ivan: IDK it just was

Well. I definitely do not feel better.

Ivan: Why?

And now he gets to ask questions?

I sigh. "Tallulah, what if they don't answer you, and then they start asking questions?"

Tallulah rolls over on the floor to look up at me, laughing. "OK, now I do believe you're texting Daisy. Did she tell you why she's mad at us?"

My face gets a little warm, but I can't tell her that I was lying now. "No."

"Just answer her," Tallulah says, turning back to her notes.

I chew my lip. "What if your answer would hurt their feelings?"

Tallulah shrugs. "Who cares? She already hurt your feelings."

OK, then. Ivan hurt my feelings, too.

Me: It seemed like you were laughing at her just because she was coded female.

Me: Or like there was something bad about a boy using a female-coded avatar. Like . . . there's something wrong with being a girl.

Me: And maybe it also felt like you were making fun of her butt?

Ivan doesn't respond for a long time. Hours. I return to studying, but with each minute that passes my heart beats louder. Then it's almost time to go home and still no reply. I'm sure I've lost him completely. Another friend gone.

When my phone finally buzzes, I jump at it.

Ivan: You're right. I'm sorry.

I'm so stunned, I almost fall off Tallulah's bed.

Ivan: I should have been better. I'm trans. I'm Black. So yeah. I know how it feels to be the butt of a joke.

Ivan: Pun not intended. 😊

I snort a laugh at my phone.

Me: Really? That's it?

I don't think I've ever gotten such an easy apology before, but I'll take it.

Ivan: Yeah, really.

Ivan: Sometimes I forget I don't have to try to be one of the guys anymore. I am a guy. I don't need to laugh at something ignorant to prove it. Not that that ever would have been OK to laugh at.

Me: I get that.

Ivan: And it can be hard for trans guys to remember that pretending to BE a girl was gross for us, but that doesn't mean BEING a girl is gross, like, for everyone.

Me: That avatar WAS gross though.

I'm going for a laugh, but Ivan takes it seriously.

166

Ivan: Yeah, but only because she was fake. Because she WASN'T a girl.

Ivan: At first, I wanted to tell you that I was laughing because she just looked so fake and ridiculous. But you know that's not the way I was laughing. And I'm sorry.

Ivan: Any chance we can forget it ever happened and stuff our faces with pizza and candy tomorrow? 🙏

Me: 😊 Yeah! The junk food picnic sounds fun.

Ivan: So you'll be there?

Me: Sure

Ivan: What's that word you use? The one that means, like, yay?

Me: Huzzah?

Ivan: Right! Huzzah! C U tmrw. 😊

I clutch my phone to my chest.

"Wait . . ." Tallulah says slowly. "That isn't Daisy after all."

I look down at her, still smiling. "What do you mean?"

Tallulah gives me a weird, suspicious smile. "Just . . . Daisy has never made you look like that."

That's when I realize I'm feeling more than relief. My face is hot like I'm blushing. My phone is pressed into my sternum like I'm giving it a hug. My lips are curled into a goofy smile that I can't stop even with Tallulah staring at me. I must look like Eloise when she texts Bobby.

As soon as it doesn't feel like Ivan's abandoning me, *boom,* my body's abandoning my own self anyway.

This isn't supposed to happen. I'm still on the medicine.

"I . . . OK, fine," I say. "It wasn't Daisy. I just . . ." I trail off, not sure how to finish.

"It's OK, Piper," Tallulah says. "You'll tell me when you're ready."

She's right about one thing: I'm not ready.

Go away, hormones.

I have to study.

The next day, I'm doing what my mom wants, taking a break. Instead of the decathlon, I'm thinking about how good hot pizza smells on one of the first cold days of fall, and how incredible it is that I can sit on the freezing cold ground in Central Park with frigid air running up the ankles of my jeans but focus my whole body on the warm parts of my arms that are pressed against Ivan's and Emma's arms on either side of me.

Our HHH meeting is over and, even though a cold spell came overnight, we're having our junk food picnic in Central Park. Except we're too cold to eat. We're huddling around the pizza we pooled our money to buy. We're pretending the hot pizza is a fire.

"Most delicious-smelling fire ever," Brice says. Then he reaches into the pizza box/fireplace and takes a slice. Part of me is a little relieved because I'm getting hungry. But part of me was enjoying the game and the excuse a pretend fire created to stand closer than we normally would.

"Bro! Don't eat our fire," Ivan yells.

"Yeah," Emma says, shoving Brice to the ground. "That fire's for all of us."

"Yeah!" Javi agrees.

Then Emma and Javi are on top of Brice, trying to wrestle the slice out of his hands as he waves it in the air.

Ivan jumps up. "Aha!" he yells, yanking the pizza free from Brice. "I've got it!"

Natalie fake-blinks her eyelashes a million times like a cartoon character. "My hero," she says, just as all the cheese falls off the pizza into the dirt behind Ivan.

Emma, Lydia, Javi, Brice, and I freeze like the game just took a turn that no one knows how to navigate. Then Ivan flashes us that adorable lopsided smile and says, "My bad?"

"Get him!" Natalie squeals, and then we're all tackling Ivan and pelting him with garlic knots and chasing each other with pizza-covered hands. Soon there's sauce streaked across my cheekbones, and gummy candies in my hair, and my stomach hurts from laughing so hard. We huddle under the blanket that we originally brought to sit on top of. It's sort of like being in Ivan's room last weekend. Sort of weirdly intimate and grown-up. But today there's nothing to interrupt the fun, nothing to make it uncomfortable. Until I hear "Piper? You ready?"

I turn around and see Calvin on the pathway in the park, looking at me with one eyebrow raised.

Heat fills my face for some reason. I'm the youngest. I still have a parent coming to pick me up. I feel weirdly young in front of Calvin, too, covered in food and dirt and unable to stop giggling.

But usually, I want to feel young.

It's all too confusing to work out in this moment. I hop up and say, "See you guys."

"Calvin?" I say, as we walk out of the park.

He turns to me like he's expecting me to say something deep and real and more honest than I'm usually capable of. His eyes are so open and ready, I almost do.

"Um . . . I know this is going to sound weird considering I just came from a picnic, but . . . I'm kinda hungry," I say.

Calvin smiles at me. "Let's get some pizza," he says. "For eating this time."

He puts his arm around my shoulders and steers me into the pizza shop for the second time today.

VOCABULARY: THE GREATEST COMMON FACTOR

In **STANDARD MATH**, the definition of **GREATEST COMMON FACTOR (GCF)** is *the largest factor that all numbers share in a given set of numbers.*

EXAMPLES

Set	Factors	GCF
12 20 24	1 2 4	4

Set	Factors	GCF
30 42	1 2 3 6	6

This is important because it allows us to simplify fractions into easier forms. It is because of GCFs that we're able to understand that

$$\frac{3}{9} = \frac{1}{3} \text{ OR } \frac{200}{500} = \frac{2}{5}$$

In **METAPHORICAL MATH** we can understand
a **COMMON FACTOR** as an essential,
unchangeable personality trait that is shared
among a set of two or more people.

In that case, the definition of **GREATEST**
COMMON FACTOR is *the common factor a set*
of people share that makes life simpler and easier
when this set of people is together.

EXAMPLES

SET	FACTORS	GCF
PIPER TALLULAH	SMART. THOUGHTFUL. SINCERE. AWKWARD. CONFUSED. GIRLS. KIDS	SINCERE

SET	FACTORS	GCF
PIPER IVAN JAVI EMMA LYDIA BRICE	THINKING ABOUT PUBERTY. HONEST. SUPPORTIVE. FUN.	FUN

{ 11 }

A week later, Tallulah and I sit side by side behind the curtain on the dark stage of our school auditorium, our shoulders pressed together, our breath in thin, excited gasps. The first day of the decathlon is finally here. I didn't know I could be so thrilled to be in my school auditorium with the seventh graders I see every day.

But my goose bumps have goose bumps.

In a minute, the panel member who's on the other side of this curtain will stop talking and the curtain will open. And in just a few hours, Tallulah and I will know for certain that we're going on to compete at counties.

Hopefully.

I know Tallulah or I can beat everyone on this stage in every specialty . . . except African American poetry. I've studied a lot, but I could use more time.

But the chances of poetry being called today are only about 22.2 percent.

"And now," the panel member says, "may I present this year's competing seventh graders!"

The curtain splits, and I scan the crowd for Mom. I'm sure she was late. It's her first day back at work. But hopefully she's here now. The lights buzz on over our heads, blocking any view of the audience before I can find her.

The panelist introduces himself as Dr. Oscar Rodriguez, a professor of philosophy at Princeton University. Tallulah and I are pressing our shoulders together so tightly, I think we may have bruises later.

Dr. Rodriguez turns away from his podium to look at us.

"Now," he says, "once I announce the first specialty, you'll have sixty seconds to decide who is the more prepared teammate. That person will come and stand on this yellow line." He points to a streak of yellow tape across the stage floor.

We all nod that we understand.

He smiles warmly. "And the first subject is . . ."

Not poetry. Not poetry.

"African American poetry."

Shoot.

Beside me, Tallulah whispers "darn" under her breath.

"OK, Piper," she says. "You've got this. I know Daisy loves poetry . . . but you're like, really smart. You'll know all the answers."

She's talking to me, but it sounds like she's trying to

convince herself. I could use my own convincing speech.

"Daisy will know them, too," I say.

"So what? If we tie, both teams go to counties. Just get them all right and it doesn't matter what she does."

"But what if—"

"And that's time!" Dr. Rodriguez says, making me jump.

I walk forward and stand on the line, right between Daisy and Caroline. I remember to be nice. "Good luck," I whisper to each of them. Caroline whispers it back. Daisy says, "I don't need luck. You do."

The first questions are easy. All eleven of us answer correctly so no one gets eliminated. But on his second question, Jack says that *On Messrs. Hussey and Coffin* was Phillis Wheatley's first published poetry collection. She was the first Black woman from the Americas to be published at all, but "On Messrs. Hussey and Coffin" was only her first poem published in the United States. She was published in Britain before that. When Caroline says *"Poems on Various Subjects, Religious and Moral,"* Jack has to sit down.

If you get a question wrong, it goes to the next person. If they get it right, you're disqualified. The maximum number of questions you can answer, and therefore points you can get, is ten. Ten is a perfect score.

I get more questions right as my classmates drop out one by one. On the fourth question, we lose Nora and Teddy. Caroline gets question seven wrong and sits when I get it right.

But there's no way I can beat Daisy. She is going to know

everything. She's known the answer to every question, whether it was directed to her or not. I can tell by the way she taps her foot against the floor as soon as Dr. Rodriguez finishes asking a question.

I didn't know Caroline's in round four (Q: *Benjamin Banneker was a Black American polymath who helped publish almanacs about the land now known as the District of Columbia. Who wrote the famous poem titled after his name? A: Rita Dove*), or Josie's in round seven (Q: *The lines 'Is the total black, being spoken / From the earths inside' open which of Audre Lorde's poems? A: Coal*).

I don't need to beat Daisy, though. Tallulah is right. All I need to do is tie.

Soon, we're the only two left.

Dr. Rodriguez asks my last question: "Each year on October 17, our country celebrates Black Poetry Day. The date was chosen to honor the man who is widely considered to be the first Black poet published in America. What is his name?"

I don't know. I know I don't know. I just shake my head.

Daisy says, "Jupiter Hammon" and then the round is over. She has a perfect score. I have a nine. She beat me.

"And round one goes to Daisy!" Dr. Rodriguez says. "OK, let me consult my notes. There are breaks between some rounds and others go right through so . . . yes. Ten-minute break today." He turns away from the stage and adds, "Parents, you can meet your scholars off stage left."

I turn to Daisy to try to congratulate her because it's the

nice thing to do, but she's running off the stage. Sprinting. She leaps down the three stairs to stage right and then takes off down the hallway.

I want to fall into my mom's arms. I want to rest my head on the angle of her shoulder while she tells me how great I did, how great I am. I want to take a minute to be grateful that I have a mom like her and not like a lot of the other TGASP moms. A mom who is only into all the TGASP stuff because I am. Who will be proud of me no matter what I do.

But when I get offstage, my eyes scan through the faces of all those other moms. Hers does not appear.

She's not here.

"Over here, Piper!" Tallulah calls. She's standing between her mom and dad. She's an only child with two parents who live with her and who both show up to everything.

I trudge over to her. She sounds so happy it's like fingernails inside my skull.

"Nice job," Edward, says.

"Yeah, you did awesome," Tallulah says.

I look at her, confused. "I lost."

Tallulah leans close to whisper in my ear. "The way I see it, you saved us, OK? You only had a month to study, Pipes, and you did exactly what you needed to."

"Yes, excellent work, Piper. You knew almost everything despite having such little time to learn a new subject," Joy says. "But why didn't you take poetry, Tally? You'd have known that Jupiter Hammon one. You'd have known them all."

Tallulah ignores her and keeps whispering to me. "All we need is a perfect score the next round. I don't think there's any other specialty Daisy and George are so prepared for. They'll get at least one wrong. And all we need is to tie. Besides, it would be fun if George and Daisy also get to counties, right?"

~~No.~~

I wanted to win. I wanted to beat Daisy. I wanted that, even if it's mean.

"Girls," Joy says. "You don't need to settle for a tie. If you work hard enough, you can win. It's all about your mindset."

Next to her, Kelly's mom is saying that she should have known that Gwendolyn Brooks was the first Black person to win the Pulitzer Prize for poetry with the collection *Annie Allen*, Eric's mom is quizzing him on botany facts even though we don't know if that specialty will be called before April, and Teddy's mom is trying to get him to put on a bow tie.

Maybe this is All Moms Stink Day.

I look at Tallulah's parents. "Have you seen my mother?"

Joy's face does this thing I've never seen it do before. It's like it breaks open while at the same time barely moving. Pity. She feels sorry for me.

"My mom's not here." I say it to make myself believe it.

"Do you want me to call her?" Joy asks.

"No," I say, mortified, even though this is my mom's mistake and not mine. "It's . . . she just went back to work . . . she probably . . . I'm going to the bathroom."

I walk down the hall, past empty classrooms and display

cases full of soccer and softball trophies. How could I have messed up the decathlon already? And how could my mom not be here to watch?

In the bathroom, I walk straight up to the line of sinks and splash water on my face. Everything is wrong. I was supposed to get onstage and kick butt. I wasn't supposed to be a quiet second-place kid. Why did I think I'd create some blaze of glory here, when I'm always a second-place kid, even to my own mom?

Suddenly, a voice calls out from inside one of the stalls. A voice that has been crying.

"Um, Piper. Is that you?"

Daisy.

"Yeah," I say.

How dare she beat me and then come in here and cry? She should at least be enjoying the moment that she stole from me.

She sniffles. "I need . . . I need help."

She sounds miserable.

"It's everywhere," she moans.

"What's everywhere?"

"I think it's . . . I think it's my period."

"What?" I whisper. My heart comes to a standstill in my chest. "Your first one?"

"Yes," Daisy wails. "He asked you that last question and . . . and I thought I was going to pee my pants, and I came in here and there's blood in my underwear. What am I going to do?"

"I'll go get your mom," I say.

"She's not here!" Daisy cries. "She had to work. I have to take these off."

There's a bunch of rustling from behind the stall door. I watch Daisy's feet disappear into her jeans and then reappear outside them.

"Do I just go out there with no underwear on?" she asks.

"Um," I say. "What if your period gets on your pants?"

"What?" Daisy wails. "It keeps going?"

Then *splash*.

Then "Oh my god! Oh my god!" Somehow, she sounds even worse. "Oh, no, no, no."

"What?" I ask.

"I just dropped my pants in the toilet!" Daisy wails.

My eyes go wide. "What?"

"That's it. I'm never leaving. I'm going to die in here wearing toilet water pants and bloody underwear."

She could just die in here.

Or not die. I don't want her to literally die. But what if she gets stuck long enough that George has to take the next specialty, even if it's one Daisy prepped?

We'd win.

"This so unfair. This is supposed to be the best day of my life," she cries.

I'm still frozen, the water running.

"Piper," Daisy whispers. "Could you maybe get your mom?"

"She's not here, either," I say.

"No!" Daisy wails. "I don't trust anyone else's mom."

And then she's not a girl who has been mean to me and Tallulah for a month. She's the friend I've had since second grade, and she's crying in the bathroom over her period during the Academic Decathlon. She's my friend living my own worst nightmare.

"I'll . . . I'll figure something out," I declare.

I look around the bathroom, in every open stall, but there's no pad dispenser. No wet wipes. No one's discarded gym pants. Nothing.

Daisy sniffles. "How?"

"Hold on. Stay right there," I say. I have no idea what I'm going to do, but I do have to do something.

I sprint out the bathroom toward Tallulah and her parents. I don't want to talk to Tallulah's mom about Daisy's period, especially after the way Daisy treated Tallulah and everything Tallulah told me about how hurt she was last week, but I don't know what other choice I have. Except right before I reach them, I crash into someone else.

Two arms grab me and hold on tight.

"Oh, honey!"

It's Mom.

"I don't know what happened. It was in the calendar but it's my first day back and—no, no excuses. I can't believe—"

"Never mind," I say. I'm not supposed to interrupt her, but I can see Dr. Rodriguez standing in the hallway looking at his watch. The ten-minute break has to be almost up by now.

"I need help. Well, Daisy does. She's in the bathroom. She just got her period and then she dropped her pants in the toilet, and she doesn't have pants or underwear or any of that period stuff."

Mom shakes her head fast like she's doing a double take.

"OK," she says, suddenly all business. "I still have my gym bag in the car from before Gladys was born. It has . . . leggings . . . shorts . . . something. Maternity, of course, but it'll have to do. And I definitely have a maxi pad in there somewhere. I'll go get it. You talk to whoever is in charge."

"What? What do I say?"

But Mom is already running down the hallway, back toward the parking lot.

I turn and look at Dr. Rodriguez. He's leaning against the door to the stage.

I didn't want to talk to Joy about Daisy's period. I definitely don't want to talk to Dr. Rodriguez about Daisy's period.

I take a shaky breath.

He checks his watch, then straightens up and tilts his head back like he's about to yell that the break is over. I rush up to him just in the nick of time.

"Um . . . excuse me?" I squeak.

He closes his mouth and looks down at me. I feel tiny with him bending over me like this.

"Yes?" he says, not exactly mean but very much sounding like I'm interrupting him.

"My friend isn't . . . she needs . . . a little more time."

He raises his eyebrows.

"And why is that?"

~~She just got her period.~~

Why do those feel like left-column words? If periods are natural and normal, like Mom keeps saying, why are they impossible to talk about, even when you really need to? Why haven't I ever heard anyone say anything like this before?

"She's not . . . ready."

His eyebrows go up so far, they almost touch his hairline. "And where is she?"

"The bathroom," I say.

"I see. Well, the competition handbook lays out the rules exactly, and this ten-minute break is about to turn into an eleven-minute break, which is not allowed."

He leans his head back as if to shout to the crowd again.

"No!"

He looks down at me. He's so much bigger than I am. I'm just a kid. A little kid who couldn't even win.

"That's not . . . that's not fair," I say.

"Of course it's fair," Dr. Rodriguez says. "Those are the rules in the rule book you all agreed to. The ten-minute break is standardized to keep things the same school to school. Rules exist to ensure fairness."

"But they don't right now," I say, trying to stall for time. I glance down the hall. No sign of Daisy or my mom.

"And how is that, per se?" Dr. Rodriguez challenges.

I see my mom dart into the bathroom carrying her gym

bag. Jeez. Daisy still needs to change. This is going to take a lot of time.

"Because . . . those rules are making it unfair," I say slowly.

Dr. Rodriguez sighs. "Young lady, explain yourself."

A crowd has started to gather around us. People are listening to me argue with the panelist on the first day of my decathlon.

"I mean . . . I mean . . ." What am I supposed to say? "This doesn't happen to everyone."

He chuckles in a way that makes me feel even smaller. "I'm fairly certain that bathroom trips do happen to everyone."

"No," I say. "I mean . . . not boys . . . not most boys."

He gives me a look that's both amused and disgusted. A look I've seen on men's faces a million times before, usually directed at my mom.

Superior. He looks superior.

"Are you telling me that boys don't use the—"

"I believe she's trying to tell you that a young lady just started menstruating," a voice says behind me. I turn and see Joy standing just to my right. I've never been so happy to see her. "But you aren't making it easy on this poor girl. Is that it, Piper?" she asks, her voice softer.

I nod.

His face remains superior. "You should have said so."

"I'm certain you can understand, Dr. Rodriguez," Joy says, "that these are unpredictable circumstances for a young woman and—"

Dr. Rodriguez holds up a hand to stop her.

"I don't want to hear about this."

I lower my eyebrows. I should have said the thing he doesn't want to hear about?

"She has two minutes," he finishes.

By now, everyone else has filed back into the auditorium. Joy turns away from Dr. Rodriguez and immediately grabs my shoulder and Tallulah's. "Listen, ladies," she says. She pulls us close to her, so we're like football players in a huddle or something. "This can't happen to you, OK? Not everyone is as nice or as fair as Piper."

Tallulah tries to wiggle out of her grasp. "Mom, what are you talking about?" she whines.

"If Piper didn't go to the bathroom, that's it. Daisy would have been eliminated over her period. I bet this has happened to other girls in other competitions. Eliminated by an act of God. You can't let it happen to you. You have to be prepared. You have to carry your supplies everywhere."

Tallulah finally breaks free. "OK, Mom. Jeez."

I take a deep breath. I don't need period supplies. I only need my shot.

I look up to see Daisy jogging toward us. She has on purple maternity gym shorts with white piping, tied so tightly they bunch out like a skirt. Her eyes are red from crying.

"Everyone's going to know," Daisy whispers when she reaches me.

Tallulah raises her eyebrows at me. I raise mine back. I grab Daisy's arm. I can't tell her that's not true—it is. Everyone's either going to guess that she got her period or that she peed her pants, which isn't exactly better. But I pull her toward the auditorium with us anyway.

I sprint for my folding chair. I'm sitting next to Tallulah, panting, as Dr. Rodriguez calls music theory. That's Daisy's next strongest specialty. I may have just ruined our chance of winning.

Tallulah and Daisy stand next to each other on the line this time, answering every single question as Eric and Jack and Josie and Kelly and the others sit down, one by one.

This might be over. Today.

Even if Tallulah gets every answer right, it doesn't matter as long as Daisy does, too.

If today is the end, it'll be all my fault for not knowing about Jupiter Hammon.

If today is the end, it'll be all my fault for helping Daisy get back to the stage.

I keep thinking Daisy will get the next question wrong. She can't be that focused, standing there in my mom's enormous running shorts. She can't be that confident. Something has to make her stumble.

I know I should probably be proud of her for facing her fear and still getting on this stage and kicking butt, but I'm not. Not if it's *our* butt she's kicking. And she didn't even tell Tallulah or me she was sorry.

On question nine, Daisy says that a dotted half-note is equal to two quarter notes, Tallulah knows the answer is actually three. Tallulah gets her last question right, too, and just like that, I'm out of my seat and cheering.

We're going to counties!

Daisy and George are, too.

But we'll beat them.

Later that night, I'm scribbling some ideas in my orange meta-phorical math notebook when Mom comes into my room and sits on the side of my bed like she's going to tuck me in the way she did before Gladys was born.

Mom pats my head, and I put the notebook down. "I'm really proud of you, you know."

I sit up and shrug. "If Tallulah hadn't gotten everything right, we'd be eliminated."

Mom plays with my hair. "Tallulah filled me on why you ended up taking the African American poetry specialty. It takes next-level empathy to accept Tallulah's position on that, and then you did all that extra work in order to be ready for a specialty you didn't know too much about a few weeks ago."

"Oh," I say. "I didn't think about it like that."

"Between that and how you helped Daisy when she needed you—"

"But, Mom—"

Mom shakes her head, stopping my words.

"No, Piper. Don't tell me anyone would have helped her because it's not true. You were willing to sacrifice your dreams in order to make something fair for your competitor. Very few eleven-year-olds would do that. Very few *people* would do that."

That's not what I was going to say.

I was going to say

But, Mom, why did I have to help her in the first place?

But, Mom, why weren't there pads in the bathroom?

And, Mom, if periods are normal and natural, why did it feel embarrassing to talk about?

"Is Eloise coming home tonight?"

Mom shakes her head. "I think she's spending the weekend at her mom's again. But you'll see her Monday, OK?"

"OK."

By Monday, something else might be on my mind. I might not remember to ask her what she thinks should have happened to Daisy today.

Mom kisses my cheek and flips the light off on the way out of my room.

I close my eyes for a minute to look for sleep but when it doesn't come right away, I open them again, crawl to my corkboard, and toss out the yellow card. It's not true anymore that none of my friends has a period.

I'm down to three reasons:

Green: *Besides, puberty and periods are about having babies one day, and I NEVER EVER EVER want to have a baby.*

Purple: *This is my decathlon year. I can't be distracted by things like hormones and periods.*

And orange: *I don't ever want to look like you, Mom.*

The purple one is more true than ever.

{ 12 }

Winter break is always boring because Tallulah goes to Georgia to visit her grandparents, and Daisy has a million cousins staying at her house. We aren't religious, so we don't do much for Christmas. Some years we have a tree, others we don't. But Christmas Day is the best, even if it wouldn't feel like Christmas to anyone else. For us, it's cozy and intimate and perfect. Our biggest tradition is breakfast. Mom gets up early and makes a feast, which we eat together on a tablecloth on the floor in front of the fireplace.

This year, Christmas falls in the middle of break, and I'm more alone than ever as I wait for it. I text Tallulah, but she's having so much fun with her family she doesn't text back often. Normally I'd be texting Daisy all day, but I guess we're still in a fight because I don't hear from her. Ivan sends me a few gifs and jokes, which is nice, but not nearly enough to distract me from what's going on at home. Mom is flustered to the point of panic because she just went back to work, and now Gladys is sick and can't go to daycare. Gladys is louder than ever. And Eloise is choosing her boyfriend over us, again and again and again.

For the first few days of break, I escape to El Jardín. And even though I'm the only person in the garden, it's a lot less lonely than being home. Sometimes I bundle inside multiple coats and shut myself into the back seat of the yellow car with a pile of books and notes to study for the decathlon. Other times I wander among what's left of this year's sunflowers and talk to them or sing them Christmas carols. You'll never catch me singing in front of people—I can't carry a tune. But plants don't mind, and sometimes it even feels like they like it. Like their energy is coming through their roots and into my feet, telling me they love my off-key rendition of *Silent Night*.

El Jardín Muerto actually looks *muerto* since it's winter and nothing's in bloom. But that's not how it works. Our garden isn't dead, it's sleeping. Peacefully. Unlike my little sister.

There's only one thing that would make these wandering, frigid afternoons better: Tallulah.

On the third day of break, a foot of snow falls, and the temperature drops to zero. I can't go to El Jardín Muerto anymore. And Gladys is screaming more than ever because, according to Mom's theory, she's angry that she had to go to daycare for all of, like, one week. I spend Christmas Eve cuddling my noise-canceling headphones. I can barely get anything done. I picture Tallulah on a sunny porch in Georgia with a book and a glass of sweet tea. I'm jealous.

Even worse, because of the ice and snow, Eloise gets stuck at Bobby's house and still isn't back by Christmas morning. When I wake up, all I want is for her to walk through our bedroom door. I don't even care about presents. I stay in bed an extra-long time, hoping she'll appear. Eventually my stomach convinces me to get up.

I step into the hallway, expecting it to smell like our traditional Christmas feast always does, frying oil or sizzling bacon. Instead, I smell smoke.

Fire.

I run to the kitchen, which isn't on fire, but two burners are on: one heating one strip of bacon to a charcoal-burnt black, the other heating a spitting pot of frying oil. I turn them off quickly and look around. The place is a mess. A bowl of raw eggs sits on the table, empty eggshells discarded all around it. A half-chopped carrot and a pile of diced celery and onion are lounging on a cutting board on the counter. Oil stains splatter the back of the stove behind the pot. The doughnut dough isn't even in the piping bag yet. A big package of bacon is half open on the counter next to the stove. Mom and Calvin aren't here and, of course, somewhere Gladys is crying. I can hear them all over the baby monitor. I can't make out their words with the way Gladys is screaming, but I recognize their tone: panic.

For a brief moment, Mom is loud enough that I hear her yell, "It's Christmas Day, Calvin!"

So she didn't just get a quarter of the way into cooking and then forget.

I walk in a slow circle, surveying the wreckage. If I had the culinary arts specialty, I could call fixing this mess studying. I don't, so fixing it will be a waste of time, but I'm the only one here, so I guess I'm going to do it anyway.

I put a clean pan on the stove and start to warm it for the unburnt bacon. I turn the oil down so that it's still hot but not spitting.

I call a bitter "You're welcome" toward the shouting happening in Mom's room, half hoping they'll hear and remember me. Remember that they left me alone on Christmas with a mess that almost turned into a fire.

I chop the rest of the carrot, then I mix the vegetables in with the eggs. I preheat the oven. Mom usually makes a quiche, which I don't know how to do. But I do know how to make egg muffins, so that's what we're having this year. I fry the bacon and chop it, then I mix it into the veggies and eggs, beat them, and pour them into muffin tins. While they bake, I knead the dough to loosen it up a little. My mom always fries whole doughnuts, but I have no idea how she drops that shape into a pot of burning oil, so I decide to make doughnut holes instead. I pour cinnamon and sugar into a bowl to roll them around in after they fry.

Soon, the eggs are smelling good, and I still haven't seen a single member of my family. Gladys is still yelling; Mom and Calvin are still debating something that I can't decipher. But I'm humming. I know these smells will pull them out of their bedroom. Soon, they'll walk into the kitchen with huge, fascinated smiles saying *Piper, did you do all this?* It'll be like when I was four, and I read out loud in front of Mom's friends, or when I was seven, and I solved an equation on the board in front of Mom's college students. For a moment, I'll be a star again.

While the first set of doughnut holes are floating in the frying oil, I decide to get even fancier. I grab the cocoa powder and mix melted butter into a bowl of sugar so that we can have three kinds of doughnut holes. Then I grab the pancake mix and the waffle iron, deciding that it's Christmas and I'm cooking, and my specialty is waffles from a box, so that's what we're having.

I put the first five doughnut holes on the cooling rack and drop some more dough into the oil. Then I spray the waffle iron and pour in some batter. By the time the egg muffins are ready, we have a whole pile of cinnamon, chocolate, and glazed doughnut holes, and a stack of eight waffles. I dance over to the fireplace to spread the tablecloth on the floor. It feels good to move my body. To create something—something more concrete than metaphorical math. Something my mom will understand and appreciate.

Gladys screams the loudest I've ever heard.

"She'll never understand what I do for her," I mumble under my breath, a joke with myself, as I cross the room back to the beeping waffle iron. "I cook the whole breakfast so she can have all of Mom's attention even on—"

"Piper. What on earth are you doing?"

An accusation.

I look up. Mom and Calvin are standing in the doorway to the kitchen, Gladys tucked between them, the three of them so close together that I can't even tell who's holding her. The looks on their faces are not the ones I've been imagining. It looks like . . . I'm in trouble?

I freeze with a waffle half unstuck from the waffle iron. "Making breakfast?"

"Why?" Mom says. It sounds like a sob.

This is not how this moment should feel.

"Because . . ." ~~That horrible baby won't let you do it.~~ "You seemed busy?"

"Is that— Piper Jane Franklin!" Mom shoves Gladys at Calvin and runs through the kitchen. She turns off the burner under the oil.

"What are you thinking? You turned on the oven?" she says. "You used the waffle iron? You heated the frying oil?" She sounds so angry. Or maybe terrified.

I stare at her.

"Do you not hear me speaking to you?" she shouts.

"Oh." I guess I'm supposed to answer. "Um . . . yes?"

"Is that a question?"

"I mean, I did some of those things," I clarify.

For some reason, I'm not following her into her anger. She's screaming but I'm calm. I'm too lonely to be angry. Does she not see that I was saving Christmas? Does she misunderstand even this?

"Do you know how many fire hazards are in this kitchen right now? Do you think we want to rush two kids to the emergency room today?"

Wait, what? "Emergency room?"

"Your sister has a fever. A high fever," Mom yells. "Did you even think of that?"

I'm speechless. Why would I have thought of that?

"Well? Did you?"

"Um, no?"

A little part of me is getting mad. But the rest of me feels powered down. So beyond lonely that I've shed all emotions. Numb.

"Of course not. You were too busy risking a house fire!"

"Anna," Calvin says, somehow softly but also at a volume where Mom and I can hear him over all the screaming.

He makes Mom stop and take a breath. I wish I had his superpower.

"I don't mean to yell," Mom says, still kind of yelling. "But this is scary. Piper, you could have been hurt. Why did you think it was OK to turn on the stove without asking?"

"I . . . I didn't," I say.

"And you know frying oil is dangerous!"

"I didn't turn that on, either, Mom."

Mom's eyes bug out. "Did you miss the part where thirty seconds ago I had to turn off that spitting oil before it burned your face?"

"No," I say. "I just . . . the oil was already on."

Mom snaps her jaw shut like she's startled. "No . . . no, it wasn't," she says. But she's not yelling.

"I smelled something burning when I woke up, so I ran to the kitchen. There was bacon on the stove and that burner was on, too," I say.

"I turned the burners off," Mom says. Then she pauses. "Wait, didn't I?"

I shake my head no.

"Oh my god." She smacks her hand into her forehead. "What is wrong with me?"

"Anna, it's all right," Calvin says. But he can speak for himself because it's not all right with me that Mom keeps yelling at me when I don't deserve it. "You need sleep. That's all."

"How am I supposed to sleep with her crying all night?" Mom is shouting again.

I'm still standing far away from her. Calvin and Gladys are all the way across the room, just outside their bedroom. Mom is halfway between them and the stove. I'm right in front of the stove, behind the kitchen island.

"I tried to fix it," I say, hoping I can make Mom feel better without telling her it's OK.

I saved Christmas, right? Can we have Christmas now?

"I threw away the burned bacon and turned off the burner. I cleaned the black stuff out of the pan. And I turned down the oil before I fried the dough."

Be impressed.

Hug me.

Eat all this food.

"Oh my," Mom whispers, shaking her head against her palm. "I'm sorry, honey."

"So . . . want to eat?" I put on a goofy smile.

Mom and Calvin don't laugh. Mom's face remains in a stake of shock.

"Gladys can eat. She should be here any minute," she says, finally.

"Gladys?" I say, looking at the baby.

"No," Mom says. "Jeez, I'm so tired. Eloise. Eloise is on her way now."

"Oh," I say, brightening. I turn away from Mom to finally remove the last waffle. "OK, we can wait for Eloise."

We're all going to be together for breakfast after all. For a moment, I don't even care that Gladys is probably going to be screaming in Mom's arms the whole time.

"Piper. Honey."

When I look up, she's back across the room, holding the baby again. She's zipping up her coat.

No.

Sirens wail in my brain. This can't be happening. They can't be leaving now. They can't be leaving me on Christmas.

"Where are you going?" I whisper.

"I told you. We have to take the baby to the doctor," Mom says. "I'm so sorry, honey, but Gladys is sick. That's why she won't stop screaming."

She didn't tell me that. She asked if I wanted them to have

to rush two kids to the ER, which is a very different thing.

"What kind of sick?" I ask.

Mom shakes her head. "I don't know. The pediatrician said that if her fever doesn't come down with Tylenol, we need to take her to the hospital. So, that's what we're doing."

I look away from Mom, out the window, because it's hurting too much to see them piling on coats and passing Gladys back and forth while I'm over here, by myself, between the fire and the feast that I just got yelled at for cooking.

"You're both going?" I ask.

Can't Calvin take her?

"She's really sick, honey. She needs us both."

"Now?"

"As soon as Eloise gets here," Mom says. She bends over to strap Gladys into the car seat on the floor. We hear a car in the driveway. "Yes. Now."

But I just made all this food.

But I was already so lonely.

Can't Mom stay?

"You're probably hungry," I say, the words falling out of me fast as they appear in the right-side column, blocking out all the left-side words I want to scream. "I get hungry when I'm tired. Maybe you can eat something quickly first." They look at each other wordlessly. They don't look back at me. I add. "Or you can take an egg muffin with you." I hold out the tin with the six egg muffins still inside it.

Calvin runs to me and takes the whole thing.

"What a great idea, Piper. We can eat these in the car."

Mom doesn't say anything. She looks up from Gladys's car seat and rushes over to me. My hands are still in front of me, like I'm holding an invisible second tin of muffins.

"I'm sorry, Piper. I'm sorry I left the kitchen like that. I'm sorry I got mad at you for trying to clean up my mess. You didn't deserve any of that, OK? When we get home, I'm going to eat every bit of leftovers from yours and Eloise's breakfast."

Mom plants a cold kiss on my forehead and then the three of them are gone, barely stopping to say hello to Eloise as she walks through the door opposite them.

I look up at my big sister, my hands still frozen in front of me. She's glowing as always, in a pretty gold sweater and a black headband and a frown, which is what this moment needs. But, for the first time ever, she's not enough.

She puts her arm around me. "Well, this sucks."

Those are the perfect words. My face breaks open and tears stream from my eyes. She hugs me tight. "Let's pack all of this this up," she says. "We'll save everything for when they're back."

I nod against her shoulder.

"And you and me? Our breakfast is going to be raw cookie dough and frosting straight from the tub. Because it's Christmas."

She laughs. I try to, but it comes out sounding more like a sob.

She tries to let go, but I hold her tighter.

"Did I ever do this to you?" I whisper. "When I was a baby? Did I ever make you feel this way?"

"What?" Eloise steps back so she can look right in my eyes. "No! You were so cute, you could do no wrong. I adored you."

I raise my eyebrows. I'm an awful big sister.

"Iper, you know this isn't Gladys's fault, right?"

But I barely hear her. I'm trying to remember if Gladys is cute. I can't picture her face. I only ever see the back of her head.

{ 13 }

Mom and Calvin are gone for hours. Something is weird when they come back: Gladys is sleeping, and they're laughing. They disappear into their bedroom, then they reappear, without Gladys. She's asleep in her crib.

Things are . . . better.

Mom restarts the fire, lays the tablecloth back on the floor, and asks me to set out breakfast even though it's 4:00 p.m. The doughnuts are tough and cold, and the nine-hour-old waffles are especially gross, but Mom, Calvin, Eloise, and I eat everything anyway.

"I know this would have been more delicious at ten thirty this morning," Mom says, gnawing on her last bite of waffle. "But it tastes amazing right now."

I roll my eyes, but I'm smiling. "OK, sure."

"I'm serious!" Mom says. "This is the first thing I've eaten since that egg muffin this morning."

"Now *that* was delicious," Calvin says.

"Thanks," I say, sheepishly.

"I barely tasted it," Mom says. Then she quickly adds, "I mean, I'm sure it was wonderful. I was just so worried, but this right here"—she picks up a mostly cooked chocolate-glazed doughnut and pops it in her mouth—"this is the perfect Christmas dinner."

Mom puts her arm around me, and I sink into her, so glad to have a hug without anything between us. It feels too good to be true, so I don't ask any questions for the rest of the day. I go to bed still not knowing ~~or really caring~~ what was wrong with Gladys.

The next day, things are even better. Gladys wakes up, of course, but she doesn't cry. She's noisy, but it's gurgling and baby talk into Mom's collar as Mom cleans the kitchen or snoring on Mom's shoulder as Mom prepares a lecture at the table. I guess whatever happened at the hospital really did help her stop crying so much. Eloise spends the whole day at our house, except for a few hours at the dog shelter, and she takes me with her for that.

I go back to El Jardín in the afternoon to sing *Deck the Halls* to the resting roots, but I don't study there. I study at home. Gladys is so much quieter that I can sit in the living room to study the way I used to. Calvin refills my water bottle before I even ask. Mom sometimes puts a snack next to me. When Gladys fusses, Mom bounces her and hums, and she quiets back down. It's the way I thought life with a baby sister would be before she was born, normal except for a tiny warm body sometimes wedged between us.

By New Year's Eve, I'm feeling pretty prepared for all four of my remaining specialties, so, in the evening, I take the *Encyclopedia of Plant Life* and *The History of Natural Disasters* and wander into the living room to ask Calvin to quiz me. The light is on under the door to the basement, so he's probably in his office. I could go down and ask, I know he'd help me, but instead, I look for Mom. Maybe I want her help even if Gladys is in between us.

As soon as I crack the door to her bedroom, Mom comes rushing toward me saying "Shh!"

She tiptoes into the hallway. The good news is she's not wearing Gladys. The bad news is she's barely wearing anything. She has on a bra, a tank top, embarrassingly huge underwear, and one leg of a pair of sheer black leggings. Also, makeup. I haven't seen her in makeup in forever.

"Mom, you're naked!"

"Oh, I'm not. I just didn't get a chance to put my dress on yet," she says, rolling her eyes. "Anyway, this is a good thing."

"Huh?"

She steps into the rest of her see-through pants.

I don't know, maybe I'm being weird. Mom changes in front of me all the time in her bedroom, but it feels different in the hallway.

"I was getting dressed and Gladys fell asleep on her own. In her crib!"

She says this the way she used to say things like "I'm the lead author on a research paper!" or "I'm being honored for my developments in algebraic K-theory!"

Those times, I said *congrats*, so I say that now, too, even though I don't see why a sleeping baby should compare to her greatest accomplishments.

"Why are you . . . ?" I gesture toward her face.

"Calvin and I are going out," she says, adjusting the straps of her bra and tank. "Gladys fell asleep at this time yesterday, and then she slept through the night. Maybe we'll get lucky, and it'll happen again."

I glance at my phone. It's 6:37.

"Really?"

Mom laughs. "Well, she slept until four."

"Four a.m.?" I say. "That's through the night?"

"It's the most sleep I've gotten in ages," Mom says, joyfully. "And now she's asleep again."

"But you're awake," I point out.

"I think I'll have Eloise wake her up to feed her at eleven. Maybe I'll get another thirty minutes that way."

"Thirty minutes?" What good is thirty minutes? Why doesn't Mom just sleep now? How does she have so much energy after waking up at four? And "Wait . . . Eloise?"

"Yup. Follow me so we don't have to whisper."

I'm smiling. I don't know why. None of the words coming out of her mouth sound like my old mom. But the way she's saying them, the way she's smiling, the fact that she's excited for a date with Calvin: all that is my old mom. And I've missed her.

"Don't worry," she says, pouring herself a glass of water.

"If Gladys is being difficult, we'll come right back, but I think we're over the hump. Can you believe we've been held hostage by an ear infection?"

"We have?"

Mom freezes and takes a deep breath. "I'm sorry, honey," she says. "I keep expecting you to pick things up by osmosis or something. I'm working on it though. When we brought Gladys to the ER on Christmas, we found out she had a double ear infection. She'd likely had it for quite some time. We didn't notice it for a while because she didn't have a fever until that day, and she went straight from the fussy five-month stage into an ear infection. But that's why she always wanted to eat. You know how sucking on something can clear your ears?"

I nod.

"That's true for babies, too. So, Gladys has been eating and eating to make her ears feel better, and that's why she's been spitting up even more. A few days of antibiotics, a few rounds of baby Tylenol, and she's a whole new kid."

"Wait . . . really?" This is a New Year's miracle. "So, she's going to be quiet all the time now?"

Mom laughs. "Well, maybe not all the time."

"Right. But are you saying . . . it's going to get easier?"

Mom tilts her head. "Am I saying what's going to get easier?"

I bite my lip because I realize this question is coming from the wrong column.

"I mean . . . are you saying living with Gladys won't always be so . . ."

hard

gross

~~awful~~

"Loud?"

Mom puts down her water and throws her arms around me. "Oh, honey. Oh, Piper," she says. "Jeez, no! I should have been teaching you how this works all along. Babies don't stay as difficult as Gladys has been forever, thank god."

"Thank god? You mean . . . you don't like it, either?"

"Piper. I hate it."

"You do?" I'm shocked.

"I love Gladys of course, but, honey, I've been miserable. I've been missing sleep. I've been missing Calvin and Eloise. I've been missing you. My gosh, Piper, did you think you were alone in it?"

I was alone in it.

I shrug.

"We're in it together. Or we should be. We have to be. I've been failing all my girls, but that ends now."

"No, you haven't," I say. And not just to be nice.

I'm glad when she apologizes for yelling. But how was Mom supposed to notice things like ear infections and notes on the calendar when she hasn't been sleeping? Why is Mom apologizing for not doing the impossible?

The reason I don't want to stop the shots is in front of me right now: My mom, thrilled that she might get to sleep past 4:00 a.m. My mom, all made up for a date, and yet unbuttoning her pumping bra and opening her laptop so that her body can make food, while her brain can make money, while her heart talks to me, all on New Year's Eve.

How can she do all this—do it all in the ugliest underpants of all time—and still not see the Wordless Chain?

I wish I could ask her, but I don't want to risk a fight when I'm this happy, and so is she.

She's clearly too busy to quiz me, but I open my books and sit next to her anyway. Even if she looks different and sounds different, she *feels* like my mom again. And I'll take it.

About an hour later, Mom and Calvin leave. Eloise, Bobby, and I sit on the couch, Eloise in the middle, and spread blankets over our laps. We pass popcorn back and forth. It's cozy.

"This was my favorite movie when I was your age, Piper," Bobby says.

I smile at him, remembering everything he said on the train ride after Ivan's birthday party. Is he another person in this lonely club? Does he really know about the Wordless Chain? Maybe I'll get another clue tonight.

"Get ready to laugh your butt off," he says.

"Bobby!" Eloise says.

"What? She's a genius."

"What does that have to do with anything?" Eloise asks.

I smile. "Because I don't need a butt, as long as I have a brain."

They both laugh. Real laughs. I don't think I've ever made Eloise laugh like this before. She laughs like I'm her friend. It sticks with me, that laugh. I can see how it's the next thing. It could be the replacement for sleeping all tangled together: grown-up laughing.

That's another part of growing up I'd be excited for if it weren't for puberty and all the strings—or chains—attached.

As soon as Bobby hits play, the baby monitor erupts with *wah wah wah*. It makes me want to pull my hair out and stuff it in my ears.

"That's my cue," Eloise says, as if this is fun instead of the biggest heartbreak in the world. She reaches across Bobby to pause the TV, then walks out the room.

I shouldn't be upset. Eloise is here to babysit Gladys, not to hang out with me. I'm eleven and I don't need a babysitter anymore. One minute ago, I was proud of myself for making them grown-up laugh, and now I want to be a baby again. It's dizzying.

"Oh, Gladys. Gross!" Eloise yells from Mom's bedroom.

I look at Bobby. "She puked. I'll bet you anything."

He smiles. "I never bet against a kid wonder," he says. He has dimples, too—not as pronounced as Ivan's, but still nice to look at. His hair is curly, and it flops over his forehead. He put on black-framed glasses to watch the movie. I can see how Eloise must see him. How she must find him cute.

She appears in the doorway of Mom's bedroom holding a screaming Gladys at arm's length.

"Told you," I say.

"I need to give her a bath," Eloise says. "It's all in her hair."

I look up and yes. Gladys barely has any hair, but the little patches of it that she has are caked in crusty green stuff.

"Would you change her sheets, babe?" Eloise asks.

"What?" Bobby says. "That's women's work."

My jaw drops. *Women's work?* That's even worse than calling my mom *Mrs. Franklin.* How could he say that? It's like all the lights in the living room dim. I'm so disappointed.

Bobby disappears and Eloise is next to me, puke-covered baby and all. "We'll start the movie again in a few minutes. We can watch while I feed her. Do you want to help me give her a bath or just watch TV while you wait?"

I shake my head. "I'll study."

Eloise laughs. "Of course. Why watch TV when you can read"—she pauses to check out the books I have spread across the coffee table—"*Advanced Euclidian Geometry?*"

I laugh with her, then she walks toward the bathroom, and I scooch to the floor and open the book. But I can't concentrate. *Women's work.*

My phone vibrates. It's ringing, which is weird. My friends only talk IRL or over text. I flip it over and my heart starts to vibrate with it. Ivan's name glows. I turn it on, and his face fills the screen.

"Happy New Year from Kiribati!" he says. There's a lot of noise and commotion in his background like he's at a party or something.

"Wait what?" I say. "Kiribati like Christmas Island?"

"Yeah. Dang, you knew that?" Ivan asks.

I shrug. It's geography. Of course, I knew it.

"What are you doing there?"

Seeing Ivan makes me smile, even though I'm still upset about Bobby.

"We go every year for the holidays," Ivan says.

"You do?" I ask, shocked. "That's like a twenty-hour flight."

"Dang, you knew that, too?" His smile gets even goofier. "Yeah, we go for the holidays. Get it? We go to *Christmas Island*?"

"Oh," I say.

"Nah," Ivan says. "I'm just kidding. That would be wild! But I wanted to call you for New Year's, and I wasn't sure if geniuses like you stay up until midnight, so I thought I'd pretend to call from somewhere that it's midnight right now. When I googled and found Christmas Island, I was like, perfect prank!"

"But . . ." I say, ~~that's wrong~~. "Oh. Funny. Happy almost New Year from New Jersey."

"Wait, *but* what?" Ivan asks.

"No but," I say. My voice cracks, giving me away.

"Don't even lie, bro. Just tell me."

"OK," I say shrugging. "It's just . . . Christmas Island is actually three hours behind eastern standard time."

"Exactly! That means it's midnight there," Ivan says.

"No, I mean, when it's nine p.m. here, it's six p.m. there."

"Wait . . . Oh! Double dang," Ivan yelps. "I did it backward. And I thought I was being so clever. Bro, it's hard to have a friend as smart as you, I swear."

I smile. When he calls me *bro,* it makes my heart heat up.

"Maybe math should be women's work," I mumble.

"What?" Ivan says, suddenly serious. "Why would you say that?"

Oh no. I wasn't thinking about how different, yet still awful, that phrase would sound to Ivan.

"No, no," I say quickly. "That wasn't about you. I was repeating something stupid Eloise's boyfriend just said. It's stuck in my brain."

"He said math was for women?" Ivan asks with his lopsided smile glowing on my screen.

I laugh. "No. He said chores were, I think."

"What?" Ivan shouts, his smile gone.

"They're here babysitting for my little sister, and he said he couldn't change her sheets because it's women's work."

"That's messed up!" Ivan says.

I'm glad he said the not-nice thing so I can just agree without saying it out loud.

"It is, right?"

There's rustling behind me as Bobby walks through the room. "Is that the guy?" Ivan asks, too loudly.

"Shh!" I say. "Yes."

"Hey you! Hey you, sister's boyfriend!" Ivan screams from the phone.

I'm embarrassed, and I feel bad for saying something not nice about Bobby, and my face is on fire, but for some reason

I also can't stop giggling.

"Shh!" I tell Ivan. I turn around. "Ignore him," I say to Bobby.

But he's already right behind me, leaning over the back of the couch to peer at my phone screen.

"Hello," he says to Ivan. "Who's this?" he asks me.

Ivan doesn't give me a chance to answer. "Why are you calling chores women's work, man?" he shouts.

I want to throw my phone in the fireplace.

"Seriously," he continues. "You don't deserve a girl at all, let alone Piper's sister."

"Ivan!" I squeal.

"What? That's messed up, bro," he says. And I can tell he means it, even though he's laughing. For some reason, I'm still laughing. And somehow, behind me, even Bobby is laughing.

"All right, I'm out. You go deal with that guy," Ivan says through a fitful of giggles. "Happy New Year!" And he hangs up.

I turn around. Bobby is standing there with an armload of baby-puke sheets.

"Piper," he says, still smiling. "It was a joke. I didn't mean it." He holds out the sheets as if to prove it.

"Oh," I say.

But it wasn't funny.

When he returns from the laundry room in the basement, I follow him into Mom's room.

I lean against the doorjamb and watch as he pulls the crib mattress up and starts to fit a clean mattress protector around it.

"Can you explain it to me?" I ask his back.

He turns and smiles at me the way I've seen Daisy's big brother smile at her when I'm at her house.

"The kid wonder needs a lesson in changing crib sheets?" he asks.

"No, I mean . . . can you explain why it's funny? Why was it supposed to be a joke? *Women's work*."

"Oh!" Bobby says. He turns back around so that I'm talking to the back of his head. "Yeah, I get your reaction. I mean, if my dad said that, whew. It'd be infuriating. But Eloise knows I don't think that way. She knows I actively work against thinking that way." Bobby lets the mattress thump back into the crib, then picks up the new lilac sheet and shakes it out. "So . . . I guess it was sort of an inside joke? It was only funny because Eloise knew I didn't mean it."

"Oh," I say. "Your dad?"

"He . . . he just . . . did you know I have four younger siblings?"

"You do?"

Bobby laughs. "How do you think I got so skilled with the crib sheets?"

"Right," I say with a chuckle.

"Yeah. My parents managed to have five kids before splitting up. I don't know how because they hate each other. And sometimes I hate my dad, too."

My eyebrows go up. "Really?" I've never heard Bobby use left-side words before.

"He's so disrespectful to my mom, and he doesn't even see

213

it. And my sisters, too. Every time we have to spend the week-end over there, he expects Beverly to take care of the three youngest ones, even though she's only fourteen. And he expects me to do what he does: sit on my butt, drink Coke, and watch football. I don't even like football. Or Coke!"

A light bulb goes off in my brain. "So, he says things like that? Like *women's work?*"

If Bobby says yes, then all I have to do is introduce my mom to his dad and *boom* she'll see the Wordless Chain.

But Bobby says, "No, not out loud. He just acts like he's doing so much more than he is. Like, my mom had to have this surgery once, right? It was just an outpatient thing, but she couldn't have all these little kids running around the next day. Beverly and I wanted to stay and help her, so she asked Dad if he would take the little kids for one night. He did, but he acted like this was a huge deal. Like it's some burden. Like he was doing her a favor by playing with his own kids. Or, like, his girlfriend will cook us a meal, and he spends five minutes doing the dishes afterward and then calls it even. He's just, like, the opposite of who I want to be. Wait." Bobby turns back to me now that the sheet is smoothly secured to the mattress. "Why am I telling you all this?"

"Because you see it, too," I whisper.

He tilts his head. "See what?"

"The Wordless—the things that . . ." I shake my head to clear my thoughts. "I feel like this stuff happens to Mom and Eloise all the time."

Bobby looks shocked. "With me? Because I'm trying hard not to be like that. I swear. Eloise deserves . . ."

He trails off, dimples flashing, like just the thought of Eloise makes his face light up.

"No, no," I say. "Not with you, or with Calvin. With . . . with the world. Everywhere we go, people dismiss my mom. When she was pregnant, they'd touch her belly without asking, as if her own stomach didn't belong to her. And no one calls my mom what she likes to be called. Stuff like that happens to Eloise, too."

"Oh," Bobby says. "Yeah, now that you say it, I know what you mean."

"But . . . it feels like I'm the only one who even notices."

"Well," Bobby says, coming close enough to knock a gentle fist into my shoulder. "That's probably because you're a genius."

"No, it's not." I'm not ready to go back to joking.

"But this stuff isn't easy to think about, Piper. I have to work to see it. It's easier to just not notice it all."

"It's impossible to just not notice it all," I say.

"Again," Bobby says, gesturing toward me. "Genius."

"OK, but then, what is it?"

He looks at me like I'm nuts. "Huh?"

"What am I noticing that other people don't? What's it called?"

He lowers his eyebrows. "I don't think it's called anything. I think it just . . . is."

I squint at him, certain he knows more than he's saying,

certain he can give me a word or words to make everything I see and feel about growing up totally clear and logical to everyone, especially my mom. But he doesn't.

"Where are you guys?" Eloise calls from the kitchen.

Bobby smiles. "Let's go," he says. "More women's work awaits."

This time I laugh.

He leans a little closer and speaks a little lower. "Hey, clear my name with that friend of yours, too, OK? I can tell he's not a *women's work* guy, and if he's ever here watching a movie with us, I want him to understand that we're on the same side."

Then he walks out the room. I stand there frozen as the image washes over me. Eloise, Bobby, Ivan, and me, all watching a movie together. It's so grown-up, so unreal, so exciting, just the idea, the picture, the fantasy. I can barely stand it.

We find Eloise in the kitchen holding a baby bottle half in and half out of a pot of hot water, Gladys smushed into her shoulder, clean and quiet.

Eloise sets the bottle on the counter. "Little help?" she says. Then she hooks her hands under Gladys's armpits and straightens her elbows so Gladys is hanging from Eloise's hands, suspended in the air. I'm expecting Bobby to reach for her, but Eloise is holding her toward me. And Bobby disappears into the bathroom.

I freeze, watching Gladys dangle.

I've held her before, of course. A few times when she was freshly born. Back when you had to be sure you were holding her head because her neck couldn't hold it up yet. I liked her little body, small enough that I could hold her feet in my left hand if her head was in my left elbow. She was always sleeping then, and she smelled like baby powder instead of spit-up, and I think I loved her.

I watch her kick her feet in the air in front of me. I don't know her anymore.

"Piper?" Eloise says.

I'm not sure what else to do, so I lift my arms. Eloise settles Gladys on my shoulder. She's like a sack of halfway baked potatoes. Heavy. Mushy. Solid. Warm and sweet smelling.

"How old is she now?" I ask.

Eloise laughs. "Seven months. I'm surprised you didn't know that, *Ma'am* Piper Franklin."

I guess I don't bother doing the math when it comes to my baby sister. I take a step back as Eloise pulls the hot pot off the stove.

Gladys puts her face in my neck and slobbers into my collar. It's gross. But for some reason, I hold her tighter. Then she grabs a chunk of my hair and shoves against my shoulders, arching her back so she can look at me.

"Her eyes are green now!"

The last time I saw them, they were blue.

Eloise stops halfway to the sink, still holding the pot. "You didn't know that?"

"No," I say, staring at them. I can see my own green eyes reflecting back. When was the last time I saw her eyes? I think and think, but I can't remember.

"They've been green for, like, months. What have you been looking at when you hold her?"

"I haven't held her," I say.

"What?" Eloise sounds shocked in a way that makes me feel like a bad sister again.

"It's not my fault. She's always on Mom. I only ever see this bald head."

Eloise stares, dumbfounded. "You're going to feed her."

I wait for ~~no way~~ to appear in my *Can't Say That* column, but it doesn't. I want to feed her.

Eloise sets me up the way I've seen Calvin set my mom up to nurse. She arranges pillows behind my back and helps me rest Gladys on my lap so that she's half sitting up. She shows me how to tilt the bottle so no air gets into her mouth. Bobby and Eloise settle into each other on the couch. He puts the movie back on.

It's funny, the movie, I think. But I'm too focused on the weight in my arms to pay attention. Her green eyes flutter: open and closed, open and closed. A soft sigh comes from her mouth when I pull the bottle away to burp her. Her cheek leans against my jaw when I pat her back. And when she burps, it feels like winning a round of the decathlon.

Maybe I don't hate Gladys.

After her bottle, I help Eloise cover her soft skin with rose-scented lotion, change her diaper, and wiggle her body into footie pajamas. She cries when she's cold, but it doesn't make me want to rip my hair out because I understand why she's crying, and how to fix it. When we put her to bed, I sing her *Twinkle, Twinkle Little Star*. Twice.

At midnight, Mom and Calvin come home and we all watch the ball drop together. We give each other hugs and then Calvin says he'll drive Bobby home. But Eloise doesn't go with them. Instead, she follows me down the hall to our room.

"You're staying here tonight?" I ask, shocked.

"Of course, Iper. It's after midnight."

There's a part of every day that's after midnight, and yet there are many, many after midnights that Eloise is not in our room.

She glances at my corkboard.

"You threw some out," she says.

I take pajamas out of my dresser.

"Yeah. You were right. I'm not jealous of Ivan."

"Good," she says.

"Except, well, I am jealous that he gets to live in New York City," I say.

And, just like I wanted, it makes her laugh the grown-up laugh again. "That one's OK. I am, too."

"I had to throw out the yellow one, too. Daisy got her period."

"So, you won't be first!" Eloise says.

"I still need the shots," I say.

"I know, Ipey. I'm on your side. Remember?"

"Thanks." I don't tell her about the thoughts that suddenly

creep up when I say that. The way it feels to imagine Ivan here watching a movie with us. The way it felt to make Eloise and Bobby laugh like grown-ups. The way growing up is starting to look . . . exciting.

I take all those thoughts and shove them into a little box and throw it away. I can't be excited to grow up. That's like being excited for puberty. That's like wanting to be subjected to the Wordless Chain. I can never want that.

I lay down with a huge smile on my face and listen for Eloise's breathing to even out. Then I climb out of bed and throw out the green card. The Gladys card. I don't know if I'd ever want to have a baby, so it's not like this affects my feelings about puberty, but still the green card is wrong now. I don't hate babies anymore.

Only two colors left. But that doesn't change anything.

{14}

The first week after break slips by in a hurricane of school, TGASP, and homework under my desk during class so I can study every second of the afternoons. Calvin quizzes me during car rides and dinner and breakfast. Tallulah and I sit together at lunch and trade study materials to quiz each other with. There's a brief warm spell in January so we meet in El Jardín in the late afternoons, google the hardest questions we can find in each other's specialties, or pull apart flowers and leaves and stems to study their parts.

The next thing we know, it's Saturday. Counties. We're at a local community college, and again we're sitting behind a red curtain on a dark stage. Dr. Patricia Gregory, today's MC, gives the introduction. The stage is crowded with folding chairs holding at least a hundred other kids. The audience is also much bigger.

Most importantly, this time I know my mom is here because she drove me.

But all that is outside this moment. Right now, the only thing real is the pressure of Tallulah's arm against mine. The cool darkness on my face before the lights come up. The way Dr. Gregory's voice rises and falls as she tells the audience how everyone on this stage has already won, how it's more important to be loved than to win.

The curtain goes up. Dr. Gregory asks us to stand.

I feel wobbly in the hot lights as I get to my feet. I smooth the skirt of my denim jumper. Tallulah has on warm-up pants and a New York Liberty WNBA T-shirt. On my other side, next to a small break in the chairs, Daisy wears leggings and a flouncy blue blouse, and George is in a polo shirt and jeans. We stand on the edges of our feet, staring out into the dark and anonymous audience. And then, *BAM!* We're smacked with a wall of applause.

This moment feels the way it should. It feels as big as it actually is. Finally.

"These are the smartest children in the county," Dr. Gregory cheers. "And I am honored to be among them. Now!" She points to the yellow tape on the floor. There are two lines today. "Contestants, please come forward and take your spot if you're competing in the specialty of . . ." She looks out at the crowd. "Drum roll please?"

There are giggles in the audience as they pound their feet on the floor until it shakes.

My hands are in fists. My whole body is tense. I'm begging the universe for a win. I like Dr. Gregory. I want her to call geometric patterns or earth sciences or even endocrinology so I can have a chance to impress her.

"Chinese dynasties!"

Tallulah makes a little "ooh!" sound like she's surprised and nervous. I try to pat her back, but she's already walking away. I fall into my seat, my fingers crossed, trying to send Tallulah luck. She's in the second row, which means she won't be up for a while. Her hair is in fresh box braids. I imagine her mom oiling and braiding her hair while Tallulah pored over maps and timelines. Her fingers are laced behind her back, and her right thumbnail is chipping silver polish off her left pointer finger. She's nervous.

So am I.

We have to win.

"The first question goes to"—Dr. Gregory pauses to read the first kid's name tag—"Harold." She smiles warmly at him, then says, "The years 220 through 280 CE are known as the period of the Three Kingdoms. Who were the leaders of each kingdom?"

The room is silent, waiting for Harold to answer. I have no idea. I've never heard of anything in that question. Harold doesn't know, either, I guess, because a buzzer indicates he's used up his allotted sixty seconds.

The girl next to him says, "Wei, Shu, and Wu?"

"Incorrect," Dr. Gregory says. "Next."

My eyes go wide. If the next girl gets this one, two teams are already eliminated.

She misses and so do the next two. The sixth kid times out.

I watch Tallulah stop chipping her nail polish and then unlace her fingers, so her hands hang loose. I watch her feet go steady on the floor and her shoulders relax. *She knows.*

The first question winds all the way to her—number twenty-eight out of fifty-seven—and she says, "Cao Pi, Liu Bei, and Sun Quan."

Just like that, twenty-seven kids take their seats, and Chinese dynasties is half over. Dr. Gregory rearranges the thirty kids left. The round continues. Five kids say the wrong answer for the second question. Then George gets it right, so they all sit down.

Daisy and I still haven't talked since the first round when she got her period. She stopped saying mean things to me and Tallulah, but she's also not saying anything. I don't know if she's still mad at me for choosing Tallulah as a partner or for assuming we'd win, and I want her friendship back a whole lot, but, honestly, I'm not worried about competing against her anymore. I have Tallulah.

By the time Tallulah gets her second turn, there are fewer than ten kids on the stage. Three others get eliminated by her. A few other kids get correct answers, but Tallulah is on fire. She barely needs ten seconds.

"Kaifeng."

"Five Hus and Sixteen States."

"Tang of Shang."

George goes out on question five, but he's one of the last kids standing, so I hope he doesn't feel too bad about it. By question six, Tallulah has already won the round. She still has to answer four more questions because the day's scores are cumulative. She stands there, alone in her spotlight and in only forty-five seconds, she secures a perfect score.

"Wow," Dr. Gregory says. "Wow."

The audience applauds Tallulah like she's a Broadway performer. Dr. Gregory announces that everyone should stay in their seats for a quick two-minute break, and the curtain falls. Tallulah runs at me, panting like she's just finished a regular decathlon. I stand to hug her, but Daisy gets to her first. She throws her arms around Tallulah. "You were amazing," she says. "And Tallulah . . . I said some awful things. I've been trying all week to figure out how to erase them from history. I don't think I can, but I am sorry. Really sorry."

Tallulah hesitates a moment, then hugs her back.

"We'll talk about it later, Daisy," she says. "This is the decathlon."

"Oh, yeah," Daisy says. "Sorry. Jeez. Still sorry."

They laugh. Daisy doesn't apologize to me. She doesn't even look at me. But, who cares, I don't want to think about how much I've missed her knock-knock jokes right now. Tallulah's right, this is the decathlon. I stay focused on the line of light under the curtain, facts from all five of my subjects flying through my brain.

When it goes up again, Dr. Gregory calls geometric patterns, and it's finally my turn with a subject I love. I go to the front row, fifth in line. I'm ready.

Apparently, I'm not the only one because all four kids before me get their first questions correct.

Dr. Gregory says, "For Piper: If two nonagons are torn apart and then reformed so that each of their sides factors into the perimeter of a new shape, what would that new shape be called?"

Easy. "Octadecagon."

"Correct," she says.

There's a smattering of applause.

Kids are more prepared for geometric patterns, so the eliminations don't happen as quickly, but all I can do is keep making Dr. Gregory say "Correct." About halfway through the round, though, the questions must get harder because the number of feet on the yellow line finally starts to dwindle.

For my seventh question, one of those how-many-triangles-are-in-this-image ones, I say "Twenty-seven triangles," which eliminates six teams, including George.

By the ninth question, only three of us are left.

By the tenth, I'm the only one. And I know the answer: "Oblate spheroid."

Dr. Gregory doesn't say *correct* this time. She says, "Wow!" the same way she said it to Tallulah. She looks out at the audience. "There are always lots of perfect scores at the school level, but at counties? Folks, one is unusual and two is unheard of."

My eyes go wide. I didn't know that.

The audience applauds me again and my face is on fire with pride and embarrassment by the time I sit next to Tallulah.

We go into round five after a ten-minute break. Dr. Gregory calls "Culinary arts."

"Oh, no," Tallulah whispers next to me.

I know she's not as confident in this one. Chinese history is one of her passions, but she just learned about cooking for the decathlon.

"It's OK," I whisper. "You only need four. We're up by six points already. As long as you get the first few right, we win."

Tallulah nods. "Right."

She takes her spot on the stage, this time in the very back row in the very last spot. If she had done that for Chinese dynasties, she may have eliminated everyone on the first question. But this round is fast, and a lot of kids know the answers. I count in my head as Tallulah takes her turns.

One right . . . two right . . . *You can do this, Tallulah.*

Three right. *Come on. Just one more.*

Four right. *That's it! At worst we tie. We're going to regionals.*

Five right. *YES! We won!*

It's technically over, but Tallulah keeps going. She gets six, seven, eight, and nine correct. And then she's alone on the stage when she says, "Ferment the cabbage with lactic acid bacteria."

"Correct!" Dr. Gregory cries. "This is stunning."

I'm standing before I can help it. It's like Tallulah's spirit invaded my body and forced me to act on her impulses. I run to her in the middle of the spotlight. I throw my arms around her and we're jumping up and down.

"Wait," Dr. Gregory says, holding her mic so the audience can't hear. "You two are partners?"

We stop jumping and nod.

My face burns. I can't believe I got out of my seat and ran to the middle of the stage without being invited to. I can't believe I displayed all my joy in front of the kids behind me who lost.

I'm expecting Dr. Gregory to remind us not to show off. Instead, she pulls her mic out of the stand and walks to us on the stage. "Parents and loved ones and teachers and supporters," she says, although she keeps looking at us. "You have witnessed history. This level is the toughest. The questions are hard. The competition is wide. And students need to be prepared to deeply discuss seven entirely different subjects. It's very difficult to prepare sufficiently in the short amount of time between the levels one and two. And yet, for the first time in the history of the Children's Academic Decathlon of the State of New Jersey, one team has gotten three perfect scores!"

Tallulah grabs my hand and squeezes hard as the applause hits us. This is what we planned but, somehow, it's bigger. So big and so perfect, it's almost scary. We stare at the obscured audience, past our shadows which are stretched in the spotlight, clutching each other across the two yellow tape lines.

This moment is bigger than I can understand.

★ ★ ★

I'm still short of breath a few minutes later when Tallulah and I meet our families in the front hall of the auditorium. There are so many hugs I can't even keep track of whose arms are around me: Mom and Calvin and Eloise and Gladys, who is strapped to Mom, but facing outward so I can see her green eyes. Plus, Tallulah's mom and dad and George and his dad and stepmom and younger brother and then Daisy's mom and her brother and then . . . Daisy.

"Piper . . ." She pauses for a split second before embracing me, and I think she's about to say something real and deep and meaningful. Like, *I'm sorry.* But she says, "Well, you didn't drop your pants in the toilet, so I'm impressed."

She gives me a goofy smile, but I don't want to joke when there's so much negative stuff built up between us.

Instead, I gesture toward the bronze medal around her neck and say, "Congrats, Daisy."

She and George came in third. Daisy was right that they deserved to be here.

I turn to go but Daisy catches my wrist.

"No, wait," she says. "I'm trying to say sorry. I'm just . . . bad at it."

I turn back around to face her.

"I . . . I'm sorry. I'm sorry about all the things I said about you and Tallulah. I'm sorry for being such a fair-weather friend. I was just . . . jealous."

My eyebrows jump. "You were?"

"Yes . . . I . . . I knew no one stood a chance against you and

Tallulah if you teamed up, and I . . . I really wanted to win. OK?"

"But that's exactly what you were mad at *me* for. Wanting to win."

"I know, I know. That was stupid of me. But it's like . . . you and Tallulah win everything. Every *Everything Bee*. Every science fair. Every time you team up, you win. And I wanted you to split up for once. I . . . I knew Tallulah would never choose me over you, but you're so nice all the time, I thought maybe you'd agree that it would be more fair if it was you and me versus Tallulah and George."

"Oh," I say. I'd never agree with that. Maybe I'm not that nice.

"But this was about winning. It wasn't about being fair. It wasn't about being a good friend. And if it was, I failed at that anyway." Daisy forces a laugh.

"Huh," I say.

The rest of my words are too tangled to be spoken. Because Daisy is right that this is about winning, but she's also right that Tallulah and I win everything, and maybe sometimes that isn't fair, even if it is fair this time.

"I do really want to win," I say. I think it's a test to see if it goes any better, saying that to Daisy, this time.

She squeezes my shoulders. "Me too. I mean, now that I'm out, I want you guys to win. I'm your number one fan. I . . . I've missed you, Piper."

I take a step away from her, out of her squeezing arm. "I've missed you, too," I say. "But I don't want to be friends with someone who talks about Tallulah like that."

Daisy hangs her head. "I know. It was terrible. I didn't mean a word of it, either. I've missed Tallulah, too."

Suddenly Tallulah is beside me.

"It's OK, Piper," she says. "I mean, it's going to be. It'll get better. Daisy's going to come over this weekend so we can talk about everything and why that can't happen again. My mom's arranging it with Kristin right now."

I look over to where Tallulah's pointing, and I see Joy talking to Daisy's mom. That makes me feel better. If the adults are handling it, Tallulah, Daisy, and I can just go back to being friends.

Suddenly there's a cold hand on my arm.

I turn. It's Ms. Gates. She has her other hand on Tallulah's shoulder.

"Girls, I need you and your parents to come with me. Dr. Gregory would like a word." The happiness zaps out of me, fast. She sounds extra serious.

Our families surround Ms. Gates, falling silent.

"Does she think they cheated?" Joy asks.

My heart thumps so loudly I can hear it.

"To be honest, I'm not sure," Ms. Gates says. "But I know they didn't. I'm prepared to advocate in any way they need."

"Me too," Joy says, standing taller. "Let's go."

My mom follows Ms. Gates but doesn't say anything. She can't even correct people who call her the wrong name, so I'm glad I don't have to depend on her to advocate for me right now.

Tallulah's eyes are wide and scared. That's how I feel, too.

When we're halfway down the hall, of course, Gladys cries. Mom tries to bounce her, but she keeps crying. My family stops as Tallulah's walks ahead.

"She's hungry," Mom says, still bouncing. She breathes in sharp, like she doesn't know what to do, and for a second, I can see the future. Mom and Calvin will debate how to feed her for two solid minutes. Finally, Mom will send Calvin with me so that she can feed Gladys. Even though I really need my mom this time, she won't choose me. In 120 seconds, Calvin and I will be running down the hallway, late to this sudden, terrifying meeting.

But none of that happens.

Mom detaches Gladys in an instant, looks at Calvin, and says, "Use a bottle."

Then she grabs my wrist, and we jog to keep up with the others.

We follow Ms. Gates back through the auditorium and onto the stage where Dr. Gregory is standing at the podium, organizing her things, and packing them into her briefcase. I notice her briefcase is embroidered with her full name: DR. PATRICIA GREGORY.

I wish my mom had a briefcase like that.

"Ladies!" Dr. Gregory says when she sees us. She shakes Tallulah's hand. She's smiling. I don't think she's about to call us cheaters. "That was stunning."

"Oh, thank goodness," Joy says as we all breathe a collective sigh of relief.

Dr. Gregory stretches a hand toward me next, and I feel like I'm shaking hands with a movie star. With the president.

Then she looks at our moms. "You should be . . . That was . . . Listen to me, I'm speechless!" She turns back to Tallulah and me. "I honestly just wanted a chance to shake your hands because I know you're going to grow up to do amazing things."

My face is hot. Tallulah keeps looking at Dr. Gregory, then looking away, quickly, like she's as bright as the sun.

"It's an honor to meet you," Tallulah says.

"Truly," Mom says, then shakes Dr. Gregory's hand herself.

When it's Joy's turn, she says, "Dr. Gregory, I can tell how much our girls admire you. Would you mind talking to them for a minute about the importance of regular study habits? How life isn't all huge competitions but it's also about the ins and outs of everyday choices to be a hard worker. To maybe . . . do your homework?"

She chuckles and so do all the adults. I don't. I step a little closer to Tallulah. I know that her mom must not mean to hurt her feelings with that question. And I get how confusing it is that Tallulah can get perfect scores today and still forget to do her homework. I don't understand that, either, honestly, but Tallulah is the kind of smart that doesn't need homework.

Dr. Gregory smiles at Tallulah. "I'm afraid you're asking the wrong person. Now, I always advocate listening to your parents, so I'm not saying a thing about homework except to tell you that I was terrible at turning it in myself when I was in school."

Tallulah brightens. "Really?"

Dr. Gregory nods. "School is so boring!"

Tallulah and I laugh.

"Listen," Dr. Gregory says. "I need to tell you all something. Just between us, in this room, OK?" All the warmth that has been present in her voice is replaced with a sudden, fierce vigor. "Do you know that, in all the years of this competition, there has never been a winning team without a boy on it?"

"What?" Edward says.

"How can that be?" Mom asks.

Dr. Gregory raises her eyebrows. "There have been plenty of all-girl or non-boy teams competing at the regional level. But only a handful have made it to finals and, from there, none has ever won."

"I don't understand," Mom says. "Are the questions somehow biased? Once they're this difficult, it hardly seems like they could be biased."

"Agreed. I don't believe it's that the questions are biased," Dr. Gregory says.

We all give her confused looks.

"I can't say too much. I'm risking my own position on the panel by—" Dr. Gregory shakes her head as if forcing herself to stop talking.

"But I don't understand," Edward says. "If it's not bias, why would that be?"

"I said the *questions* aren't biased," Dr. Gregory clarifies in a tone that is not open to more inquiry.

"What?" Mom says.

"So the questions aren't biased but . . . something else is?" Joy asks.

Dr. Gregory sighs. "I wish I could say more, but my removal from the board would only make this more difficult for your girls."

It doesn't matter. I know already. I know what's biased. It's not the questions, and it's not even the competition.

It's us. It's our bodies.

Seventh-grade girls are way more likely to be in puberty than seven-grade boys. Half will have their periods by the end of seventh grade. That means half the girls on this stage are trying to compete with, as medical journals say, brains "awash with hormones that can cause side effects of both physical discomfort and brain fog." Boys are more likely to complete seventh grade without even beginning puberty, and if they do, it doesn't require extra equipment like pads and period underpants. It doesn't pull them off the stage the same way it did Daisy.

I know—I *know*—that girls are (at least) as smart as boys.

So puberty is the only answer.

The purple card glows in my memory. I can't let puberty capture my brain.

"My point wasn't actually to worry you wonderful parents," Dr. Gregory says. "Because with these two, I don't think there's anything to worry about. I just wanted to be sure you all understood the stakes." She steps toward Tallulah and me and, instinctively, we lean in as if she's going to tell us a secret. "Tallulah and Piper, I believe if anyone can break this pattern, it's you," she whispers. "And so, I want you to know, in the strictest confidence of course, that I'm pulling for you."

My heart is pounding.

It *is* even bigger than I could understand on that stage. It's bigger than us.

It's not just a competition. It's not just a summer program.

It's a mission.

DEFINITION

PRIMES

TRADITIONAL MATH

Definition: A **PRIME** number has no positive whole divisors except for 1 and itself.

Examples: 1, 2, 5, 7, 11, 13, 17, 19, 23, 29

Opposite definition: A **COMPOSITE** number is one in which two or more whole divisors can be multiplied together in order to create it.

Example: 24

$2 \times 12 = 24$

$3 \times 8 = 24$

$4 \times 6 = 24$

Importance: Because they can't be broken down, prime numbers are often called the building blocks of all math. If we tried to build something on the number 24, it would fall into all those parts. But we can build a lot on 29.

METAPHORICAL MATH

Definition: A prime number is one that becomes a foundation for a new pattern.

Example: (If it happens) Tallulah and I will be the prime number 2. As in the 2 girls who first won the Children's Academic Decathlon of New Jersey.

We will not fall apart.

We will be the prime 2 that other girls can use as a foundation until the results are actually fair.

{ 15 }

ood morning, Piper!" Mom says the next day. She's in my room way before she ever should be on a Sunday. She opens my shades so that light invades and attacks me through my closed eyelids. "Time to get up."

I rub my eyes. "Why?"

"They changed your HHH meeting this month. It's today."

"Wait . . ." Now my heart is racing. I sit up fast. "But it's January."

Mom tilts her head at me. "Uh-huh?" she says.

The next HHH meeting is supposed to be twelve days from now.

It's supposed to be a Friday.

It's supposed to be after my next shot.

It's been a month since our last failed conversation about the shots, and Mom hasn't brought it up again. Which means

I'm getting my January shot.

Right?

"Is something wrong?" Mom asks.

"No. Never mind."

I can't risk bringing up how this new HHH meeting schedule means two trips to New York this month instead of one. After yesterday, I need my medicine more than ever.

"Get dressed." Mom leaves the room.

Half an hour later, Mom straps Gladys into the car seat beside me. "Calvin isn't feeling well so the baby's coming with us."

"OK," I say. I squeeze Gladys's chunky leg to hear her giggle and pretend I wasn't excited for something as basic as a car ride alone with my mom. Something that used to be a chore.

On the drive, I'm thinking about what Dr. Gregory said yesterday. I open my phone and google the list of winners in decathlon history. It dates back to 1975. The gender of the winners isn't stated, but the first names make it pretty easy to tell: *William, Richard, Thomas, Patrick, Tony, Diego, James, Alexander, Joseph, Christopher, Justin, Bill, Daniel, Braeden, Cooper, Rudolph, Emmet, Charles, Marius, Elijah, Cecil, John, Edward.* I count all the way to 1992, thirty-four winners, before I find one name that could even possibly belong to a girl: *Devon.* I pull an index card out of my backpack and make a quick chart. In the end it looks like this:

Male winners: 91
Female winners: 2

Tiffany (Teammate, Dan), Eileen (Teammate,
Gregory)
Undetermined: 4
Devon (Teammate, Stuart), Ari (Teammate,
Brian), Angel (Teammate, Ronald) and Jordan
(Teammate, Nathaniel)

I gape at what I've written. Not only has an all-girls team never won, but only between two and six girls have won at all, even with a boy as a partner. Quickly, I google the Children's Academic Decathlon of the State of New York. Then the Children's Academic Decathlon of the State of Pennsylvania. Ohio. Nebraska. Oregon. Alaska. It's all the same.

In fact, no all-girls team has won ever, anywhere, any year, in any state.

This proves my theory. After all, the questions and procedures are different in every state, but puberty happens earlier on average for girls everywhere.

Joy keeps saying we need to be prepared, but we need more than maxi pads. Or, actually, we need less. We need it to not happen. We need to win this decathlon as kids and worry about being women later, once we get back from college.

That's still what I'm thinking about when I say goodbye to Mom and Gladys and join my HHH friends in the church basement.

"Bro!" Ivan says, as soon as I arrive. "Saved you a seat."

His smile is crooked, and my face is hot. I giggle.

Ugh! Stop it, Piper.

I sit.

"I knew you were a G&T kid, but you're, like, the smartest kid in all of New Jersey?" he asks.

I stare. *He knows about yesterday?*

"I saw your picture," he says.

"What?"

Ivan pulls out his phone and there I am, holding Tallulah's hand on the stage. It's the exact scene I've been replaying in my subconscious for almost twenty-four hours, except from outside my own eyeballs.

"We're in the news?" I'm stunned.

"It's so cool," Ivan says. "It says you're the first kids in Jersey to ever get three perfect scores in a row."

"Let me see," Emma says, coming up to us and yanking Ivan's phone out of my hands. "Dude! That's you!" She points to the screen.

I nod, my cheeks pinking.

Javi joins us, reading aloud from their own phone. "'The two young ladies set an unbeatable county record by scoring a perfect thirty points.' Yeah, you did!" Javi says, slapping me a high five.

My face is on fire now.

"How did you know all of that?" Lydia asks, gazing over Javi's shoulder at my picture on their screen. "Chinese dynasties?"

"Well, my partner did that one," I say. "I only did geometric patterns yesterday."

"Still. You're, like, twelve, right?" Lydia asks.

I smile. "Eleven, actually."

"I'm eleven, too, baby, and I don't know *any* of that," Javi says, snapping rainbow suspenders against their chest for emphasis.

"Me neither, and I'm thirteen," Emma says. "Hey, I'm supposed to share today, but you should instead. You should talk about this."

As soon as she suggests that, Dr. Knapp tell us the official meeting will start in five minutes. I can imagine it, sort of. Talking to everyone at this HHH meeting about how wild it is that girls have never won together. How Tallulah and I have to be the first girls to win. How precocious puberty and the threat of my treatment ending are making all of that harder.

But I'd have to say *precocious puberty* out loud. I'd have to talk about embarrassing stuff in front of everyone. I can't do that.

"Nah, I want to hear from you," I tell Emma.

She shrugs. "OK. But this is so cool, Piper. When's the next part of it or whatever?"

"Regionals are in March," I answer.

"Can we come?" Emma asks, yanking on Lydia's arm to indicate she means the two of them.

"Oh," I say again. "Um . . . I guess?"

I've never thought about this before. It's making me a little itchy, the way my worlds are colliding in this moment. But I'm feeling something else with all this attention, too, somehow. Something warm and clear and bright. I'm feeling *known*.

"I'm going," Ivan says. I turn to him, startled. He's still looking at his phone, at my picture.

"You are?"

"Yeah. Natalie and me. We already talked about it."

"Ooooh!" Brice and Javi say. "Natalie. The giiiiiirlfriend!"

Ivan shoves Javi playfully. "Shut up!"

I'm laughing with everyone, but Ivan looks serious as stone when he turns back to me. "My dad's going to drive us. I have to be there, Piper. You're going to win this whole thing."

He says it like it's true already. Like it's obvious. Like he can see how big a deal it is.

"If we do," I say. "We'll be the first pair of girls to win, ever."

"Really?" Ivan yelps, with predicted surprise. I'm assuming everyone else will feel and sound the same. But instead, all our friends who have been burying me in attention are suddenly shifting on their feet and looking away.

Finally, Brice says, "Awkward!"

Then, I get it. My face is hotter than ever before. How could I say that? How could I not think it through first?

"Huh?" Ivan says. "What's awkward?"

"I think Brice means . . . we don't actually know, right? We don't know if all the kids who won before are boys," Lydia says.

Emma already has the same list of winners I was reading earlier open on her phone. "Yeah, it's not like William and Richard could have admitted they were trans in 1975," she says, pointing at it.

"Right," I say. I'm feeling a lot. Shame, because I should have thought about how gender isn't binary before someone had to point it out to me. But something else, too. Something that may be even sharper than the shame.

"There could be many girls on this list of almost all-boy names," Emma says

"The list could actually be no boys. *All* those Patricks and Josephs could have been girls," Brice laughs.

Normally, I don't mind when someone corrects me on this stuff. Normally, I appreciate it because I want to get it right. But today I'm swallowing left-side words.

~~It doesn't matter if they were actually girls.~~

That's not true. I know it does matter. I know I'm awful for even thinking that.

But still, I feel wiggly and gross, the way I do with Dr. Grand. Like I'm having an entirely different experience of the world than everyone else.

Is winning the Academic Decathlon as two girls not important, after all? Does it not matter because we can't ever confirm that we're actually the first girls to do it? Is it true that being a girl doesn't matter, even when all the people who get all the awards and all the credit for everything always turn out to be boys, or people who look and act like boys, even if it's only because they're forced to in 1975? Does that mean that even if, officially, we're the first girls to do something important, we can't talk about it, because we can't know for sure that we're the actual first?

"Guys," Ivan says. "So what?"

Everyone freezes and looks at him, surprised.

"So . . ." Emma says slowly. "That means if *you* won back in 1975 or 1984 or whatever—"

"They would have listed me as a girl?" Ivan says. "Yeah. And that really sucks for William and Richard if that is what happened to them. If they weren't boys, and they were girls."

"Or neither," Javi says.

"Yeah, or neither," Ivan says. "But it doesn't actually matter for Piper's point. I mean, if one of these winners isn't a boy, then this ridiculous list erases trans history. Or nonbinary history. But no matter what, this list erases *girls'* history. If the only way a girl ever won is by pretending to be a boy, that's bad for girls and for trans kids. Just because the year 1975 stunk for the entire LGBTQIA+ plus community, doesn't mean it was fair to girls."

Yes. That's what I've been thinking.

"You're right," Javi says.

Ivan shrugs. "Plus, your partner's Black, isn't she?"

I nod. "Yeah, Tallulah."

"And I'm guessing Black kids aren't fairly represented among the winners, either?" Ivan says.

"They definitely aren't," I affirm.

Ivan smiles. "But Tallulah's going to win. Because you're going to win. You have to. And I have to be there when you do."

I beam at him.

The meeting begins, and I sit and listen to Emma talk about puberty and periods and being raised by her aunt instead of her mom. She's open just like Ivan is.

These friends all just told me that I'm amazing, but I can't do what they do—share my inner thoughts and private moments so clearly, in a way that builds connection and makes HHH such a safe place. I just memorize facts. They organize the world.

They're a different kind of genius.

{ 16 }

When I get back in the car, Gladys is awake, gurgling at me from her car seat. I'm overwhelmed by a desire to touch her, tickle her, make her laugh. Mom watches in the rearview mirror as I nuzzle my head into the soft folds of her neck and giggle with her before buckling my seat belt.

Mom turns on the blinker and pulls out into the Manhattan traffic. "Let's go to the Tea House."

~~No.~~

But I say, "Why?"

Gladys giggles.

"Oh, we should do something fun," Mom says. "We're already in the city."

"But . . ."

That's our place. Yours and mine.

"Come on, Piper. This is a girls' trip, right?"

So?

Who cares if Gladys is a girl?

"Let's pass this tradition on to the next generation," Mom concludes.

No!

"Gladys is in my generation," I say. "And we don't really know if she's a girl, yet."

Mom sighs. "OK, listen, honey. I have to talk to you about something, and I'm trying to make it fun. I wasn't imagining Gladys here with us today, but she is. We still have to talk. And I think the Tea House is the place to do it."

No.

You'll ruin it.

Choose anywhere else.

"OK."

When we get there, Mom looks extra ridiculous in the four-sizes-too-large armchair because she's holding a baby. We order a pot of orange ginger tea and the triple-decker tray of scones and mini sandwiches. I take a sip and try to enjoy it. I'm at the Tea House with my mom. Finally. It should feel better than this.

Gladys reaches a fat fist toward me and yanks a handful of my hair.

"Ouch! Watch it, baby." I laugh. At least she's not screaming.

She lets go and gurgles, as if to apologize.

"It's OK," I tell her. "You're the only person who's allowed to pull my hair."

I look at Mom, expecting a smile, but her face is unreadable.

"I think she's starting to like me," I say.

"Piper!" Mom says, shocked. "Gladys loves you."

"She does?" I'm surprised, not so much by my mom's words, but by her tone. Like she's stunned this isn't something I already know. Like it's as simple and true as basic arithmetic.

"Don't you see how she follows you with her eyes whenever you're in the room? Don't you see how she always watches you?"

How would I have noticed that when you only ever let me see the back of her head?

"She does?"

Mom bounces Gladys and coos at her. "And no one makes you laugh like your big sister."

Gladys belly laughs, so Mom looks at me with a smile that says *See?* That laugh actually proves the opposite of her point. Gladys is laughing at Mom, not me. It still makes me feel good, though.

The food comes, and Mom and I each put a tiny cucumber sandwich and a maple scone on our huge plates.

"So," Mom says. I take a bite. "I have to tell you something. And I know you don't want to hear it."

My jaw drops even though my mouth is full of cucumber and aioli. My heart stops.

No.

No, no, no.

"Honey, we're here to celebrate the end of your puberty blockers."

A sob slips out of me before I can help it.

"I know you don't see it, Piper, but it's time to be finished. And after years of those needles, calling it quits is a big deal. You deserve to celebrate the occasion."

"No!" I say it out loud this time. "No. That's not fair."

Mom swallows. "I'm not sure it's about fair. It's about—"

"You're making me *celebrate* it?"

Mom pauses. "Honey, growing up should be joyful."

"Joyful?"

"Yes, Piper. That's how most kids feel about it. That how you should feel about it."

So now the problem isn't the shots. It's me.

It's not like I don't know what she's talking about. I've had slivers of that joy when Eloise laughs at my jokes or when Ivan smiles at me. But if that joy is the only thing that most kids feel about growing up, then most kids don't know about the Wordless Chain. How can I hold on to joy about something that will make strangers look at me or touch me or laugh at me in ways I don't want? How can I be joyful about growing up when growing up means rolling your eyes and pretending that the things that rip your heart to shreds are no big deal? How can I be joyful when growing up means being called the wrong name? When it means my feelings are an inconvenience to the world? How can I be joyful about growing up when it doesn't just mean getting smarter, but it also means cramps, painful breast buds, and getting stuck places with no pad when I really need one?

Why should all that come with a serving of *joy*?

"Don't you feel at least a little happiness at the thought that puberty will come, and then it'll be over?

"But . . ."

I trail off. I can't say any of what I'm thinking. It's all stuff that Mom has called ridiculous or pitter-patter.

"But I'll get my period," I say, finally.

"Eventually, you will," Mom says.

"Don't you see? We're gonna lose!" I cry.

Mom winces. "You mean the decathlon?"

I nod.

"What does that have to do with anything?"

I give her a look. "You heard Dr. Gregory. No girls have ever won together."

Mom shrugs. "Maybe you and Tallulah will be the ones to change that."

Maybe.

The word punctures my heart like a bee sting. I sit back in my enormous chair, putting more space between my mom and me.

Maybe.

Like she doesn't believe in me.

Like the Academic Decathlon is metaphorical math all over again.

She's probably taking away my shots because she never believed I'd win in the first place.

"We could have been the ones to change it," I say. "But not anymore." ~~Thanks to you.~~

Mom lowers her eyebrows. "I don't see how all of this is

related. If anything, you'll have more time to study without having to see Dr. Grand."

~~Wrong.~~

"Um, no," I say. "That's not how it works."

"Honey. What does your eventual period have to do with the decathlon?"

"Tell me," I say, slowly and quietly, trying to make my voice sound nice and patient. "What do you think Dr. Gregory was trying to tell us yesterday?"

Mom looks totally lost.

She has to be pretending.

She's not stupid.

I keep talking. "More seventh-grade girls are in puberty than seventh-grade boys. That's why girls lose."

"What?" Mom says. She adjusts Gladys on her lap. "Honey, you're a little mixed up."

"No, I'm not."

"Winning has nothing to do with puberty."

"Well, what else could it be? Do you think boys are smarter than girls?" I demand.

"No—"

"Do you think boys work harder?"

"Of course not, but—"

"And you yourself said that the questions weren't biased."

"Well, yes—"

"So, it's not brains and it's not bias. There you go. Puberty. Periods."

Gladys yelps like she doesn't like what I'm saying any more than Mom does.

Mom shakes her head. Even though I'm yelling and interrupting, she's staying so calm. I know any minute she's going to tell me to be nice. For now, she says, "I don't think it's puberty, either."

She picks up a cucumber sandwich and tries to take a bite, but Gladys's bouncing knocks it out of her hands.

"Then you explain why there's never been any girls team to win from any state. Or why in New Jersey, only between two and six girls have won, even with a boy teammate."

"How do you know all that?" Mom asks.

"I googled it. Some of the names make it hard to tell but it's mostly obvious. A minimum of two and maximum of six. That's all the female winners in our state since the decathlon started all the way back in 1975."

Now she's going to say *be nice*. There's no way she's going to let me keep being this rude.

"Well, first, in 1975, there were no girls," she says.

I raise one eyebrow. "In the entire state of New Jersey, in 1975, there were no girls?"

Mom lifts another sandwich to her mouth to hide her smile. "No. I mean that it used to be the *Boys* Academic Decathlon. There were no girls in the competition until, I think, the late eighties or early nineties."

My heart stops. My jaw drops. Hearing this piece of history feels like being slapped in the face.

"They . . . girls . . . we weren't allowed? No matter how smart we were?"

"Yup."

"But—but—" I stammer, shocked. Heartbroken. Unclear why my heart is broken for anonymous girls from almost fifty years ago. "But what about the summer program?"

Mom laughs. Like this is not a big deal. "I'm sure that was all boys, too. The entire University of North Bend was all boys until sometime in the seventies."

"What?" I yelp.

"Just be grateful you get to grow up now and not back then, honey."

Grateful? But things now aren't all the way better. And they're a lot more confusing. At least girls in 1975 understood *why* they weren't winning.

I shake my head. I have to stay focused. "OK. But shouldn't girls make up half the winners since whenever they were included?"

Mom nods. "And you think puberty is why that's not the case?"

"It *is* why that's not the case." Is she listening to me? Is this working? Can I keep my shots now?

Mom sighs. "I thought you'd notice how even when Daisy had her period, she did quite well. And Tallulah seems to be entering puberty, yet she still won."

"Daisy lost!" I say. "And Tallulah . . . no way. She better not be, anyway."

"Honey, you can still win if you and Tallulah—"

"Mom! If you're right, if she is entering puberty, that's even more reason I need to stay on the shots. We can't both be hormonal and stupid."

"Piper," Mom says, "hormonal does not mean stupid."

~~Wrong~~.

"It means illogical," I say. *And that means stupid.* "Can I please stay on the shots? Mom, please?"

Mom shakes her head. She turns Gladys around and clutches her as if she's her comfort animal. "My mind is made up."

I gape at her, shocked. She's going to do it. She's going to ruin the Tea House and it won't even matter because she's also ruining the rest of my life.

Gladys fusses and Mom bounces her.

"So you're totally fine being the reason I don't win?" I say, fast and loud and angry, and not caring how many tea-sippers turn to look at us.

"Honey—"

"It'll be all your fault! You realize that, right? If you take the shots away and then we lose, it'll be *you* who kills my dreams."

Mom recoils, like I slapped her.

I don't care.

"Let's be nice, Piper," she says. I knew she'd say it.

I use the meanest voice I've ever heard come out of my mouth. "Let's. *You* can start by not stealing my body from me."

Tears spring into Mom's eyes. She reaches for my hand, but I pull it away.

"That isn't what I'm doing, honey. I hope one day you'll understand that I'm empowering you. I'm thinking about your eventual relationship to your adult body. I care so much about all my girls feeling empowered in their own bodies. You and Eloise and Gladys."

"Well Eloise—"

~~Isn't actually your daughter.~~

"Eloise—"

~~Also abandoned me.~~

"Is already done with puberty. And you don't need to worry about precocious puberty with Gladys. So this is your one and only chance to demonstrate how deeply you care about empowering us when it comes to our own bodies and guess what? You're failing."

"You never know. Gladys shares half your genetic material," Mom says.

"It's not about genes," I spit.

Mom lowers her eyebrows like she doesn't understand. Does she care so little about where my precocious puberty came from that she didn't even google it? One quick search and she would know.

Scientists have three main theories as to what causes precocious puberty. Mine couldn't have come from an environmental hazard, because then there would be many more girls from Forgotten Corner, New Jersey, in Dr. Grand's office. And it couldn't have come from my food because we all eat in the same cafeteria. So that leaves one answer.

Precocious puberty is overrepresented in girls who do not live with their biological father.

It is further overrepresented in girls who live with a different, unrelated, adult man.

Calvin's not my dad, but he's enough of a dad to me that I know the kind of dad he is. I know he's never, ever going to leave Gladys. He's never going to leave either of us, any of us. But that'll protect my baby sister from the precocious puberty it caused in me.

"What do you mean, it's not about genes?" Mom asks.

I open my mouth to start yelling about Calvin, to let my mom know that she's directly responsible for my early puberty. But it turns out I can't. Even this angry, I love them each too much to say that part out loud.

I wish she could see the Wordless Chain.

I change tactics. "You never even wanted me to win, did you?"

Being nice doesn't matter now or ever again. She can't punish me more after stealing my entire life.

"Honey, why would you—"

"You never thought I could," I say. "You never believed it me. You still don't."

"Piper, what—"

"You're treating the decathlon the way you treat metaphorical math. Like it's silly. Like it doesn't matter to you."

"Oh," Mom says, in a voice that's clear and steady and not angry. A voice she used all the time before Gladys was born, but one I haven't heard for a long time.

Gladys fusses.

"You're partly right, Piper."

That's surprising enough to make me be quiet. I'm not sure what she was supposed to say, but not that. I don't want to be right that she doesn't care if I lose. That's like the one thing I've said in this conversation that I thought probably wasn't true.

"You don't want me to win?" I whisper.

"Of course, I do," Mom says. "But only because that's what you want."

"Huh?"

She sighs. "You know, ever since you tested into TGASP, I've felt this need to be careful."

"Careful?"

Mom starts shifting Gladys from hand to hand as she adjusts her shirt.

No.

"I think I overcorrected," she says.

She reaches into her collar and loosens a part of her bra.

No. No. No.

"Piper, I think your ideas about metaphorical math are creative and fascinating . . ."

She shimmies as if to pop a boob out.

NO!

"But I struggle with how to let you know that, how to encourage you, because I don't want to be the kind of parent who—"

"Mom!"

"What?" she snaps.

"Please don't do that here," I beg.

"Huh? What? Breastfeed?" Mom says, her tone changing to convey how ridiculous she thinks I am for something as unreasonable as, I don't know, expecting my own mother to keep her shirt on in public.

"Yes," I say.

"I don't have a choice," Mom says. "Gladys needs me for food. You need me to talk."

"I can take a break from talking," I say. "Can you go to the bathroom or something?"

"Why would I do that?" Mom asks, like I'm being silly. "There's no reason I shouldn't feed my baby at the table."

"It's embarrassing. That's the reason."

Gladys starts sucking. Everyone was already looking at us, and I swear they stare harder now. My mom looks like a doll at a tea party, breastfeeding another doll at the tea party.

My face is so hot.

"Oh, honey, this isn't embarrassing. Or at least, I'm not embarrassed and I'm not trying to embarrass you," Mom says. "But I'm not going to hide just because I have a hungry kid. That's part of my own bodily autonomy. I'm feeding a kid in a restaurant. It's not gross or unnatural or even private. I'm not going to miss out on life just because mine is the body that makes the milk."

That stops my breath. It's another example. Another link. But this time, *I'm* the Wordless Chain.

"That's why I need the shots," I say, quietly, giving it one last try, even though most of me knows it's pointless.

"This?" Mom says, gesticulating to her boob.

"Yes," I say, looking away. "That and . . . and how Dr. Grand never calls you the right thing. And how Eloise has cramps. And—"

"Oh, come on, Piper," Mom says. "Just because you go through puberty doesn't mean you have to breastfeed a baby in a restaurant thirty years from now. It doesn't mean any of those things."

"But some bad things will happen to me."

"Honey," Mom says. "Bad things happen. That's true. But puberty doesn't stop them or cause them. And good things, those happen, too. I mean, look at you guys," Mom says.

"What guys?' I ask.

"You and Gladys and Eloise," Mom says. "Look at how beautiful you are. Look at how beautiful all of this is, our family. None of that would have happened for me without puberty. And look at how miraculous my life is."

When I look at her life, I see it wrapped in heavy chains. The same ones that are starting to weigh on my shoulders already. I feel puberty coming.

The shots really are over.

Mom takes a bite of cucumber sandwich. Some mayo drips out and plops onto her boob where Gladys is sucking.

And I must be a part of the Wordless Chain. Because that is *embarrassing*.

"Piper, I need you to know I've never once doubted the power of your intellect."

I look up at her, fast. She sounds so sincere. Fierce.

"I think metaphorical math is brilliant. I believe you and Tallulah are *the* two smartest kids in all of New Jersey, I really do. I know I sometimes I seem standoffish about your gifts. But that's not because I don't believe in you."

"It isn't?"

I sound open and honest now, too, even though part of me is desperate to go back to arguing. To convince her to change her mind. To insult her if she doesn't.

The bigger part of me knows I need to hear this.

"No," Mom says. "I just want those gifts to be *yours*."

"Huh?" Of course, they're mine.

"The way I see some of the other parents in TGASP invest in their children's successes and get crushed by their failures . . . it's not, well, that's just not the kind of mom I want to be. I don't want to remind you to study all the time. I want you to study because it's what you want to do. I don't want to ask you too many questions or challenge you on metaphorical math. I want that to be yours, too. But it's not that I don't care, honey. I'm fascinated and awed and curious about everything you do. I've been . . . I've been overcorrecting. And I'm sorry about that."

"Oh," I say. I'm chewing all those words over in my brain, slowly.

"Deep down, Piper, deep down I truly believe you and

Tallulah are going to win. And when you do, you'll be unique winners, and not just because you're girls. You've had no tutors, no extra classes outside of school, no parents scheduling your hours of studying and punishing you if you don't do it. Tallulah's parents may do a few things differently than us, but I know they make sure she's the engine in her own intellectual life, too. So, when you win, you'll be unique in two ways: because you're girls, and because you did it *on your own*."

That all sounds so good, for a split second I'm smiling. Then I remember. "But . . . we're not going to win. Not if I'm in puberty."

"I don't believe that, Piper. That is not what I believe."

I know she's telling me the truth. She really does believe in me. She really does think I'm going to win.

Too bad she's wrong now.

It's over.

I'm not going to change her mind. I'm not going to get another shot. I'm not going to win.

Mom puts her shirt back on and asks for the check. "It's been a long day. Let's go home," she says.

On the walk back to the car, I let her put her arm around me. Even though I'm pretty mad at her, it still feels good. As soon as I buckle my seat belt, my phone buzzes.

Tallulah: A transformative event has just transpired.

Tallulah: Your acceptance of the facts are most unlikely!

Tallulah: (I mean, you're not going to believe it)

It's hard to imagine that anything could cheer me up right

now, but at least it sounds like Tallulah has something happy to say.

Me: Please bestoweth the details upon me.

Tallulah: Es la peor semana de mi vida.

Translation from Spanish: *It's the worst week ever.*

Translation from code language: *It's the best week ever.*

Me: What events have transpired to bring on such a unique reality?

Tallulah: I GOT MY PERIOD!

Then, just like Gladys, I cry the whole way home.

{ 17 }

It's only a few weeks later, only five days after my missed shot, that they wake me up in the middle of the night: two quarter-sized burning lumps of pain wedged between my rib cage and the mattress where I've been sleeping on my stomach. Two balls of fire sharp enough that I jump to my knees and grab my chest. My palms are met with two zapping, electrocuting reminders that my body is not mine anymore.

Breast buds.

{18}

The next day, a dark February afternoon, I get home from school and find Gladys alone in her high chair. She babbles at me over her tray of avocado cubes. I give her a quick hug.

"Where's Mom?"

Part of me wants to see her, and part of me doesn't. Part of me knows it's not her fault that I have breast buds or that Tallulah has her period now. Part of me knows she could never have protected me from the Wordless Chain. Not forever.

But I'm still mad at her. It's easier to blame it all on her than to admit that she's as powerless as I am.

Mom doesn't appear right away and my phone buzzes, so I sit down at the table next to Gladys and remove it from my pocket.

No nos encontremos en el jardín por la mañana?

I'm not sure if she's trying to translate *Let's not meet in the*

garden in the morning or *Let's not meet in the garden tomorrow*.
So, I'm not sure what she's saying in code. Either *Meet me in
the afternoon* or *Meet me yesterday*. Or maybe she means *You
didn't meet me yesterday* . . . because I didn't. Not yesterday or
the day before.

The truth is I've been avoiding Tallulah. Not completely.
I've just been avoiding being alone with her. She keeps trying
to tell me the Story of Her Period, whatever that means. But I
don't want to hear it. I don't want to hear all the details about
yet another reason we're doomed. And I haven't been studying
much outside of school and TGASP for the past few weeks.
There's no point anymore. We set a record with three straight
perfect scores in counties, and *boom* puberty for both of us.
Now we're going to lose anyway.

I don't even ask her what she means. I text back something
that could be an excuse to not go to the garden tomorrow or
today or one for not being there yesterday.

Me: Apologies aplenty.

Me: Mi casa ha sido muy aburrida.

Literal meaning: *My house has been very boring.* Code
meaning: *My house has been very busy.*

**Me: My kin have consistently placed demands upon my
time.**

That's a lie. I've barely spoken to my mom since the Tea
House. She certainly hasn't asked anything of me. And now,
I guess, she doesn't even greet me when I come home from
school. She lets Gladys do it.

"Bah!" Gladys shouts, startling me.

Then I hear Mom's voice coming from her bedroom. She sounds panicked.

"You what . . . You broke down? Are you OK, El?"

It's Eloise.

I give Gladys a quick kiss, and rush to my mom's open door. She's standing in the middle of her bedroom, half dressed like she always is these days. Her bare feet dent the bedroom carpet. Her jeans are unzipped and unbuckled. The tank top that was supposed to go on top of her bra is hanging from her neck like a scarf that's too tired to do its whole job. Her cell phone crushes her ear.

"Honey, I'm so sorry," she says into the phone.

"Mom?" I say, softly.

She holds up a finger, telling me to wait.

"Oh, of all days."

"What's wrong with Eloise?" I ask.

Mom holds up her finger again.

I lean out the doorway to check on Gladys. She's mashing avocado into her barely there hair, oblivious.

"I know . . ." Mom is saying. "Listen, honey, is it OK if I send Calvin? It's just that I've been waiting for this appointment for . . . I know you understand. OK. Calvin is on the way."

She hangs up without saying goodbye and wiggles the rest of the way into her tank top. She rushes past me saying, "Get your coat. Need your help. Will explain on the way."

"My coat is already on," I say to her back.

I guess I didn't lie to Tallulah after all.

Five minutes later, we're in the car and Mom is filling me in. Eloise was on her way to babysit Gladys because Mom has a doctor's appointment, but Eloise's car broke down, so she called, panicking. Meanwhile, Mom still has to go to the doctor, so Calvin is helping Eloise—

"And you're here," Mom concludes. "Because I need someone to hold Gladys during my appointment."

"Oh," I say, looking at my baby sister. She still has avocado mush right around her hairline, but she smiles at me, and somehow the mess makes her cuter. "OK."

"I know that's not fair, and you have things to do," Mom says. "I'll increase your allowance or something. I . . . I'd normally cancel, but I really need to see this doctor. I've already rescheduled at least four times because Gladys had an ear infection, or there was a snowstorm, or Calvin had a meeting, or there was a decathlon—"

"Mom. You don't have to pay me to hold my sister."

Mom lets out a breath.

"Thank you, honey. I love you."

I feel good about helping her for about one minute. Then she pulls into the parking lot, and I see the line of pine trees down the median and the red door to the building.

Oh, no. I know this place.

The sign on the door reads *Forgotten Corner OB-GYN.*

You can't take a baby here.

This is the Vagina Doctor.

"Um . . . I could watch Gladys in the car?"

"Oh, don't be ridiculous. It's freezing," Mom says.

After a long wait in the lobby, we find out it's also against office policy to leave us there, so I end up in the examination room with Gladys in my lap, as Mom undresses her bottom half, wraps herself in a paper sheet, and then lays down on the table with her knees propped in front of her.

Weirdly, it feels like this is another place that's about to get ruined. I have good memories here. I liked this place when Gladys was on a screen, a fuzzy image made of light and sound. I'd stand next to Mom and clutch her hand, waiting for the baby to appear, Calvin's palm on my shoulder.

"Look," Mom would whisper at the ultrasound. "That's your sister."

I watched right here as Gladys grew from a beating blob to an adorable alien and then to a shadowy baby who even sucked her thumb. Back then, Gladys seemed like a promise. Like a metaphorical math impossibility: all addition and no subtraction.

Once she was born, her impossible-ness shifted. She became a boundary. A road block. An invader.

But now she's just a person. A person on my lap who presses her feet into my thighs and bounces while I grip her chubby armpits.

"Bah!" she says.

"That's right, you're jumping."

Mom sighs on the table and pulls out her phone to check

the time. After a long wait in the lobby, we've been in this room almost ten minutes.

"My appointment was more than half an hour ago," Mom mumbles.

I focus on Gladys's jumping, so I don't have to think about where we are.

Several minutes later, a doctor flies into the room. He's old and white with gray hair and clear-framed glasses, the kind that make the bottom of his eye sockets look all big and wobbly because they're half for reading and half for distance. He's wearing high-top Air Jordans under his white lab coat like his feet are a different age than his head.

"OK, then Mrs.—"

He pauses to check the folder in his hand.

"Ms. Franklin," he says.

I guess, since he corrected himself, Mom doesn't say anything about he just wasted forty-five minutes of her time like it was nothing. He doesn't even acknowledge it.

"Bah!" Gladys says.

The syllable breaks my heart. The Wordless Chain will come for her after it traps me. Will I be able to help her? Or will it become both invisible and wordless, the way it is for Mom and Eloise?

I don't know the words for the Wordless Chain, but I do know one word that makes the links a little bit looser, at least for me.

I put my hands on Gladys's face so that she's looking right

at me, keep my eyes steady on hers and say, "Doctor."

The doctor turns to me, surprised. "Yes, young lady?"

My face burns. I didn't realize it would sound like I wanted his attention. "No, um," I stumble. "Nothing. I was just telling my sister that my mom is a doctor, too."

"Piper!" Mom says.

I'm embarrassing her.

But maybe I don't care. Maybe, now that I'm not getting my shots anymore, I want to try things the more-honest-than-nice way.

"I just want to be sure Gladys knows, Mom. She wasn't there to see how hard you studied for your doctorate. She didn't get to attend your dissertation defense. She didn't get to cheer when they called you *Dr. Franklin* at your graduation."

All three of them stare at me.

The doctor says, "OK, well, Dr. Franklin, that is good to know." He smiles.

There's a wiggly half smile on Mom's face, too.

"Bah!" Gladys jumps, then cuddles into me, like she understands.

"So, it is normal to experience some continued discomfort postpartum," the doctor says.

Huh?

I know that *postpartum* means after giving birth, but Gladys is almost nine months old. That's a long time to be uncomfortable.

"Well," Mom says. "it's been over eight months since—"

"That's still within the normal range," the doctor says, setting up his computer.

I'm staring at him.

Discomfort is normal when you're going through puberty and your breast buds are hot coals of pain. It's normal every single time you get your period. *And* it's normal after you have a baby? For more than eight whole months?

"We consider discomfort normal for up to a year."

A *year*?

Mom is supposed to work uncomfortably, and go to a million appointments uncomfortably, and feed her baby uncomfortably, and take care of me uncomfortably for a whole *year*?

The chains are tightening around me so fast it's hard to breathe.

"This is a different feeling," Mom says slowly. "New."

"When did you first notice the pain?" the doctor asks, his face on his screen.

"I don't know. Three or four weeks ago?" Mom says.

He finally looks at her. "So, it's not new, then?" He says it like he's caught her in a lie.

I hold Gladys close. I want to cover her ears. I don't want her to hear anyone talk to my mom this way. I don't ever want her to hear the weakness, the defeat, in my mom's voice when she answers.

"Um," she sounds like she's trying not to cry. "I meant that it's . . . I've been trying to get into this appointment for, um, a few weeks, but I just got back to work, and there isn't enough time in the day, and the last time I had one, you canceled it due to snow . . . even though it didn't snow very much that day."

The doctor only says "We'll have a look."

I turn Gladys toward me. I bury my face in her belly, making her giggle. I want Mom to know we aren't watching, we aren't listening. I want her to have bodily autonomy . . . even if she took mine away.

I lean back and say, "A boogeta boogeta BOO!" On *boo* I use my nose and forehead to shake Gladys's belly while she scream-laughs. When I stop, she freezes, anticipating the next one.

"A boogeta boogeta BOO!"

More giggles. It's perfect. I can't hear anything Mom or the doctor are saying.

"A boogeta boogeta BOO!"

But this time, Gladys lurches toward me, giggling already before I get to her, and her hard head whacks right into the burning coal of a breast bud on my left side. Before I can stop myself, I'm wailing, "Ow!"

"Piper, please," Mom says, like I'm embarrassing her again.

"Sorry," I mumble. I want to put Gladys down and curl into myself until my own normal discomfort isn't so sharp.

"I'll call in a prescription," the doctor tells Mom.

She needs medicine? That means she was right. Her discomfort was *not* normal.

No wonder Mom thinks *normal* is a bad word.

"You can get dressed, Dr. Franklin."

I wish it felt better to hear him call her that.

Once we're back in the car, Mom turns around in the driver's seat to look at me.

"I didn't mean to yell," I say, before she can start lecturing me on being nice. "It just hurt."

Mom flinches like my words smacked her.

"What hurt?"

"Gladys's head. It banged me."

"Oh, no," Mom says. "She banged your head?"

I shrug and look out the window. I don't want to talk to Mom about this. I don't want to think about how it's normal for breast buds to be painful and how it's going to be normal for everything to hurt all the time and how, even when it isn't normal, you have to work really hard to make anyone believe you, the way Mom just did.

"No," I whisper. "My chest."

"Oh, honey," Mom's voice cracks. "Are your breasts tender?"

I want to hold my hands over them and cradle them back to regular.

I nod.

"I'm so sorry, Piper."

I shrug.

Why won't she apologize for not telling people to call her doctor? For ruining the Tea House? For stealing my shots?

Why does she only apologize for things that she could

never do anything about?

"I embarrassed you," I say.

Mom shakes her head. "No. You didn't."

"But you said *Piper!*" I say, imitating her tone.

"Yes. At that moment, I was embarrassed, but what you said about how Gladys should know that I'm Dr. Franklin . . . you're right. I'm going to be thinking about that for a long time. And I did cringe when you sassed the doctor like that, but—"

"I wasn't trying to sass the doctor."

"I know. I know," Mom says. "But . . . maybe you should be sassing doctors. Maybe I should be. The truth is I'm not embarrassed by you, not ever. But . . . sometimes I'm embarrassed in front of you."

"Huh?"

"I want to be able to correct people who call me the wrong thing, like you do."

"Why don't you then?" I ask.

"Well . . . I always have a million things on my mind. Like: Will this doctor believe that I need some medicine? Will Gladys stay quiet enough for me to make it through this appointment? Are Eloise and Calvin OK? Will we need to pay through the nose to get her car fixed? What time are we going to get home? How am I going to get everyone's dinner on the table if I need to go from here to the pharmacy and then give Gladys a bath and get her to bed on my own because Calvin is helping Eloise and—"

"Whoa"—my eyes are bugging out of my head—"how do

you think about all that? It's so—"

~~boring.~~

"Much."

Mom sighs. "Usually, I'm too exhausted to take on the mantle of *Call me doctor and treat me with respect*. I know that's what you're looking for out of me . . . and I know I should be able to do that for you. And when I seem embarrassed . . . that's why."

"Oh," I say, stunned.

But I don't want her to remind people she's a doctor for *me*. I don't want her to want respect so that I can see it. I want to see *her* want the respect in the first place. For herself.

I feel like I'm a part of the problem again.

My phone buzzes.

Tallulah: OK, but do you have any time so we can talk?

My heart races. It somehow didn't occur to me that Tallulah might actually need to talk to me. That her texts might be about something more than the Story of Her Period.

Me: Of course. Are you OK?

We're not texting in code, and that makes me feel like a terrible friend.

Tallulah: Yes. And it's OK if you aren't there yet, Piper. But I am, and I'd really like to share it with you.

So, it is about her period. I don't understand why she's pushing so hard for me to hear the Story of Her Period. I heard her telling it to Daisy and Josie already in TGASP and Kelly during school lunch. Isn't that enough?

Tallulah: Just meet me in El Jardín.

Me: OK. I can be there in half an hour.

Tallulah: Malo.

That means *bad* in Spanish. A relieved breath rushes out of me. At least we're back to texting in code.

If being her best friend requires listening to the Story of Her Period, I guess I'm all ears because I never want her to text me out of code again.

{19}

Thirty minutes later, I'm shivering in El Jardín Muerto. Everything still looks like it's *muerto*. But it's not. When I lay on the ground where our sunflowers used to be, I can feel the dormant life inside the earth. It hums through the layers of dirt, vibrating with potential, as if the roots recognize me as their caretaker, or their friend.

Above me, clouds float lazily across the pale winter sky. Soon Tallulah will be here and, from the footsteps in the frozen ground, I can see that she also was here earlier today. It's cool how we get to have this place both alone and together. How the garden can belong to each of us as individuals, but also to us as a unit. How completely we can share it because it needs us and loves us without knowing anything about us, not even whether we are two or one at any given moment.

I close my eyes.

It's only February, but I swear El Jardín Muerto is almost ready to burst into life again. I can feel the new, green sprigs of spring stretching through the frozen soil beneath me, warming it. It happened last year, too. Long before the trees surrounding us had found their leaves again, our garden was radiating colors and fragrances.

"Oh, hi," Tallulah says, startling me. I open my eyes and find her standing above me. "Ready?"

No.

I jump to my feet. "Sure."

We huddle in the back seat of the yellow car, bundled in ski jackets, with those breakable hand warmers stuffed into our mittens. It's usually bearable to study here, even in winter, if we layer up and shut the car doors against the wind. But it's too cold to be even slightly bearable today.

Tallulah says, "I'm glad you didn't mind coming here even though it's freezing because I really wanted to be here when I first try this."

"OK," I say. I still don't know what she's talking about but it's clear she thinks I should know what she's talking about. I really hope it doesn't have anything to do with periods.

I watch as she wiggles around, her hands darting in and out of all the pockets in her puffy coat and snow pants.

"Found it," Tallulah says, pulling a wrinkled piece of paper from the butt pocket of the sweatpants under her snow pants.

"Found what?"

"My self-expression," Tallulah says, smiling.

My jaw drops. I forgot. I completely forgot I was supposed to be working on the tenth round at all.

"Ms. Gates said we should prepare them again in February, right?" Tallulah asks. "So she can choose one?"

My heart thuds. "Right," I say, as if I'm not surprised.

But I am. Somehow, Tallulah is the responsible one this time. Somehow, I forgot.

But it doesn't matter. We won't win anymore. Our bodies are making sure of that.

"You be the audience," Tallulah says. "Remember, Ms. Gates said they want audience participation, so participate."

"Got it," I say.

"Then you can present yours to me if you want."

I don't know what to say. It's so unlike me to forget an assignment. Tallulah, of all people, should understand. But for some reason, I don't want to tell her.

"Sure."

"OK, here we go," Tallulah says. Then she begins reciting from her paper. "One thing you should know about me is that if you met me anywhere else, you probably wouldn't think I'm that smart."

"What? You can't say that!"

"Shh. Just listen."

"You told me to participate," I point out.

"Yeah, participate when I ask for it."

"OK. But Tallulah . . . you can't lie."

She lowers her paper. "I'm not lying."

"Everyone who meets you knows you're smart. It's the most obvious thing ever," I say.

She shakes her head. "I'm not like you."

"Yeah! You're smarter than me." I'm not putting myself down. I know how smart I am. It's a fact that Tallulah is even smarter. Still, I expect her to argue because if someone like Daisy or Teddy or Kelly told me that I was smarter than them, I'd say it wasn't true, even though I am.

"*Being* smart isn't the same as *seeming* smart," Tallulah says. "And Ms. Gates said we have to be vulnerable."

"Right," I say. I think about the presentation I prepared for Ms. Gates when we first worked on our creative self-expression, back in November. "I don't think I did that."

"I'm starting over," Tallulah says. "One thing you should know about me is that if you met me anywhere else, you probably wouldn't think I'm smart. I know that's hard to believe when I'm standing in front of you as one of the four smartest kids in the state of New Jersey, but it's true. If you met me in a grocery store, or at a birthday party, or in a lot of other places, you might even think that I'm stupid."

"Tallulah!"

She ignores me.

"Until I met my teacher, Ms. Gates, and my partner-slash-best friend, Piper Franklin, I would have agreed. I used to think I was stupid, too."

"Tallulah!"

"Here's why: If you said *hi* to me somewhere, I probably

didn't answer. Or if I did . . . Well, why don't we try it?" She pauses her reading and looks up at me. "Then, I'm going to, like, pantomime walking along in the grocery store while someone from the audience says *hi* to me, and instead of saying *hi* back, I'm going to say what's on my mind."

"Like what?" I ask.

"Huh?" Tallulah says.

"What will you say is on your mind?"

Tallulah smiles. "Oh, no, I want it to be genuine. I'll say whatever's on my mind in that moment."

I squint. "Won't this presentation be what's on your mind in that moment?"

"Well, yeah. But there's never just one thing on my mind."

"Really? Even when—"

She cuts me off. "Nope. Never. Like, right now, I'm talking to you, but I'm also thinking about how when we sit in this car in summer, we'll be able to eat strawberries. And at the same time, I'm listening to Mozart's Divertimento in D major."

I look around.

"There's no music," I say.

Tallulah taps her temple. "There's music in here. A whole symphony. Anyway, to continue." She begins reading from her paper again. "I said something smart to you in this imaginary grocery store, but you'll probably walk away thinking I'm stupid because I didn't say the thing you expected. I'm smart, but my brain is slanted. It works a little off-kilter. It can't reprioritize according to the people around me, and that's why I'm standing on this stage as one of the four smartest kids in all of New Jersey, but I'm also in danger of failing seventh grade."

"Tallulah!" I say, so loudly the car almost bounces.

She shrugs. "It's really hard to prioritize school and homework when there's a decathlon, which is so much more interesting."

Tallulah starts rooting around in her pockets again.

"So then I did some drawings," she says.

"You draw?" This, like a lot of what's happening in this car, is news to me.

"When I realized how I wanted the panel to visualize my brain, I took a few cartooning classes online."

"You did?"

I've never been so repeatedly shocked in my life. Tallulah has so much fascinating stuff going on. Why has she spent so much of the past few weeks trying to tell me about her boring period?

"And I drew, like, pictures of my brain in different environments. It's actually a thing I did with the school counselor a long time ago. But then I learned . . . darn it," she interrupts herself. "I forgot them."

My heart deflates. I really want to see how Tallulah visualizes her brain.

"Oh, right! I have pictures of my drawings on my phone."

"Yay," I say.

She opens her phone, scrolls, then hands it to me.

I'm expecting to see an image of a cartoon brain, maybe

with glasses and box braids. But instead, it's a triangle, a right triangle with the slope on the right-hand side. It's outlined in black and shaded deep purple in colored pencil. It's labeled *Tallulah's Brain When She's Asleep*. Next to it there's a blank space that's labeled *Piper's Brain When She's Asleep*.

"What's that?" I ask, pointing at the blank space.

"I don't know. I can erase that part if you want. But I thought a point of comparison may be good, and then we get a little bit of you in it, too. Ms. Gates asked me what shape your brain is, but you'd need to tell me that, right? I think most people's brains are oval shaped, almost like an actual brain, and that's why they can sort of roll in and out of different modes according to different expectations, like how we're supposed to act and think one way in math class and then roll into a completely different brain space for art class or gym class or lunch or whatever. You seem to roll so much better than me. Maybe even better than average. Maybe your brain is a perfect circle?"

I don't answer right away because I can't form words. I'm gaping at Tallulah over the purple triangle on her phone screen. Of course I knew she got in trouble at school, and of course I've heard about how she doesn't always do her homework or whatever. But I never knew she felt this . . . out of place. This alone.

"Piper, you look sad," Tallulah says suddenly, as if sad is the wrong emotion for the moment. "If your brain is an oval, it's a very smart oval. I wasn't calling you normal."

"No," I say. "That's not . . . I . . . Tallulah, I'm sorry."

"Sorry?" she says.

"I had no idea you saw yourself this way," I say.

"No!" Tallulah shouts, making me jump. "Don't feel sorry for me. That's not what I'm going for. Scroll."

So I do. The next picture is labeled *Tallulah's Brain When She's at School*. It's a triangle again, but upside down from the sleeping one. It's not purple this time; it's a million colors all mixed up on top of each other in polka dots and checks and lines that are straight and angled and curvy. At the very top there's a tiny blank space labeled *remembering homework and classroom procedures and all the other things I have to know for school*.

This one makes me sadder. Tallulah carries this much chaos in her head for six-and-a-half hours every weekday. But I also laugh. Talking to Tallulah does feel like talking to this colorful and chaotic triangle sometimes.

The next picture is *Tallulah's Brain When She's at TGASP*. The triangle is back in the shape it was for the sleeping picture. It has the same colors and patterns as her school brain, but this time they're organized inside the triangle. It looks like a comfy, cozy, triangular quilt.

"Wow," I whisper.

"Look at the next one," Tallulah says.

I scroll again, and when I see the next image, I gasp. The shape of the triangle has changed so it's equilateral, with the point right at the top, balanced. The patterns are organized like they were in the previous image, but this time they're all purple and all pointing toward the top of the triangle in a way that, after the last two images, looks organized and relaxing. And there's more: growing out of the tip of the triangle are lilies and cucumbers and lilacs and roses and tomatoes and pumpkins and watermelons. It's labeled *Tallulah's Brain When She's with Piper*.

I'm still staring at it when Tallulah says, "Piper! Why are you crying?"

I hadn't even realized I was crying until she said it, but now I feel them: hot tears in my eyes that freeze the instant they hit my cheeks.

"It's so good, Tallulah," I say. "You have to do it. You have to do the creative specialty. I can't come up with anything this good. You have to believe me about how good it is."

"OK, OK," Tallulah says with a pantomimed look of submission on her face. "If you insist, I'll take the creative round."

"Really?" I ask. I'm relieved, but the tears won't stop.

"Yeah." She shrugs with a giggle. "I sort of ended up working really hard on it." She tilts her head. "Why are you still crying?"

And maybe because I'm with Tallulah, and it takes the corners of her triangle to knock all the brain columns out of my head, I answer honestly. "Because you got your period."

I look at my best friend, my brilliant best friend, and my heart shatters. Even she doesn't see the Wordless Chain I see. After a childhood with a chaotic-triangle brain, she's now going to have that chaotic-triangle brain inside a body that she can't control.

"Huh? My period is a good thing," Tallulah says.

I whisper, "It means we're going to lose."

"What?" Tallulah yelps. "That doesn't even make sense. The judges won't know I got my period. I'm not going to get onstage and announce it."

She giggles, but when I don't, she stops.

"Wait," she says. "Is this why you didn't want to talk about it? Because you think it means we'll lose?"

I shrug.

"Oh. Daisy and I thought you were jealous that we hit puberty before you, and—"

"You didn't," I say.

It's time to tell Tallulah.

"Didn't what?"

"I mean, I started puberty first. I was only six. I had precocious puberty."

Tallulah looks confused for a millisecond, then her eyes light up. "Oh, the doctors! The appointments!"

I nod.

"And that's why you know so much about endocrinology."

I nod again. "You don't sound angry."

"Huh? Why would I be angry?"

I look down and study the chipping purple nail polish on her now-pubescent fingernails. "Because I kept a secret."

"No, you didn't," Tallulah says. "There's no such thing as a secret with your own self. That's just called privacy."

I raise my head, surprised. "Oh."

"And Daisy was down to talk periods, so don't worry about it. I don't have to tell you how it happened to me. But anything you want to tell me, you can," she says.

And now, suddenly, I do want to tell her. It feels weird to talk about the thing I've tried to hide for so long. It feels risky to say the words *precocious puberty* in this sacred garden, like it could ruin El Jardín Muerto the way the Tea House is ruined now. But it doesn't.

"So . . . you're officially in puberty again?" she asks when I'm finished.

I nod, miserably. Here we go. She's going to be like Mom or Eloise or anyone else and try to convince me that puberty is a good thing.

But she says, "I'm sorry, Piper."

"You are?" I ask.

She nods. "I'm happy about my period because my body is growing the right way, you know? I mean, not right. But predictable. I'm happy that my body is being predictable because my brain often isn't. But your body has never been predictable, so I get it. It's different for you."

My eyes go wide. Yes, that's true.

"But why would puberty make us lose?" Tallulah asks.

"You heard what Dr. Gregory said. About how hard it is for girls to win."

"So?"

"So, I bet no one with a period has ever won before."

"So?"

"So! Do you know what puberty does to your brain? It washes it in hormones. It makes you so emotional you can't think. It makes you more impulsive and . . . it's . . . it's not good, OK? I mean you're not even a girl, anymore, right? You're a *woman*. You could have a baby! Do you know how scary that is? No one who can have a baby should be in the *Children's* Academic Decathlon."

"Yeah, maybe," Tallulah says, calm and quiet even after all my wailing. "But who cares?"

"Who cares?" I squeal in disbelief.

"Piper. We're going to win anyway."

She says it with such a confidence it makes me drop my hands, sit up, and listen.

"If being in puberty makes it harder to win, so what? If that's why no all-girls team has ever done it, who cares?"

"What do you mean, so what, who cares?" I argue. "It's unfair."

"The decathlon hasn't ever been fair." Tallulah says this like it's obvious.

"It hasn't?" I ask.

"Of course not!" Tallulah says. "Nothing is fair. This one is just more obvious because it's unfair to you. But you know what else? No two kids of color have ever won together. Black kids are underrepresented on that winner's list like girls are. I'm a girl, a girl with ADHD, a Black girl, and now I have my period. That's just one more thing. It was always going to be hard. I don't care if puberty makes it harder."

I'm stunned. My mouth opens and the words that come out are "You're, like, really smart."

I knew that already but this is a different kind of smart. A smart that's deeper than the decathlon. A smart that's deeper than school or homework or TGASP. A smart that I'll probably work the rest of my life to emulate and never be as much as Tallulah is right now, without trying.

"I know," she says. "I am."

I laugh. She doesn't.

She grabs both my hands in hers, and, even though we're wearing mittens, I can feel the determination leaving her body and entering my hands and then growing inside me and flowing back into her hands. "We're going to do it anyway," she whispers. "We're going to do it no matter how hard it gets." She squeezes. "We're going to win."

And just like that, my hope is back.

METAPHORICAL MATH

HOPE IS EXPONENTIAL

In all mathematics, there are several operations that make numbers grow:

Counting

Addition

Multiplication

Exponents

__EXPONENTS__ make numbers grow fastest.

Proof

Addends	Multiples	Exponents
$10 + 2 = 12$	$10 \times 2 = 20$	$10^2 = 100$
$10 + 3 = 13$	$10 \times 3 = 30$	$10^3 = 1,000$
$10 + 4 = 14$	$10 \times 4 = 40$	$10^4 = 10,000$

In **METAPHORICAL MATH**, most positive emotions grow via something like addition.

Example: If happiness = 10

Happiness + Peacefulness = 20
Happiness + Peacefulness + Belonging = 30

BUT HOPE IS AN EXPONENT.

$$\text{Happiness}^{\text{hope}} = 1,000,000*$$
(*Note: out loud you read this like "Happiness to the power of hope equals one million.")

{20}

When the day of regionals arrives, I'm not feeling hopeful anymore.

It's not nerves. It's not because Ivan and my HHH friends are in this auditorium somewhere. It's not because of everyone else who's here: Mom and Calvin and Eloise and Bobby and Gladys. It's not because Gladys is screaming on Mom's chest, and Mom might have to step out to feed her right when they call one of my specialties.

I'm not thinking about the fact that we're in a huge auditorium on a real college campus with over one hundred kids from all over northern New Jersey. I'm not thinking about the news cameras or reporters, and I'm not counting how many times someone has come up and asked if I'm Piper Franklin before Calvin can shoo them away.

I only have one thought: *Where is Tallulah?*

She was supposed to be here half an hour ago.

She's not answering her phone. She hasn't answered any of the texts I've sent her.

Me: No estoy aqui (I'm not here)

Me: Kindly inform me of the coordinates of your current locale?

Me: Dude, llegaste muy temprano! (Dude, you're very early!)

Me: WHERE ARE YOU?

I even did my best to text *This feels like a life-or-death situation* in Latin.

Me: Hoc sentit sicut vita vel morte situ

As the minutes tick by, more and more competitors go backstage, and more and more audience members fill the seats in the auditorium. Mom and Calvin step closer and closer to me until their shoulders are pressed against mine like Tallulah's should be.

Today, we only compete in two specialties. There are only four academic specialties left total, and three of them are mine.

"Anything but athletes," I mumble.

"What's that?" Mom says.

She leans in close and Gladys, who's strapped to her chest, grabs a handful of my ponytail. I barely notice.

"They can't call female and nonbinary athletes. That's Tallulah's. If they call it, I won't know anything."

Calvin puts his hand on my shoulder, grounding me. "She's going to be here, Piper. I'm sure of it."

He's not so sure. I can see it on his face.

Just then, an announcement blares over the PA. "All contestants should be on the stage."

"I'll call them again," Calvin says. "Get up there."

My feet are heavy as I search for my seat. It's easy to find. There are only two empty seats left and the signs hanging on the back of them read *Piper* and *Tallulah*. I sit down. Everyone is staring at me. I feel naked without my partner.

The panelist begins introductions from the other side of the curtain. The boy to my right leans toward me.

"Are you the one who got all those perfect scores?" he whispers.

My hands are shaking. My heart is trying to crawl down my rib cage and settle into my stomach. I nod. I can't remember what that felt like. Success? Confidence? It's about to all be over if Tallulah doesn't show up.

I wish Daisy were here. I wish someone were here.

"Where's your partner?" he hisses.

If I answer, I'll cry.

"Mom! Back off."

That's Tallulah voice behind me. Thank god.

"They almost didn't let you back here, Tally. I can't back off until you find your seat."

Her mom is using this overly patient voice that Tallulah really hates.

She sits next to me. I don't look at her because if my mom were walking me onto the stage like a kindergartener, I'd be so embarrassed. But my shoulder finds hers and presses.

"I'm in my seat," Tallulah says. "You can go."

"Tally, I don't understand how this happened. I reminded you so many times."

"I know," Tallulah says through clenched teeth.

What did she forget?

"If this decathlon is as important as you say, one would think you'd remem—"

"Mom," Tallulah hisses. "It's going to start."

"But sweetie . . ." Joy says, softly. "Do you really think you're ready to spend six weeks on your own in Indiana after what happened today?"

What did Tallulah do?

"I don't know," Tallulah whisper-shouts. "But get off the stage anyway so that Piper can go to Indiana."

"Oh! Right," Joy says. For a split second she makes a face almost identical to the one Tallulah makes when she realizes whatever she's saying or doing is out of context for what's going on around her. "Good luck girls. I love you both. You can do it. You *must* do it."

Tallulah whimpers.

"Tally. It's OK now," Joy whispers. "Forget about everything. Enjoy this. This is why you've been working so hard."

Tallulah looks a lot closer to tears than enjoyment.

Her mom finally leaves the stage.

On the other side of the curtain, Dr. Jeff Coleman is saying, "And now, may I introduce you to the smartest one hundred and eight children in northern New Jersey!"

The curtain begins to open.

Tallulah pants. She's sweating.

"You didn't answer your phone," I whisper under the applause.

"I'm grounded from my phone," she says.

"Why? Where were you?"

When Tallulah looks at me, I see tears behind her smudged glasses, reflecting the bright stage lights. Somewhere, the audience is clapping. Somewhere, TV cameras are pointed at us. Somewhere, the mostly empty hopper is rolling, ready to spit out its fourth-to-last ball.

I can't follow what's happening but everyone around us stands and we stand, too, like our bodies are on autopilot.

But I'm not on the stage. Tallulah and I are alone in this moment, this moment right before our Academic Decathlon regionals, when she's crying, and her mom is angry.

"You were right, Piper. We're going to lose," she whispers.

"What?" I ask, suddenly terrified.

"I got my period again and I . . . somehow I just . . . My mom says this never happens to her and this can't be what happened, but it is. I totally forgot about it. I got in the car without a pad or anything. And we had to go to a store and . . . and then I had to find somewhere to change, which was a gross public bathroom in a gas station. And when I got back in the car, Mom said I had to use hand sanitizer, but I somehow opened it upside down and it spilled everywhere and messed up her car. She was so angry and we were so late, and it was all my fault."

"Oh," I whisper.

"You were right. Hormones washed away my smartness or whatever. We're going to lose."

I press my shoulder deep into hers, lost for words. Lost for everything. "Maybe they won't call your specialty. There's only two today."

Tallulah doesn't look up from her high-tops. "I can hope," she says.

"The fifth specialty is"—the panelist pauses to roll the hopper—"female and nonbinary athletes. Please, step up to the yellow line."

I take a deep breath, and, on the exhale, words come to me.

"Never mind. Listen. You can do this. If I were this upset, I'd never be able to do it. But you . . . remember you can think about more than one thing at once. You can answer every question and be upset at the same time. No one else could, but you can."

"It's hard," she blubbers.

I bump my shoulder against hers. I use her words. "So what? We do it anyway."

She sucks in, like she can suck back the tears even though they're still flowing. She nods. And then she walks to the yellow line.

I watch her hands behind her back, wringing out each finger. I watch her shoulders shake. She's still crying. I want to hug her and smack her at the same time. A dread fills my stomach and climbs, sickly, up my esophagus.

We're going to lose. We're going to lose because we're girls after all.

The first kid answers the first question correctly, but the next three are stumped. And then it's Tallulah's turn.

Dr. Coleman repeats the question. "In 1991, FIFA hosted what is now considered the first Women's World Cup, but at the time they didn't want to give it the same title as the men's competition. What was it called instead?"

Even from behind, I can tell Tallulah is still crying.

I hold my breath, ready for it to end. If she gets the first question wrong, we have no chance of making finals. The world will never hear about Tallulah's triangle brain. I'll have to stand up there and do whatever specialty they call next. I'll have to pretend it's OK, even though our dream will be over.

Tallulah's tear-soaked voice says, "The FIFA World Championship for Women's Football for the M&M's Cup."

"Correct," Dr. Coleman says.

My jaw drops as three kids take their seats.

I sit on my hands to keep them from shaking as the questions wind back around to Tallulah. I expect one of two things will happen: either she'll stop crying, or she'll get something wrong. But neither does.

"Who won the all-around in the Gymnastics National Championships in 2013?"

"Simone Biles." Sob.

"At which Olympic Games did Babe Didrikson break four track and field records despite only competing in three events?"

"1932." Sob.

"In 2021, Ruthy Hebard helped her WNBA team win the national championship. Which position did she play?"

"Power forward." Sob.

She doesn't stop crying until the seventh question when only a few kids are left on the yellow line. On her eighth, she takes them all out by knowing that it was Representative Patsy Mink of Hawaii who cowrote the law that became Title IX and totally changed women's collegiate athletics.

We're officially winning again.

She gets her last two questions right, too.

"That's a fourth perfect score in a row for this team from Forgotten Corner!" Dr. Coleman tells the applauding audience.

Tallulah falls into the folding chair next to me like it's a couch at home.

Without a break, Dr. Coleman announces the last specialty of the day: "Earth sciences."

"You got this," Tallulah says.

I ignore the butterflies in my stomach and say, "After what you just pulled off, I better."

I move to the line. No one stands next to me. It feels like it's taking a long time for everyone to get settled. When I turn around, I realize that my competitors are finagling to not stand in front of me. They're afraid of me. They're afraid I'll take them out on the first question.

It doesn't matter who ends up next to me, though. By the sixth question I'm the only one left. By the tenth, I've gotten us our fifth perfect score.

The audience gives me a standing ovation. I turn and gesture for Tallulah to come and stand with me again. "Take a good look at these two," Dr. Coleman says. "They're going places."

Tallulah squeezes my hand.

The scene is similar to the one after counties, but I feel different, and I can tell she does, too. We know now. The competition—the studying and preparing and answering questions—that's the easy part.

If we don't win, it won't be because we aren't smart or because we aren't prepared. If we don't win, it'll be because we weren't ready for growing up. For life.

But that hasn't happened. Slowly, together, we're tackling both the hardness of life and the hardness of the decathlon. We can do this.

A few minutes later, Tallulah and I are standing outside in the sunshine with our moms, smiling for a million cameras, and answering questions for a lot of reporters. When they clear away, Ivan, Natalie, Emma, and Lydia are standing right behind them. Emma and Lydia give me a quick hug before they have to go, but Ivan and Natalie linger.

"Bro, that was awesome," Ivan says, shooting me his adorably lopsided smile. He's wearing a Knicks baseball cap and a black T-shirt. "And I was ready for it to be boring."

"He was convinced it would be boring," Natalie says, her eyes twinkling. She shoves the bill of his hat down on his face.

"Hey," he says, laughing. "I'm not a genius, all right? I didn't know if I'd understand what was going on."

Natalie takes the hat off his head and fits it over her own blond ponytail.

"Bro!" he says, an admonishment this time. The durag he had on under his hat is askew on his braids. He holds it on his head with one hand while grabbing for his hat with the other. Natalie ducks away from him.

Something wiggles inside me. It's a weird, new feeling. It's almost like jealousy, except it feels . . . pleasant.

Ivan turns back to me. "I knew you were smart, but whoa. Not that smart." His hand is still on his head, like he's afraid Natalie will steal his durag, too.

I shrug, smiling at the way she's laughing at him.

She's definitely laughing *at* him. It's on the verge of mean. But he's enjoying it too much for it to be mean.

Tallulah appears beside me. "Hi." This is the moment. HHH meets Tallulah and the decathlon. I always thought I'd be uncomfortable and sweaty if this happened, but I'm not. I'm too distracted by Ivan's hat and this new wiggly feeling inside me.

"Hey, Tallulah," I say. "These are my friends Ivan and Natalie."

"Nice to meet you, genius teammate," Ivan says. "Excuse me

one moment." He pulls his durag straight and tries to grab his hat back, but Natalie dodges him again.

The wiggling continues. What can be jealous, but good?

"You were awesome," Natalie tells Tallulah. "I read ESPNW every morning, and I still didn't know half that stuff."

"Thanks," Tallulah says. "Um, how do you guys know each other?"

"I go to HHH with Piper," Ivan says.

"You go where?" Tallulah asks.

"You know, the group in the city," he says. Meanwhile, Natalie doesn't notice, but Ivan's hand starts slowly reaching toward her head again.

"Like New York City?" Tallulah turns to me. "Piper?"

But I can't answer. I have to see the moment when Ivan knocks the hat off Natalie's head.

"Don't even bother asking questions, Tallulah," Natalie says. "That group is all confidentiality this and confidentiality that." But she starts explaining what she knows about HHH, and then Ivan makes contact. His hat flies off her head and lands about three feet away. She squeals and runs after it. He runs, too, and tackles her—but gently—before diving for it.

Wiggle, wiggle, wiggle.

"Ivan, we have to go," someone calls from across the pavement. I look over and see Ivan's dad handing Gladys back to my mom. My worlds really are colliding, and it's not itchy and uncomfortable at all. Instead, it's sort of fascinating.

"OK," Ivan calls.

Then, suddenly, his arms are around me. "I'll be at finals," he whispers in my ear.

Chills go through me.

"You will?"

"Us happy, healthy humans stick together, right?" We laugh as he lets go.

"What does that mean?" Tallulah asks.

"I'll explain it all later," I tell her. "I promise."

And I will. It's just that the hug is over in real life, but it's happening on repeat in my brain, and I want to enjoy that a little longer.

When I get home, I'm exhausted. But before I go to bed, I pull the purple card off my corkboard, rip it up and throw it in the trash. I'm in puberty now. Officially. So is Tallulah. And we're going to win anyway.

I have only one card left. The orange one. It's the only one that really mattered in the beginning, and it matters just as much as ever, even if I can win the decathlon during puberty.

Mom, I don't want to look like you.

{ 21 }

At school on Monday, everything is different. Everyone is looking at us, talking to us, talking about us. Even the kids who don't usually pay attention to the decathlon know what happened because we were all over the news. Everyone is talking about how we didn't just win the regional title, we *squashed them*, we *killed them*, we *wiped the floor with them*.

The attention feels good. Incredible. Nice girls don't *squash* and *kill*, those are left-side words. But I don't cross them out. I can want to win more than I want to be nice.

Our teachers tell us not to do homework. They let us sit in the back of class, studying and quizzing each other. They excuse Tallulah for every assignment she's forgotten all year, and she goes from almost failing to straight As in one day. After lunch, the principal calls us into her office to congratulate us. "You're the first kids from Forgotten Corner to make the finals," she says. "You're an honor to educate. And all this press is so good for our school."

We don't know what to say because we did it for ourselves, not the school, but before we can answer she's busy giving us things: books and calculators and bagels and orange juice.

The weirdest thing about all the extra study time is that we don't need it. Last week we were busy cramming for four possible specialties. Now I have only my two most familiar ones left—botany and endocrinology—and I've already had months to prepare for them. Tallulah only needs to practice her creative self-expression presentation. By the end of the day, we aren't even studying. We're chatting.

"OK, so tell me now. How'd you meet Ivan?" she says.

I giggle as I explain what a Happy Healthy Human is and then I tell her about his birthday party.

"Wow." She gives me a goofy smile I've never seen before. "He's cute, right?"

My face gets a little warm, but I decide to choose privacy for now. "Um, I don't know," I say.

She sighs. "I wish there were more Black guys in this school."

I do, too, but just because I wish there were more Black kids at the school in general, partly so that being Black could be one fewer way Tallulah has to be alone all the time.

But I don't think that's what she means.

"I mean, I wish there were more Black kids here every day," she continues.

"Me too," I say.

"But I'd be even happier if these imaginary Black kids were cute guys like Ivan."

"After finals, Tallulah. You can go boy crazy after finals."

She brightens. "So, then you'll introduce me to all your New York City teenager friends?"

"Sure," I say.

She leans in to whisper even lower. "Although, don't tell anyone, but I sort of think George is even cuter than Ivan."

"After the decathlon, Tallulah. After!" I say, but we're giggling.

I still wish I could have the shots, but there's a weird freedom in knowing it's over now. I don't have to resist all the signs of growing up the way I used to. I can giggle with Tallulah as she talks about cute boys and actually sort of enjoy it.

In TGASP, Ms. Gates declares a "Free Day" for celebration. The room is decorated with orange and purple balloons, our favorite colors. The classroom speaker plays pop music. There's chips and pretzels and cupcakes.

"Can we play *Everything Bee* on your computer?" Caroline asks Ms. Gates.

Everything Bee is the trivia game we usually play on TGASP free days.

"What's the point," Josie whines. "It's not even fun. No one ever beats Tallulah and Piper."

"How about you be on Tallulah's team?" I ask her. "I want to partner with Daisy this time anyway."

I watch Daisy's face light up as she runs over to me.

308

Tallulah and Josie win, of course, but it doesn't matter.

It's a perfect day.

Until I get home.

I let myself in the back door. I don't see anyone, so I go down the hallway to my room and throw my backpack on my bed. It knocks something off my bedspread. Actually, three somethings. Three ugly, strappy, satiny somethings.

No.

~~*Gross.*~~

"Mom!" I scream "Mom! *Mom!*"

She appears in my doorway in less than one second, out of breath and in just leggings and an undershirt, with half her hair wet and the other half dry.

"Piper, what's wrong?" She sounds like she's worried I'm being murdered or something. Let her worry. That's how it feels to see those things in my room.

I point at the floor next to my bed where they've fallen. "What are those?"

But I know what they are. Training bras.

Because for some reason I'm supposed to train my breasts into being big enough to need a bra? Because I need to train my body to look like my mom's? Because I need to train to become a person I don't want to be?

Mom visibly relaxes, her shoulders untensing. "Jeez, honey. I thought you were hurt." She walks into my room and puts her hair dryer on my desk chair. Then she picks up the three bras and lays them on my bed in some display. Like they're supposed to be some happy surprise.

She sits, shaking the wet side of her hair. I don't know how she can possibly look so casual when I'm this angry.

"Let's talk. Come sit, Piper."

~~No.~~

She pats the bed next to her.

~~I don't want to be that close to them.~~

I need to make it through finals. I need a few more weeks in a kid body. Once we win, then I'll face the Wordless Chain. Then I'll let myself grow up. Not yet.

I walk to my bed and sit, like she asked.

Mom speaks. "I . . . well, I was in the store, and I thought to myself, *You know what? Piper's probably going to want a bra soon. Right?*"

~~Wrong!~~

"When I was your age, Gram made a day out of it. We went to the mall, ate lunch together. Then we went to the lingerie section of a department store, and I felt so . . . so grown-up. So special. Gram announced it to the saleslady: 'My daughter needs her first bra.' I just about burst with pride."

"Pride?" This story is ridiculous. "About underwear?"

Mom nods. She looks like she's about to burst with pride again now.

"When Eloise was ready, I did the same. I even let her skip school."

"What? Who would want to skip school for bras?"

"Hey, I remember that," Eloise says, suddenly appearing

in the doorway. "We went to the Bridgewater Mall, and you let me pick out anything I wanted. I bought a hot-pink bra from Target and a tie-dye one from Uniqlo." She laughs her big open laugh and sits on my other side.

What is this, an ambush?

"But something told me you wouldn't want all that fuss, Piper," Mom says.

Finally. A sentence that makes sense.

"I don't."

Mom and Eloise laugh, which makes me more upset. I'm being honest, not funny.

"So, as much as I'd love to spend a special day alone with you, I decided I'd better do this your way."

My eyes are wide. Is that what it takes to get a day alone with Mom? Bra shopping?

Mom is beaming. She's proud of herself. "This way you can go through this milestone in private, where you're comfortable."

I'm the opposite of comfortable.

"So, what do you think? Do you like any of them?"

~~No.~~

I can't say that out loud. Clearly, I'm supposed to be grateful that Mom considered my feelings, even though she considered the wrong ones. I feel misunderstood and invisible and angry.

Mom holds out a white bra with pink polka dots on the straps. "Here. Try one on."

My face is hot. My hands are clenched between my knees.

I shake my head, just slightly. Mom and Eloise are finally both here, both with me, with no Gladys, and now I want them to disappear along with the bras and the budding breasts that sent them.

"Maybe this one?" Mom says, holding out a different one.

I take a deep breath and force nice words to come out. "Thank you for getting them for me, but I'd prefer not to try that on."

"OK," Mom says, slowly. "Well, if you don't like any of these, we can certainly go to the store and pick out some together. Or maybe we look online?"

I clench my teeth. "No, thank you."

"Do you have another idea?" Mom asks.

~~Here's an idea: You can leave me alone.~~

I shake my head.

Eloise's eyebrows are low, like she's worried. Mom deflates. "Piper, I'm trying. You don't have to make this part difficult, too."

Me?

~~I'm not making it difficult.~~

~~I'm just noticing that it is difficult.~~

"I'm doing this your way, and even that's not working," Mom says.

That's it. I can't hold back anymore.

"My way? How is this my way?"

"You just said you didn't want to go bra shopping with me."

"That doesn't mean I want to come home and find my bed

buried in some gross old-people underwear. Look at this." I pick up an orange bra and shake it at her. "Yuck!"

"Piper, I'm not—"

But Mom stops talking when I throw the bra across the room. It lands in the garbage can like I intended. *Whoosh.*

Mom gasps.

"I don't want any of these," I say.

I know she thought that bra was perfect. I can imagine her in the tween section of some store spotting an orange training bra and thinking, *Oh my goodness, Piper's favorite color.*

But an orange bra ruins the color orange.

"This is my way," I say, spinning to face Mom and holding my hands out to display my perfectly braless body in my pink T-shirt and black overalls.

Mom raises one eyebrow like I'm the one being ridiculous. "Your way is to wear overalls every day for the rest of your life?"

"What?" I say. "What do the overalls have to do with anything?"

"Piper," Mom says, softly. "I want to make this as painless as possible . . . and you may not like it but . . . you need a bra now."

"No, I don't!" I explode.

It's not like anyone can see my stupid breast buds. They're red-hot charcoals of pain, but no one outside my body would ever know about them.

Right?

I keep yelling. "And, even if I did, I wouldn't want one. I don't want anything for my stupid puberty body. I only want to pay attention to my brain."

"Oh, honey," Mom says quietly. "Your body is important, too."

"Not right now. It's my brain's turn."

Eloise tilts her head like she's trying to understand me. Mom says, "Huh?"

"I'll worry about my body after the decathlon," I say.

"But Ipey—" Eloise says.

Mom interrupts her. "Honey . . . I didn't want to say this, but when you were onstage on Saturday . . ."

She trails off and I freeze standing in front of her, my eyes wide, my heart ice, not even beating, waiting for the next word. Because it can't be what I'm afraid it's going to be. She can't be about to tell me that when I was at regionals—when I was standing under those bright lights answering impossible questions, impressing the world with my brain—it can't be that my own mother wasn't thinking about any of that. That instead of what I was doing, she was thinking about how I looked.

She was thinking about my body.

"What?" I challenge, no brain columns left at all. "On Saturday, what?"

Mom looks at Eloise who looks back at Mom like they're having a whole conversation with their eyes and leaving me out of it.

"Are you saying that you could *tell* I need a bra? Are you saying that the entire *world* could tell I need a bra?"

"You don't have to be upset," Mom says, too quickly. "But the spotlight was bright and . . . and . . ."

She *was*. She was thinking about my body instead of my answers. My own mom. She *is* the Wordless Chain.

"No one else noticed. I promise," Eloise says, rushing to my side. She puts her arm around me. "Moms notice this stuff first. No one else would even be thinking about bras. Moms can't help it—they notice things."

But I wanted my mom to be noticing other things.

"I was competing," I say.

"I was listening, too, honey," Mom says. "I told you how impressed I was. The bra is just . . . I only want to protect you."

"To *protect* me?" I yell.

"Well, yes." Mom says.

"You think a *bra* is going to protect me?"

"Bras do protect you, in a way."

"Do you even live in the world? Do you notice anything else, ever? Do you ever see anything except for my messed-up body?"

Mom gapes at me. "Piper, what are you talking about?"

"Do you know what was actually protecting me? The only thing that ever actually protected me?"

They stare blankly.

"The puberty blockers!" I scream. "If you hadn't taken them away, there would be zero chance anyone would be thinking about my bra status while I was winning regionals."

"OK," Mom says. "I've had enough." She stands and turns her back to me to pick up the discarded bras. "I tried to understand about the godforsaken shots. You never told me anything, and I had to make the best decision possible with the information that I did have from the doctor and other professionals. I was always willing to listen to you, but when you wouldn't talk, I was forced to make the decision on my own. And you know what I did then?"

I shake my head.

"I imagined which decision I would be more comfortable explaining to you when you are an adult. That's how I decided. I was always thinking of you, Piper. Through every step of this journey, I've always been thinking of you. And I'm done with you punishing me over all of this, all right? I'm not some magical being forcing you to go through puberty—everyone has to. It's not my fault that it came early for you. I didn't—"

"Well, you did marry Calvin."

"What?" Eloise says.

"What?" Mom yells.

I don't say anything. She should know. She should care about me enough to google.

"Are you going to explain that comment, or is it going to be another one of those maddening things you hold over our heads without ever telling us what they mean?" Mom says.

"Yeah," I say. "That."

I don't think I've ever been this angry.

"Fine," she says. "You know what, Piper? You were worried that puberty would ruin your chances of winning this competition. But look, your treatment is over, and you're still winning. So, unless you have some other reason that—"

"Maybe I do," I say.

"What?" Mom says.

"Maybe I do! Maybe I did have another reason I wanted the shots. Maybe I do have another reason that I go to bed every night begging my body not to change. Not to get a period. Not to ruin everything."

"If you have another reason"—Mom is screaming now—"why didn't you tell me?"

"Because . . . because . . . because I was *trying* to be *nice!*"

"Who cares about being nice?" Mom yells, and if I weren't so angry, I'd be shocked. She's the one who has given me at least 497 lectures about being nice in my not-yet-twelve years of life. "I've been begging you for months now to tell me why you're so scared to grow up. Tell me, Piper. Tell me!"

I glance at my stupid corkboard with only one stupid orange index card pinned to it. I take a deep breath to blow the last whisp of brain columns away, and then I say, "Because I don't want to look like you."

Mom's face freezes, then it shatters.

After an eternity of staring at me with that shattered face, she runs out of the room without another word.

I am empty.

I am pointless.

I turn to Eloise. She looks shocked.

"That was . . . wow, Piper." She walks past me out our bedroom door yelling my mom's name.

I collapse onto my braless bed and soak it with my tears.

METAPHORICAL MATH

INFINITY IS THE LONELIEST NUMBER.

There's an old song* that makes this claim: *One is the loneliest number that you'll ever do.* But in metaphorical math, one is a very un-lonely number. It's the first number, so everyone relies on it for everything. In metaphorical math, ones are way too busy to be lonely.

The loneliest number is the furthest away from one:

INFINITY.

No one understands that guy.

(*NOTE TO MA'AM PIPER FRANKLIN: Add in the name of the song once I remember it.)

Problem:

Imagine a number line with every possible number marked. Not just the popular numerals everyone thinks of, but every kind of number. All the fractions. All the decimals.

Q: In your imaginary number line, are there more numbers between 1 and 2 or 1 and 5?
A: 1 and 5

Q: How many numbers are between 1 and 5?
A: ∞

Q: How many numbers are between 1 and 2?
A: also ∞

Q: But are there more numbers between 1 and 5?
A: Yes, all of the above is true. Both answers are ∞, but also, one ∞ is bigger than the other ∞.

I bet you want to stop reading. I bet you're uncomfortable. I bet that level of abstraction makes you itchy and queasy. I bet you want to run right away from infinity.
I told you, she's lonely!

(Plus, infinity is the number that looks the most like a bra.)

{ 22 }

Mom and I barely talk for the entire next week.

I know I need to tell her that the orange index card wasn't supposed to be hurtful. That it's not about how she looks really, it's about what happens *because* of how she looks . . . or something? After all this time, I still don't have the words.

On Sunday morning over breakfast, Mom finally speaks to me. "Calvin will take you to HHH today."

I look up, shocked. "I still get to go?"

"I'd say, if anything, you've demonstrated how desperately we need someone else to teach you how to be happy and healthy because clearly I am incapable." Mom walks out of the kitchen.

After a long and silent car ride with Calvin, complete with extra traffic, I get to the church basement just in time to see all my friends settling into their folding chairs. I missed the part where we catch up and goof around, I guess.

To make matters worse, Dr. Knapp walks up to me and whispers, "Linda is absent today, so I'm going to ask you to share, Piper. I'm sure you're ready by now."

My eyes go wide.

~~No!~~

~~I can't!~~

Before I can find a polite way to object, Dr. Knapp has started the meeting, and all the kids around me are giggling over an icebreaker that I'm too distracted to learn how to play. Then suddenly they're all quiet and staring at me as I stand in the middle of the circle of folding chairs. I'm silent. My tongue feels thick and lazy.

"Um, I'm not sure what to talk about. . . ."

"Just share what's on your mind," Dr. Knapp says.

More awkward silence.

"Talk about how you kicked butt at the Smart Kid Summit or whatever," Ivan calls out.

I can't even smile. "You mean the Academic Decathlon." My voice sounds weird.

"She won!" Lydia cheers.

"We were there," Emma says.

"Yeah, we were!" Ivan says.

I should be smiling but instead I feel like crying. There are too many eyes on me. Also, I'm not wearing overalls today. Maybe it doesn't even matter what I say. Maybe everyone is only thinking about how I look. I guess if I ever want to find out if the whole world was thinking about my underwear choices instead of my answers last week, this is the place to do it. No judgment and confidentiality and all that.

"Um, can I start my share with a question?" I ask.

Dr. Knapp nods encouragingly, even though I've never seen anyone do that before.

"So, like, did any of you guys get distracted from the competition because of my, um . . . my clothes?"

"What? Your clothes?" Emma says.

"Like, your outfit?" Lydia asks.

I sigh. "No. I mean, because it looked like I needed a bra?"

The cheering and goofing halts, and they stare at me like I've suddenly sprouted antennae. Dr. Knapp's jaw drops open.

"Um, *no*," Ivan says, finally. "I was busy watching you kick butt."

"Yeah. Why? Did someone tell you that?" Lydia asks.

I shrug.

"That sounds kind of like bullying," she says.

"Anyway, you don't *need* a bra," Javi says. "No one *needs* a bra."

No one else says anything, and I don't either, even though I'm standing up and I'm supposed to be sharing.

Finally, Dr. Knapp takes over. "I agree," she says. "You know, Piper, a lot of people who have breasts never choose to wear bras. So, if anyone told you that—"

"It wasn't just anyone," I say. "It was my mom."

She closes her mouth, then says. "Oh."

My friends all sit back in their chairs. Ivan whispers, "Dang, bro."

Then, suddenly, I really am sharing. Everything I'm feeling comes spilling out in front of everyone. "My own mother was distracted from my competition because, she said, it looked like I should have been wearing a bra. She thinks a bra will protect me. Like two little cups of fabric can keep all the bad things that happen to people who have boobs away from me. But I don't want to wear a stupid bra. And I want something better to protect me from all that stuff once I have boobs. Which, I guess, my mom thinks is now."

My words stop as quickly as they started.

That shouldn't be my whole share. When other kids go, they have a nice story. A clear beginning, middle, and end. They leave off at a place that makes us whoop or cry or *aww*. But I have nothing else to say.

Javi pipes up. "That's like me and belts." I turn to them and they're smiling at me.

"Javi, this is Piper's time," Dr. Knapp reminds us.

"But I want to hear," I say.

Dr. Knapp squints at me.

"Plus, I sort of need some help," I admit with a self-conscious chuckle.

Dr. Knapp nods at Javi.

"So," Javi continues. "My mom kept buying me belts even though I hate them. Belts are so boring. She just kept saying I need one no matter how many times I told her I hate them.

It started to feel like I was somehow disappointing her by hating belts. I'm like, does my mom want me to be boring? You know?"

I nod. Javi's mom wants them to be boring, even though Javi will never be boring. My mom wants me to grow up, even though it's the last thing I want to do.

"And every day she's like 'Javi, put on a belt. You need a belt.'"

Javi rolls their eyes.

"Does she think belts protect you somehow?" I ask.

Javi smiles. "Well, that's my point. When I was finally like, 'Why ma? Why is a stupid belt so important?' It turned out, she just thought my pants were too big."

Javi pauses and then everyone in the room bursts out laughing.

"Now." Javi stands in front of their folding chair and opens their cardigan to reveal a pair of green-and-yellow suspenders. They snap the straps against their chest and do a little spin on the tile floor. "We never fight anymore. At least not about belts."

Even I can't help laughing.

When the room settles, Dr. Knapp turns back to me. "Do you relate to Javi's story, Piper?"

"Not really," I say. "I mean, at least belts *do* help with pants that are too big, but how the heck is a bra supposed to protect me? It's not, like, bullet proof."

"Did you ask your mom that?" Dr. Knapp says. "I think that was Javi's point."

They nod.

I pause. "Not exactly."

"What did you say?"

I take a deep breath and tell the truth but quickly, hoping the words will run together enough to mask how awful they are. "ItoldherIdidn'twanttolooklikeher."

It doesn't work. There's a lot of yelling.

"What?"

"*What?*"

"You said that to your *mom*?"

"Bro, if I said that to my mom . . . oooh."

Once they've died down, Dr. Knapp says, "Let's remember that puberty causes mood swings, which sometimes make us say things we don't mean, and when that hap—"

I interrupt her. "No. I meant it. I don't want to look like her."

"What?" Javi yelps again.

"Is she ugly or something?" Brice asks, laughing. No one joins him.

"No!" I say, losing my patience. "I don't want to look like any of your moms, either."

The room erupts a third time, but Dr. Knapp holds a finger to her lips, asking for everyone to be quiet. When it's calm, she says softly, "And me?"

My face is hot, but I nod. "You too." I say it like it's a confession. Like it's heartbreaking. And it is. I love Dr. Knapp. I love my mom. I want to *want* to be like them.

"So, you're saying," she says. "That you don't want to look like a woman?"

The room is hushed now.

"Yes, but it's not about gender," I say quickly. "I'm a girl, I'm totally a girl. And I want to be a girl, but . . . I want to stay this way."

"What way? A kid?" Ivan asks.

I shrug and nod at the same time. Is that so strange?

"But why?" Javi asks.

"I don't know!" I say. I almost shout it. "I mean I do know, but I've been trying to explain it for months now, and I can't. Even after months of thinking and thinking, I don't have the words for this. And I'm supposed to be so smart. It's a bunch of pictures and memories in my head. To me, they're all related. They're all part of the same thing. But I don't know what that thing is, and whenever I try to talk about it, people think I'm being ridiculous."

"What pictures and memories, Piper? Maybe give us an example," Dr. Knapp says.

I shake my head. "You're going to say it has nothing to do with me."

"No, we won't. Not if you tell us that's the wrong thing to say," Emma says.

"Yeah. This is a safe space. Remember?" Javi says.

"Exactly," Dr. Knapp says.

I stare at her.

She nods to encourage me.

I take a deep breath. "OK." I shudder. "One example: my mom has a doctorate in mathematics. But no one ever calls her *Dr. Franklin*. Even when I remind them to. And other people call her by my stepdad's last name, even though that's never been her name."

"I get that," someone says.

"Yeah, that's messed up," Brice adds.

"That's the thing," I say. "Usually, people understand the examples, but they don't see the link. They don't see what it all has to do with me."

"OK, give us another," Dr. Knapp says.

"There are so many," I say. "Like . . . my mom has a baby, you know, my baby sister? And now she's so busy. She never gets to rest. She never even gets to do just one thing at a time. She's always working and cooking and breastfeeding and cleaning and dealing with me . . . her life looks so exhausting."

"I get that."

"Me too."

"Another one's about my big sister. Whenever she gets her period, she's in so much pain. Everyone says it's normal, but it shouldn't be. Then there's the way people, especially doctors, talk to my mom like she's stupid and doesn't even know what's going on in her own body. Like they don't believe her. And lots of men look at my mom like she's not even there, but they look at my big sister like she's *too* there. Plus, there's like how hard it is for women to ever become federally elected officials. And did you know that every single one of the personified vehicles in my baby sister's picture books uses he/him pronouns?"

I stop, out of breath. Everyone is staring at me.

"That's why I don't want to go through puberty," I finish.

"You're wrong," Lydia says, loud and forceful.

"I am not!" I say. "All of those things are true."

"No," Lydia says. "I mean you're wrong that we wouldn't see how all those things are linked. Or what they have to do with you. I see it."

"Me too," says Emma.

"Yeah," says someone else.

"You do?"

Lots of people in the room are nodding.

"Then someone please, please tell me what it's called?" I cry.

"What *what* is called?" Ivan asks.

"The big thing. Whatever connects all those examples. What links the way people treat my mom, and the statistical lack of women in Congress and, you know, me."

Everyone stares at me. No one is telling me I'm ridiculous, but no one seems to have the answer, either.

"I don't think there's a word for it," Javi says eventually.

"There has to be," I say, almost crying now because I'm so desperate to be able to explain this, explain myself, explain the world.

"Why?" Brice says. "I mean, what's a word going to do? You can't just not grow up because there are no female bulldozers in baby books."

"True," Dr. Knapp says. "But words are powerful."

She stands and walks to the blackboard that's been wheeled to the back of the room. She starts to pull it toward us.

"Still. There's no word in the world that can give Piper what she wants. She can't just not grow up," Brice says. "That's scientifically impossible."

"No, it isn't," I say.

Brice freezes. So does everyone else.

"It is possible. It's why I'm here, at HHH. Because I wasn't growing up. Because for years I haven't been growing up."

"Huh?" someone says.

My heart is doing a tap dance in my chest. My hands are shaking. Part of my brain is begging me to be quiet. But I'm going to do it. I'm going to say it out loud. Here I go.

"I had precocious puberty, so I was on blockers," I say.

There's a collective *Oh!* in the room.

"My mom decided that I don't need them anymore. That I'm old enough for puberty now. But she doesn't get what we talk about in here. She doesn't get that it's my body, that I should have a choice in who I want to be."

Dr. Knapp has finished wheeling over the blackboard. She's looking at me quizzically but then she shakes her head as if to clear it.

"Let's return to that," she says. "For now. Your word."

My jaw drops. "You can name the Wordless Chain?"

I didn't mean to say my metaphor aloud, but Dr. Knapp doesn't ask. She turns to the blackboard and writes. Everyone is silent, watching the letters appear in chalk below her hand.

Systemic Oppression

And just like that . . . the Wordless Chain is no longer wordless.

I mouth the words: *systemic oppression.*

A few kids around me are saying *oh* again. I'm smiling.

"You know," Dr. Knapp says. "Part of how systemic oppression persists is by insisting it's not real while at the same time victimizing us all. We talk a lot about how systemic oppression targets people of color and disabled people and gay people and all LGBTQIA+ people. And, as Piper has just demonstrated so eloquently, it also targets people who identify or present as women. A lot of people deny the existence of all of these forms of oppression, which is why it can be hard to find the overarching word for it when you see example after example like that. But I think this is the one you're looking for, Piper?"

"Systemic oppression," I repeat, just so I can hear these magical words in my own voice.

"Yup," Dr. Knapp says. "And you make an interesting point, Piper. One that I'm betting a lot of girls feel, even if they don't quite recognize it, or don't have the bravery to call it out."

I lower my eyebrows. "What's my point?"

"Well, let's add these things together."

Then, without knowing it, Dr. Knapp does her own metaphorical math. She writes:

Growing up means bodies change shape

+

Growing up is exciting!

+

Women are often systemically oppressed
because of the shapes of their bodies

=

She pauses writing and we all stare at the chalkboard, slack jawed.

"Any ideas?" she says finally.

"If you're excited to grow up . . ." I say slowly. "It can look like you're excited to be oppressed."

"Exactly!" Dr. Knapp says, filling in my words on the board. There's a lot of *whoa*s being murmured around me.

"Told you she was smart," Ivan says.

"But," Dr. Knapp says. "You're allowed to enjoy growing up, to be thrilled by it, without welcoming the oppression. Your body is yours. You can love it no matter what."

She's looking at me, so I say "Yeah," even though I'm not really listening. I'm repeating the words in my head.

Systemic oppression. Systemic oppression. Systemic oppression.

I need to talk to my mom.

Dr. Knapp's eyes twinkle. "A lot of girls face puberty with excitement, and they're surprised about the downsides. I have a feeling the opposite may happen to you, Piper. I think you'll be surprised to find that it's mostly awesome to be a grown-up."

Oh, come on. That can't be true.

"You're on my mom's side now?" I ask.

"No." Dr. Knapp chuckles. "I can't be. There aren't any sides. There's no choice here. You challenge me, Piper, because I'm all about choice in this room. I'm all about empowering you young people to make your own choices in gender expression and who you love and who gets to touch your bodies and who you get to be. But, Piper, you've proven that even I have a limit. You've found the one thing even I'm going to tell you that you have no choice in."

"I did?" I ask.

Dr. Knapp smiles. "Growing up. You get to choose *how* you do it, but not *whether*. The actual growing, that part's not a choice." She puts her arm around me. "You gotta grow up, I'm afraid. But. You don't have to do it wearing a bra."

And everyone laughs.

{23}

As soon as I get home, I want to talk to Mom, apologize, and give her my new words. But she's in her room with Gladys and the door is closed. I go to my own room. Eloise is there, changing out of her dog walking clothes.

"Hi!" I say.

"Hi, Piper," she says coolly. She uses my full name. She hasn't talked to me since Bra-magedden, either. She has her back to me, stepping into a pair of jeans.

"Oh, right, you're mad," I say.

She doesn't turn when she speaks. "What you said to your mom, that was cruel."

"I know," I say. "But I didn't mean it that way. I didn't mean she looks bad. I don't want to look like you, either."

"What?" Eloise yells, turning to look at me.

"No! No— Hold on. That's not what I mean, but I have the word now."

"What word?" Eloise asks.

I take a deep breath and say it, loud and clear. "Systemic oppression."

Eloise raises one eyebrow. "I'm sorry. What?"

"That's the real orange card. That's why I don't want to look like you or Mom or any grown woman. I like how you look. But it's the way the world looks at you. It's systemic oppression."

Eloise's face softens. "Oh. Well, that is a lot less offensive."

"I didn't know the word for it before today." I sit on the edge of my bed hoping that Eloise will come sit next to me. She does.

"But Ipey . . . it still doesn't make any sense."

"Yes, it does," I say, taking a deep breath. "You might not see it, but it's there. Dr. Knapp says it's designed to be invisible."

"What are you talking about?"

"Systemic oppression! That's why all those unfair things happen to Mom, and she still couldn't see that I needed my shots."

Eloise's eyes go wide. "You *still* think you need the shots?"

"Yes! They kept me from being systemically oppressed."

Eloise is looking at me like I have three heads.

"It's real," I say. "System oppression is real. Dr. Knapp said so."

Eloise snaps at me, which is weird because she never does that.

"Of course, it's real, Piper."

My full name again. I close my mouth.

"And honestly the fact that you think I don't know about

systemic oppression is offensive all over again. I know systemic oppression. Duh. I'm a girl, and I'm fat."

"You . . . you've noticed it?"

"I may not be a kid wonder, but I'm not stupid," Eloise says. "The part that doesn't make sense is what you said about the shots."

"Huh?" I say.

"You're already systemically oppressed."

The idea hits me like a gong. I freeze, swaying on my bed, the truth of it vibrating through me.

"Like . . ." Eloise thinks for a second. "Like you said yourself: no girls have ever won the Academic Decathlon."

"But that's because seventh-grade girls are more likely to be in puberty than seventh-grade boys." Even as I say it, I'm not sure I believe it anymore.

Eloise gives me a look. "Seriously?"

"I don't know why else girls wouldn't be winning. It's not the questions. It's not that boys are smarter."

"It's the creative round, silly. The whole thing is designed so at the very end there's a tiny bit of subjectivity, right? And there you go. That little bit means that almost all the winners will be white boys. I don't think the judges are purposely choosing white boys. It's just . . . that's who we're accustomed to seeing win. So, boom, they win."

My eyes go wide. Maybe she is the kid wonder. "Oh."

"You really believe kids don't suffer from systemic oppression?"

"Not all kids," I say. "I know Ivan does. I know Tallulah does. She's Black and she has ADHD, so people don't realize how smart she is. But—"

"And she's a girl," Eloise says.

I think about how much Tallulah gets in trouble at school. How she's called rude when she's being honest. How, often, she gets in trouble for things the teachers tolerate in the boys. How it's oppression, even if it's not quite clear if it's happening to her because she's Black or neurodivergent or a girl. How all the oppression she faces is deeper and thicker and harder to prove or see through because of all these different dimensions of who she is.

"Yeah. I guess you're right," I say. "And she's a girl."

"Plus, how about Gladys?' Eloise says.

"What? Gladys doesn't even know if she's a girl," I say.

"And yet . . . you're always complaining about her picture books."

"Whoa. Even Gladys. Already." I drop backward so that I'm lying on the bed, a little numb. Everyone is trapped in this, not just Mom and Eloise. All this time I've been so frustrated that they can't see the Wordless Chain, when, really, I'm the one who has been refusing to see what's trapping me.

"Exactly," Eloise says. "Honestly, Ipey, if anything puberty makes this better."

I sit back up. "What? How?"

"Because kids are also systemically oppressed. We have no power. We can't vote. We can't make our own medical decisions. And as much as I love Anna, I really wish she'd stop telling you to be nice all the time. That's because you're a kid. And a girl."

No, it's not.

Oh, my god.

It is!

"Even that stuff you said about Calvin is because of systemic oppression," Eloise says.

"Huh? What stuff about Calvin?"

Eloise rolls her eyes. "About Calvin causing your precocious puberty."

"No." I pause. "Everything else you've said is true, and I love Calvin, and it's not his fault, but I'm right about that part. That's science," I say. "The research says—"

"I read that research as soon as you mentioned it. I googled it right away. I know what it says. I still can't believe you're blaming Calvin," Eloise says.

"I'm not. It's not that he did anything wro—"

"Calvin has nothing to do with your puberty, Piper!"

"But that's the only theory that fits for me. Girls who live with a man they aren't related to are more likely to go through early puberty."

"Ipey, come on. There are a million non-causal reasons for that, like maybe girls who don't live with their dads are more likely to live in chemically rich environments? Or maybe girls who don't live with their dads are more likely to have experienced trauma?"

"But it says—"

"I know what it says, but I don't believe it! Systemic oppression is everywhere, Iper, even in science. I bet that study was funded by a group of women-haters who are terrified of their daughters growing up or something."

"Oh," I say.

"Your puberty has nothing to do with Calvin. I'm insisting on this one. And not because Calvin is great, and we love him." She grabs my face to make me look at her. "Your puberty, your body, is *yours*. It's not about our dad or Calvin or any man."

"So I'm a part of the problem," I say slowly.

"Yeah, but that's OK, Iper. Everyone is. That's what makes it systemic."

She puts her arm around me, and I crash into her middle, tangling myself up in her, just a little bit.

Eloise speaks softly. "I have to say something else you're not going to like."

I shrug against her because I don't like any of this.

"I've changed my mind. I think your mom did the right thing by taking away your shots. Ipey, you deserve to grow up."

I'm still thinking about that when I hear her say. "Oh, hi, Anna."

I look up and see Mom coming into our room. "Hi, girls." Her face is relaxed in a way it hasn't been all week. Her tone is patient. I have a feeling she may have been eavesdropping on us. I don't care. I need to apologize.

Mom sits on my bed on my other side.

I open my mouth and wait for the words to come. "I . . . I'm . . . You're beautiful, Mom."

"Well, thank you," Mom says. She sounds surprised, not angry.

"I've always thought that. I didn't mean you were ugly. I didn't even mean that I didn't want to look like you. I was talking about this thing called systemic oppression."

"Wait, what?" Mom says. Her face looks amused, the way she looks at Calvin when he makes a joke right in the middle of a fight.

"Those are the words. I finally have them. They're why I don't want to go through puberty. People don't treat you right, Mom. They call you the wrong thing, or they ignore you. They constantly make you doubt yourself. And that's why I don't want to look like you. It just seems really hard."

"Oh, honey," Mom says. "You . . . noticed all that?"

I nod.

She puts her arm around me. "That's a pretty grown-up thing to notice."

"I'm sorry I said it in a mean way."

"Piper," Mom says. It isn't until she wipes my cheek with her thumb that I realize tears are falling, slowly, down my face. She wraps her arms around me and rocks me. "Baby girl." She hasn't called me that since Gladys was born. It feels good. "It must be hard to have such a big brain, huh?" She strokes my hair. "I think I owe you the apology, anyway."

"What?" I pull away. I thought I was the only rightful apologizer in this conversation.

"If you were noticing all that . . . well, I said some things I shouldn't have. Like when I said it has nothing to do with you that there's never been a woman president."

Eloise smiles. "But if there ever is a one, I guarantee she'll have gone through puberty before that election."

Even I can't help laughing.

"Still," Mom says. "Piper's right. There are things about puberty that make life more complicated."

My eyes go wide. "You admit it?"

Mom smiles. "I never meant to not admit it. I guess . . . I didn't want it to be true. I want your life to be easy, so I wanted puberty to be easy."

"Easy?"

How is that possible?

"Yes, Piper. But you're right. Having a period is not easy. You'll be OK when it happens, but it's annoying and inconvenient and sometimes painful, and you knew that."

I smile. "So . . . I'm allowed to dread it now?"

Mom chuckles. "Absolutely. Also, I've been thinking. Puberty is inevitable, but systemic oppression doesn't have to be. I'm going to do what I can to make some of this better, starting right now."

"What do you mean?" I ask, because it's not like my mom can build a time machine and go through history to reverse the building of the Wordless Chain.

"I mean, I'm going to work to make this part of the world a little better. Like you've been wanting, Piper."

Eloise and I exchange a look.

"What?" Mom asks.

"In all your free time?" Eloise says.

"Yeah, you're pretty busy, Mom," I agree.

Mom laughs. "Well, true. It won't be enough, but there are some things I can do. Like, I'm Dr. Anna Franklin from now on. I'll correct people who don't call me that. And I'm going to acknowledge all the unfairness you notice. I'm going to stop brushing it off. Or do my best to stop that, at least."

"Oh," I say. I'm smiling because those things do sound small, but they feel pretty big to me. And Mom's right that she can do that stuff even when she's so busy.

But she's not finished. "And then, one day, once you've already won and once Gladys is a little older, I'm going to volunteer to be a judge on the decathlon panel. I'll put myself in a space where you three will hear me called Dr. Franklin all the time."

My eyes go wide "Really?"

"I have an idea, too. Something I can do," Eloise says. "We just got free pad and tampon dispensers installed in the high school bathrooms, like, last year. But now that I think about it, they're even more important for younger girls. My friends and I will petition the school board with you guys."

"Wow," I say. "I actually feel better." I frown. "But TBH, since I'm allowed to say it now, I still hope I don't personally need those pad dispensers until after the decathlon is over."

I mean it as a joke, but they take it seriously, and that's good because I mean it seriously, too.

"If I'm being honest, honey," Mom says, "that what I hope, too."

"And me, Ipey," Eloise adds. "Me too."

{24}

The hope pays off. The next weekend when I climb out of the car into the parking lot of the Trenton Community Theater at the final round of the Children's Academic Decathlon of the State of New Jersey, I'm wearing a mom-approved tank top under my T-shirt, no bra, and I have no period.

I'm still a kid.

Calvin's hand is shaky on my arm as he leads me toward the main entrance. Mom's voice is a little shaky, too, when she wishes me good luck before I go backstage. But I'm not nervous. I know exactly which specialties I have to tackle today. I'm so prepared I could get perfect scores in my sleep. Tallulah and I watched the YouTube cast of the Monmouth County Championships and the South Jersey regionals. We're up against two boys whose scores in those competitions were eight, eight, nine,

nine, and eight. Between my two strongest specialties and Tallulah's triangle brain, today is our easiest event.

It's familiar by now. Dr. Patricia Gregory is on the other side of the curtain again. Tallulah's arm is pressed into mine. Introductions are longer. We learn that Landon Hu has been composing music on the accordion since age four and that Charlie Beck has three pet tarantulas. Charlie, Landon, and the audience learn that Tallulah and I are the highest scoring team to ever enter the finals. The audience is already applauding, hooting, and screaming as the curtain rises.

Dr. Patricia Gregory calls endocrinology. Instead of yellow lines, today there are two small yellow Xs. I stand on mine and the spotlight zaps on over me, hotter than ever.

Endocrinology was always going to be everyone else's weakest subject. Back in October, I was the only TGASP kid who even knew the word. And Charlie Beck, standing next to me, hasn't gotten a perfect score the entire competition. I can do this.

Dr. Gregory's first question comes to me: "Piper, which human organ is part of both the endocrine system and the exocrine system?"

Easy. "Pancreas."

"Correct," she says. "Charlie, to which class of hormones do epinephrine and norepinephrine belong?"

I watch him shift from one foot to another and run a hand over his blond crew cut. Next to us the clock ticks. For a moment, I think this might be over already. I know the answer: amino acid derivatives. If I eliminate him this quickly, it takes a lot of pressure off Tallulah in the last round. Not that she needs it.

But with only twenty-five seconds left, Charlie suddenly says, "Oh! Amino acid derivatives."

He gets the next question right, too.

Then, Dr. Gregory says: "Piper, hormones are fundamental in the regulation of bodily processes, reproduction, and human development. What is the scientific term for this regulation?'

"Homeostasis."

"Correct."

It's OK. I'll get him in the next round.

Except he knows that polypeptides are a class of hormones that include glucagon and he knows that the anterior pituitary is composed of the pars distalis and the pars intermedia.

He gets his first perfect score. The audience booms a loud applause at him before Dr. Gregory even asks my last question.

"What is the antibody that the thyroid produces in an individual who has Graves' disease?"

I know the answer, of course, but I can't speak because I'm panicking.

This isn't real. I'm asleep. This has to be a dream. A nightmare.

I wait to wake up. I force my eyes to open as wide as they can, but I'm still here, frozen on the stage, too scared to move.

My feet are glued to the X.

My heart is thundering.

All because a little something, a tickle of a feeling, has slipped into my underpants. And it's not pee.

It's happening here. Now. At the worst possible moment.

The clock ticks.

"Piper?" Dr. Gregory prompts.

"Sorry," I say. "Thyroid-stimulating immunoglobulin."

I don't wait for her to shout "Correct" before sprinting off the stage. I can tell from the applause that chases me that I got another perfect score. My third.

Now must be the break. Ten minutes to solve this.

I run into the empty hallway, my sneakers echoing on the tiles as I dash toward the bathroom in the front. It's empty, thank god. I run to the last stall, tear off my pants, and there it is. A little coin of blood right in my underwear. I stare at it, not believing for at least a full minute. It's so small. Just one tiny, brownish spot. This can't be it. That isn't my period. That's something else. Anything else. I can totally just pull up these only slightly dirty underpants and march right back onto that stage and get my fourth perfect score.

I wipe to prove it, but there's red goop on the toilet paper.

I throw it into the toilet, then lean over it, afraid I'm going to puke. Instead, only tears of frustration fall into the bowl. What am I supposed to do? Yes, Mom made me a little period emergency bag to carry around, but it's in my backpack, which is not in this bathroom or even in this building. I can't go back onstage with blood in my underwear.

But I need to. I need to get back on that stage before they

start botany because Tallulah didn't prepare for botany and, more importantly, I didn't prepare for creative self-expression. If I don't get on that stage before the end of this break, we'll never win.

I look through the crack next to the stall door to see if this bathroom has a pad dispenser. *Yes!* There's one on the far wall. I squint. *No!* It costs twenty-five cents. I don't have any money. Maybe I can break it?

I pull up my pants and open the stall door. Immediately, a huge rush of blood releases into my underwear. I look down, horrified. There's a stain on my jeans.

What am I going to do?

The door to the bathroom bangs open.

I slam my stall door shut.

"Iper?" Thank god.

"Yes," I say, miserably.

Eloise doesn't answer. Instead, I hear her call into the hallway, "She's in here!" And then a lot of feet appear in the space beneath my bathroom stall.

"Honey, I was so worried," Mom says. "Why aren't you out there?"

"I'm going back," I say. "I just need . . ." It's mortifying to say this to all those anonymous feet. "Like, a pad. Or something."

There's a loud microsecond-long sob from the other side of the stall. Mom.

"Honey, you . . . you . . . ?" she asks. "Now?"

I think she's trying for a soothing voice but failing, yet

somehow her panic is actually soothing. She's not going to tell me this is normal and natural and that I should be happy.

"Yeah," I say. I watch under the stall door as at least a dozen feet shift. Who am I talking to?

"Ipey, I'm so sorry."

"Don't be sorry. Help!"

Mom takes a deep breath. "OK," she says, "open the door."

I open the stall door and there's a collective gasp that takes away any hope I might have had that the stain on my jeans wasn't that noticeable.

The gaspers are Mom and Eloise, plus Joy; Daisy; Daisy's mom, Rachel; Natalie; and Ms. Gates. Thankfully, Gladys isn't strapped to Mom's chest. And weirdly, Tallulah isn't here.

They all stare at my crotch.

"Is this your first time, Piper?" Ms. Gates asks, softly.

"Yes," I sob. Then, when no one says anything, "What am I going to do?"

Mom looks around helplessly.

"I have Tallulah's period kit in my purse," Joy says. "I'll run and grab it."

As soon as she's gone, Rachel says, "Oh! I have a quarter." She runs to the machine on the wall.

"Um, excuse me?" Natalie says, looking around. You'd think I'd be embarrassed that she's seeing me like this, especially since I don't know her very well, but I'm not. I'm not embarrassed at all. I'm grateful to every girl and woman in front of me trying to help me solve this. "But Pipe—Piper—doesn't need a pad as much as she needs, you know, pants."

Everyone looks at each other, but there's pure silence until Rachel curses. "Sorry," she says. "It's out of order."

"What?" I say. "How?"

"Those things are always broken," Ms. Gates says.

"They are?" I cry.

"Yes, they are, Piper," Mom says. "And yes, that's another thing that shouldn't be. But right now, we need to focus on what should be, which is you on that stage."

I nod, still miserable but buoyed by all the girls and women nodding around my mom. By the team ready to get me through this moment.

"I have a pad," Joy yells, coming back through the door, brandishing a green plastic square.

I look down at the stain. "What do I put it in?"

"Oh!" Ms. Gates says. "I just had a thought. . . . Um, I was swimsuit shopping this morning. . . . I have some bikini bottoms in my car. Brand new, never used. I'll go get one."

Daisy gives me a look that I can't wait to return once the decathlon is over. *Ms. Gates wears bikinis?*

"What about pants?" I say. "I can't go do botany in just my teacher's bathing suit."

The women look at each other, wide-eyed. They look like they're waiting for someone to come up with a great idea, and they also look like they're saying something to each other. Something I don't understand.

Then Daisy walks up to the open stall door, puts her hands

on my shoulders, and shoves me.

"Hey!" I say, startled.

She pushes me into the stall and shuts the door behind us.

"What are you doing?"

"This," she says. She unties the drawstring of her sweatpants.

"Huh?"

"You wear my pants, and I'll stay here and wait," she says.

My eyes bug out.

"Sweetheart, how will you get home?" Rachel calls over the stall door.

"We'll figure that out later, Mom. Gosh!" She puts a hand on my shoulder "Are you going to win?"

"Yes," I say, not a speck of doubt in me.

"No matter what?" Daisy asks, her pants now hanging from her fingers in front of me, like a threat. I never knew anyone in pink-and-yellow polka-dotted underwear could look so fierce.

"No matter what," I repeat, just as floral printed bikini bottoms come flying over the top of the stall door and the small green plastic package that is a maxi pad comes skittering underneath.

"Then I'm sure," Daisy says. "Get dressed." Then, she calls "Hey, Mom? Can I use your phone while I'm stuck here in this stall?"

They laugh while I wiggle out of my dirty jeans and Daisy unwraps Tallulah's menstrual pad and secures it into Ms. Gates's bathing suit. I step into them and tie Daisy's black sweatpants around my waist.

Daisy looks at me. "You promised, remember. No matter what." She opens the stall door and shoves me out.

"Huh?" I say as I crash into my mom.

"Honey." She breathes in sharply. "There's one more thing."

"But it's OK," Eloise says.

"We all know you can do it," Ms. Gates says.

Then, Mom puts her hand on my shoulder and before she can speak, there's accordion music somewhere.

"No." I rush to the bathroom door and throw it open. "No!"

It's the tenth round. The creative round.

I missed botany.

We lost.

After all that, we lost.

Landon Hu's music fills the hall. And, even worse, it's beautiful. I didn't even know an accordion could sound so beautiful.

"Piper?" someone says, from beside the bathroom door.

I jump.

It's Ivan. "What's wrong? What happened?"

"Did they go out of order?" I ask, desperately. "Do I get to do botany after Tallulah does her self-expression?"

"No," Ms. Gates says, behind me. "Dr. Gregory was calling for you to come back as you were running off the stage."

"She was?" I ask. I didn't hear that.

Ms. Gates continues. "She was explaining how, since today's program is aired on television there are no breaks. The rounds just follow each other. They waited a few minutes, but then they had to proceed."

"So?" I say, unable to put the pieces together. Unable to comprehend.

"So, Tallulah did botany. Otherwise, you would have had to forfeit," Ms. Gates says.

"But she didn't prepare."

"I went back in and watched," Ivan says. "She got a nine."

"She did?" Joy says. "Wow. And without studying."

"What about the boys?" I ask. "Are we winning?"

"Well, no," Ivan says. "Landon got a ten."

"What?" I wail.

"You're only down one point, Piper. You can still win," Ms. Gates says.

"But Tallulah is supposed to do the creative round."

"She can't," Calvin says, suddenly beside me. I guess he's been waiting outside the bathroom with Ivan, and a thankfully quiet Gladys. Bobby is with them, too. "Dr. Gregory said it has to be you."

"Tallulah has already competed in the maximum of five specialties," Ms. Gates says.

"But that's so un—"

"Yes! Yes, Ipey," Eloise says, rushing to grab both my hands. "You're right, and you've always been right. That's not how it should be. A lot of things should be different for girls and women, and this is a big one. And if you don't win, I'm going to do everything I can to make it right, to make sure you get to go to North Bend for the summer anyway, OK? I'll fundraise. I'll argue for you to the end of the earth. But even though this isn't how it should be . . . this is how it is. And right now, you *can* still win."

"Actually, you have to," Daisy's yells from inside the bathroom. "I demand it! You have my pants."

The accordion music swells to a crescendo making us all go wide-eyed. It's so beautiful.

"You wrote a self-expression piece back in November," Ms. Gates says. "I never got to see it, but I'm certain it was more than sufficient. Just go do your best, Piper. I believe in you."

"Me too," Mom says.

"Me too," Calvin says, walking up beside Mom with Gladys on his chest. Gladys gurgles her own encouragement.

"Me too," Joy says.

"Me too," Eloise says.

"Me too," Daisy calls from inside the bathroom.

"Me too," Ivan says. "I'm not even worried."

"Me too," Bobby says. "Now go be that kid wonder."

I open my mouth to protest his nickname because it's not accurate anymore.

Mom beats me to it. "Bobby's right. You still get to be a kid. No matter what your body has to say about it. Now go!"

I stall for a half a second. I should be miserable, and most of me is. But for some reason I'm trying to memorize this miserable moment. I'm looking at twenty eyes all looking back and me, and I'm feeling . . .

The opposite of wordless.

I turn and I run.

I crash into the folding chair next to Tallulah just as Landon is taking his bow. The audience is on their feet—a standing ovation.

"What happened?" she hisses in my ear.

I look at her. "Everything."

"And just in the nick of time," Dr. Gregory says into the microphone once the applause has died down. "Our last contestant has returned to the stage. Piper Franklin, at the sound of the buzzer, you'll have ten minutes to creatively express yourself through whatever outlet you choose."

She nods at me.

I stand. Tallulah reaches up and grabs my wrist.

I give Tallulah a look that I hope says *I'm sorry.*

TBH, we probably won't win now. We aren't going to college this summer. TBH, I'm going to cry so hard when this is over. But things have changed, too. I'd miss seeing Gladys grow every day. I'd miss out on opportunities to make Eloise laugh like a grown-up. I'd miss going to the town pool with Calvin and Daisy and Josie and Caroline. I'd miss Ivan's dimples and the smart things he says at HHH. I'd miss having this community of women and girls who team up against an unruly period.

I'd miss Mom.

Plus, who would take care of our garden?

We probably would have won, Tallulah and me, if she had talked about her triangle brain. We probably would have won if it weren't for my period. Two things I've been terrified of are happening at once: puberty and losing. And even though everyone kept insisting they had nothing to do with each other, I was right that they'd be linked. But somehow neither of those terrible things is as bad as I thought.

I walk to the X on the center of the stage where a mic stand has been set up along with several other things that I guess Tallulah was planning to use: a projector, a whiteboard, markers. The spotlight flips on and heat rains down on me. Then there's a buzzing sound and what feels like a million people stare at me, waiting for me to express myself to them. The stage is silent. The audience is silent. I've never heard such deafening silence. My knees shake inside Daisy's sweatpants.

"H-h-hello," I say, but I can tell they can barely hear me. I take a step closer to the mic stand. "Hello." My voice cracks. "I'm Piper Franklin, and, um, this is unusual, but my biggest passion in life is math."

That was supposed to be a joke, but there's barely a reaction.

"See, I'm a girl, and I'm a gifted kid, and a friend. I'm a decathlon competitor, a daughter, a sister," I say. "It's hard to be all those things at once, so I think about who I am in percentages."

Behind me, Landon coughs. Tallulah clears her throat. In front of me, the audience makes similar noises. This isn't working. I wrote this in the fall, but that feels like forever ago. It's not the self I want to express anymore.

I throw up my hands. "Hold on. I'm starting over." I take a deep breath. "My name is Piper Franklin, and I'm not supposed to be doing this."

The room goes still and silent. I can feel Tallulah's eyes shooting daggers into my skull.

"I don't mean the decathlon. I am supposed to be doing this," I say, spreading out my hands to indicate that I'm covering more ground. "But the creative specialty, that was supposed to be my partner. Tallulah."

I turn to point at her and, sure enough, her eyes are narrow and angry.

I jump back around.

"She's mad at me. And she should be, really, because I was supposed to do botany, and if I had, then we'd be tied instead of losing right now," I ramble. "Actually, you should all be mad at me because, now, none of you gets to hear about how Tallulah's brain is shaped like a triangle. Her presentation was stunning. It even shocked me, and I've been her best friend forever."

I sort of thought the perfect words would come to me once I got rid of my brain columns, but I can't seem to find my way back to the point. And my words won't stop.

"So, I guess that's two bad things. You don't get to learn about Tallulah's fascinating triangle brain, and we're going to lose."

One of the boys behind me laughs.

"Piper!" Tallulah says.

I open my mouth to continue but now there are no more words. I can hear people in the audience shifting. I can feel eyes leave my face to check phones and watches.

I guess that's it. I guess I sit down now.

"Piper!" Tallulah hisses again. "Remember. Who cares? So what?"

We do it anyway.

My voice is stronger when I speak again. "OK. One more time. My name is Piper Franklin, and I was supposed to compete in botany, but I didn't because . . ."

I breathe in. There are a million people in this room. A trillion ears in this room. A video camera in this room.

I can't do this.

But I'm going to.

"I got my period."

All the shifting and coughing and phone-checking stops. My heart jumps all over my chest. The eyes are all on me again.

"Yes, my first period. Here. Today. And I've been scared to get my period since I was six."

I pause, feeling the right reaction from the audience, finally. They're leaning forward, even more still.

"That sounds weird because what six-year-old is thinking about a period? But the answer is"—I take my two thumbs and point to myself, Daisy-style—"this guy!"

Now, they laugh. They actually laugh.

"That's because I had a condition called precocious puberty. That means that I was six, but I was also ten, and for a different reason I was also fifteen, all at the same time. You probably think that's impossible, and right now it is, but soon it won't be."

Oh! Tallulah said this is supposed to be interactive.

"Has anyone here ever heard of Sir Isaac Newton?"

Several hands go up.

"Does anyone know what he is famous for, mathematically?"

Someone toward the front yells, "He invented calculus in order to explain the rules of physics."

"Thank you, Eloise!" I say. Then I lean into the mic like I'm sharing a secret with the audience and whisper, "That's my big sister."

I get another laugh.

"Sir Isaac Newton is my hero," I say. "And, like him, I'm inventing a whole new kind of math. That's what I've been working on since I first hit puberty." I pause. "Yes, you heard that right. At six years old, I was both in puberty and trying to follow in the footsteps of Sir Isaac Newton."

Another laugh.

"So let me introduce myself yet again. I am *Ma'am* Piper Franklin, first time period-haver, and future inventor of metaphorical math. You see, Newton's invention of calculus made it possible for humans to understand things they'd been working on forever, like gravity and velocity. Without it, he couldn't have written the law of universal gravitation or developed the three laws of motion. But my math, metaphorical math, will solve an even bigger mystery: human emotions."

There are mumblings of interest in the audience.

"Maybe *solve* is the wrong word. Because that's not what math does. Math explains. It's a fully logical explanation of the world around us. In fact, math is about creativity. One of the reasons I love it is because, in math, if you can imagine something, then *bam* it's real, as long as it doesn't break the rules of logic. Like . . . let's talk about square roots. We all know that the square root of nine is three, right? Because three times three equals nine. Or, the math way to say it is, the square root of *b* is *a* when *a* multiplied by *a* equals *b*.

"The trouble comes in with negative numbers because the only way to get a negative answer in multiplication is to multiply a positive and a negative number together. In other words, they are never the same number. So, there can't be a square root of negative one. Right?"

I look at the faces in front of me. Some are thoughtful like they're following or trying to. Others are sort of glazed over. But Dr. Gregory is nodding like crazy, so I keep going.

"Wrong! Because we can *imagine* a new sort of number, and as long as that doesn't contradict any of the logic we've already proven, mathematically, that number can exist. So, the square root of negative one is . . ."

I write a lower-case italic *i* on the board.

"Imaginary! Imaginary numbers exist because they don't cause any contradictions with the logic we already have: two plus two is still four, eight times nine plus twenty-eight is still one hundred. So, numbers can be imaginary. Imaginary doesn't mean illogical. In fact, if you really think about it, all numbers are sort of imaginary. *One* has no meaning unless there's one *of* something. All numbers are at some level of abstraction. That makes math creative. And *that* opens up a whole new world for mathematicians, like Sir Isaac Newton. And like Ma'am Piper Franklin."

I pause as the audience chuckles.

"But the thing is, even though math is supposed to be completely rational and one hundred percent logical, it doesn't always work when you factor in human beings. Like, you know that old phrase *time flies when you're having fun*? Have you ever felt that way?"

I raise my hand and so do several people in front of me.

"But it's mathematically impossible, right? Because the rules for time work by following precise logic. Every hour is exactly sixty minutes, and every minute is exactly sixty seconds. So, time can't actually fly. And yet, it *feels* like it can. What if math could explain this stuff? What if an equation could explain why thirty minutes feels long at the dentist but short when you're with your triangularly brained best friend? And what if math could explain how, four years ago, I was simultaneously age six, age ten, and age fifteen?"

They're silent now, curious.

I walk over to the whiteboard. I erase the *i* and draw three circles, side by side, not touching.

I turn back to the audience. "I know you're expecting a full explanation. You're expecting me to tell you how metaphorical math can explain everything, right?"

A few people nod, looking eager.

"Well, I can't. In case you haven't noticed, I've been very busy studying for this thing called the Children's Academic Decathlon of the State of New Jersey, and, of course, I'm not prepared to teach you everything I've discovered because I'm only talking right now because I just got my first period ever, and they don't bend the rules here for *anything*."

Laughter. Lots of laughter. It feels so good. Dr. Gregory even whoops.

"So, instead, I have an easy math question. I'll ask Charlie. What's eleven plus two?"

I turn around to face the back of the stage. Tallulah doesn't look mad anymore. The look on her face reminds me of how I felt when she presented her piece to me in El Jardín Muerto.

"Huh?" Charlie says. "Thirteen."

"Always?" I ask.

Charlie pauses. "Yes?"

"OK," I say. "Landon, do you agree?"

He takes so long to answer, I wonder if he's trying to wear out my time. He says, "I think so."

I glance at the clock. I startle. It's at zero. I've already been talking for ten minutes. I'm out of time. But no one stops me, and I have on pants and a pad, and I promised Daisy I'd try to win, so I keep going.

"Does everyone agree?" I ask the audience.

A different voice calls out this time. "Sometimes it's one."

Mom.

There are tears in my eyes as I say, "Right." I turn back to the whiteboard.

A lot of the audience is mumbling in confusion as I scribble inside one of the circles. When I step back, they see a clock.

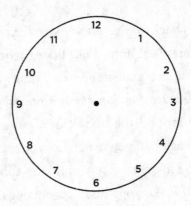

"Oh," a gazillion mouths say at once.

"Eleven o'clock plus two is one o'clock." I demonstrate by using my pointer finger like an hour hand. "In math, we call this mod 12. And congratulations, you're all already masters in mod 12! In metaphorical math, we have a lot of ages at once, and they all progress differently through time. Of course, your chronological age just keeps marching forward; it's a regular number line."

I draw a line on the board next to the circles.

"But your body doesn't work like that. If we think of the age of a body as related to its abilities to do things like walk and talk and run and, I don't know, regulate hormones, then I think we can see that body ages don't consistently progress forward. Instead, they work like a clock. And for a lot of lucky people, these two ages line up. When you're one on the number line, your body is at about a one-year-old's ability." I demonstrate by pointing one finger to the chronological age one on the number line and another finger to the one on the clock. "When you reach the bottom, six years old, you're about halfway through childhood, according to your body.

And then you get back to twelve, and, what happens? Your body goes berserk. Your chest hurts. Your bones ache from growing too fast. And you lose your mind every time your mom even speaks to you because *dun dun dun* hormones! You've reached your first circle around the body clock: puberty. When you get back around again, if you match up, you're chronologically twenty-four: time to actually start thinking about having children, which will make your body go nuts again. Believe me. In addition to a brand-new period, I have a brand-new baby sister. So, I've seen this first-hand."

The second I say that I'm afraid it was mean. But when the audience laughs, my mom is louder than anyone.

"Then you go around again and when you hit the top, you're fifty. Menopause."

I stall a moment, letting their confusion sink in.

"You're probably saying, wait a second, that's not right. Twelve plus twenty-four doesn't equal fifty. And you'd be correct. But that's because the body-age clock doesn't move perfectly in sync with the chronologically aged number line. So that's how, four years ago, I ended up with this combination."

I put a dot next to the six on the number line and draw the hour hand of the body-age clock pointing to eleven.

"Plus, there are more ages. Another thing happened when I was six. My teachers talked to my mom and said maybe I was gifted. They gave me an IQ test and it said I was as smart as your average fifteen-year-old." I draw an intelligence age clock in mod 60. I draw an arrow pointing to the fifteen.

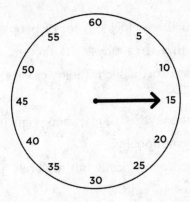

"So, six years past the day of my birth, my body thought it was eleven, and my brain thought it was fifteen. You'd think that intelligence would have helped me, but it didn't. I understood everything that was happening to me, like, scientifically, and that made it harder emotionally. And that's because I understood way more than I wanted to. I mean who wants to fully understand something like how babies are made when you're only six? Everything made me so uncomfortable. In comes the last clock."

I draw this one in mod 30, with thirty as the highest possible number, and label it "Emotional Age." Then I point the arrow to six.

I turn back to the crowd.

"I was as smart as a fifteen-year-old and my body was trying to turn me into an eleven-year-old, but my emotions were only six years old. And, if that's not enough, an even more unusual thing happened to me. It's especially weird if you understand metaphorical math, which only I do, so I guess I'll have to explain it. You see, a lot of times people don't quite match up on all these clocks. A lot of people may be more emotionally mature than physically mature, or very imma-ture in both ways so their chronological age doesn't match. Right?"

"Right!" someone yells. "I'm twenty-eight chronologically but forty-seven emotionally."

"I'm sixteen chronologically but my body age is only, like, twelve," someone else calls.

"I'm twelve," Landon says behind me. "But my body is nine and my intelligence is, um, I think forty."

Everyone laughs. But I barely hear. *They get it.*

"But the thing is," I continue. "No matter at what speed, these clocks and number lines are all supposed to move in the same direction. Sometimes they slow down or speed up or even stop, but they don't go backward. Unless you're me. Once my parents figured out I was in precocious puberty, I started on a medicine that made all of this wonky."

I add a second arrow to the original mod 12 clock, point-ing to six.

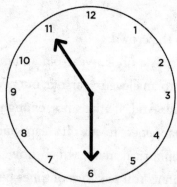

"My body age went back in time. And then it just stayed there. My intelligence moved forward. My chronological and emotional age went to eight and nine and ten. But my body stalled at some weird mash-up of six and eleven until this January when the medicine stopped, and I flipped right to the top of the clock without doing all the things in-between."

I erase the other arrows and draw in a new one, pointing at twelve.

"Today, I'm chronologically eleven, and even though a few months ago my body was six, now it's twelve. Intellectually I'm, I don't know, twenty? And emotionally, I'm on target. Eleven. So, that's what I can express about myself in this moment: I am Ma'am Piper Franklin, the mother of metaphorical math, and I'm three ages at once. And one more thing. I'm going to say it again because it was scary the first time, but it seems like the biggest truth about me in this moment: My name is Piper Franklin, and I just got my period."

I pause to look at the audience as they cheer. I hang on to the moment. I freeze it. I need to replay it when I'm stuck in a bathroom stall at the University of North Bend with blood in my underpants. I need to replay it the next time Gladys bonks her head into my breast bud, and when I finally figure out what I want to do about a stupid bra. I need to replay this moment over and over again because, from the way the audience was still and focused and thinking, and from the way they kept me talking much longer than ten minutes, and from the way the boys behind me are scuffing their shoes, and the way I can hear Tallulah jumping out of her seat and knocking over her chair, and the way Dr. Gregory is smiling at me, and the way Mom is already in the aisle running to me, I know the thing I've been afraid of didn't happen at all.

The opposite happened.

I have my period.

And, because of that, we won.

THREE MONTHS LATER . . .

I have one foot out the back door when Mom says, "Piper Jane Franklin!" from the kitchen table behind me. I turn.

She's sitting at her open laptop, working, thankfully fully dressed this time. The briefcase that we got her for her birthday is at her feet, the embroidered DR. ANNA FRANKLIN face up for the world to read.

"Yeah?"

Mom uses a fake-stern voice. "If you think—"

She pauses because Gladys is giggling in a way that makes us all giggle. She's with Eloise and Bobby on the couch, listening as they read the picture book they made for her, *Good Luck, Monster Truck*. TBH, it may be for babies, and it may not even look like a book because it's just a bunch of laminated pages of clip art in a three-ring binder, but it's now my favorite book of all time. The main character is a monster truck named Sally, and the monster truck characters use the full range of pronouns.

"Piper Jane Franklin!" Mom repeats once it's quiet. "If you think my eleven-year-old is about to leave for the evening the day before we drop her off at college, you've got another think coming."

I smile. "I'm just going to see Tallulah quickly. She needs help packing."

It's not a lie. I am going to see Tallulah, and she does need help packing. But the two aren't linked.

"All right." Mom's eyes twinkle. "I'm not making your favorite dinner for nothing."

"I promise!" I call as I skip out the door.

Tallulah is already in El Jardín Muerto when I arrive. Colors explode out of the cars around her. Strawberries drip from the vines that hang out the window of the silver car, lilacs climb out the moonroof, blossoming pumpkin vines crawl around the tires, and the sunflowers in the middle light up, highlighter yellow.

"Hey. Are you sure she'll find us?" Tallulah asks as I approach. She tosses me a strawberry.

"I shared my location on my phone," I say. I shove the whole fruit in my mouth and let the juice run down the back of my throat. It's like magic touched our garden this year. The strawberries are so juicy, you have to eat them in one bite, or you'll end up stained pink down to your shoes.

I join Tallulah on the roof of the minivan and we wait, our shoulders pressed together. Tomorrow, we go to college. I should be nervous about that, but I'm not. I'm ready. I've packed. I've read the welcome packet about one million times. I've been texting with my assigned roommate, who isn't Tallulah because the program wants to be sure we make new friends. Plus, I started my third period yesterday, and I didn't even cry. That makes me basically invincible.

But I am nervous about today. About saying goodbye to our garden.

We sit, breathing in the smells and the colors and this feeling of being on the edge of an ending—not the ending of childhood, we have a lot more time for that it turns out. But the ending of something, even if I'm not sure what the word for it is.

Then we hear a hushed, "Whoa."

Tallulah jumps off the car. "Daisy! You found us," she squeals. They hug. Daisy's eyes slowly take in the flowers and litter and fruit and cars and vegetables.

I hop down to join them.

It was Tallulah who figured out that Daisy's gated community is just beyond the other side of El Jardín Muerto. That she can get here by jumping a different fence. That maybe we should ask her to take care of our project this summer. That maybe we should share it with her, too.

"What is this place?" she asks, hushed.

"We call it El Jardín Muerto," I say.

"But it's so . . . alive."

"That part's a secret," Tallulah smiles. "And now you're in." She hands Daisy a strawberry, but Daisy doesn't eat it. She looks at the yellow car in wonder, then moves on to the minivan.

"All of this is not supposed to grow at the same time," she says.

Tallulah and I shrug. We know that's true, but El Jardín has always been beyond truth.

"Things grow according to metaphorical math here," Tallulah says.

"Right," Daisy says, like that makes perfect sense.

Maybe it does. I'll have to think about it later.

"We were wondering if you would take care of it for us this summer?" I ask. This is the part I'm nervous about. "Basically, just budding and planting and also hanging out here and keeping it company. If you want, it's yours now, too. It can be all of ours next year."

Daisy is nodding, so I continue.

"My sister, Eloise, can help if you go on vacation or something. Or you can ask George or Josie or Caroline or whoever. There's only one rule."

"No adults," Tallulah continues for me. "El Jardín likes it that way."

"So what do you say?" I ask.

Daisy stops surveying the cars and turns to us. Her eyes look a little watery.

"I say, knock knock."

I smile. "Who's there?"

"Daisies."

"Daisies who?"

"Daisies belong in the garden," she says. "In other words, yes."

We all laugh and fall into a giant three-person hug.

"I'm glad you guys won," Daisy says. "But I'm really going to miss you."

"I'll miss you, too," Tallulah says.

"Me too," I say. And I mean it. But all the missing that will happen this summer—for my mom and Calvin and Eloise and Gladys and Bobby and Ivan and Daisy and Ms. Gates and Dr. Knapp and TGASP and HHH and El Jardín Muerto—it doesn't feel sad.

That's my next metaphorical math puzzle.

Missing people makes one sad, while paradoxically, having people to miss means one is happy.

"We'll be back for eighth grade," Tallulah sings.

"Yeah. Everything will be so different, though, huh?" Daisy says.

I think about how Daisy's right, but also how everything is different all the time. I think about giggling at the pool yesterday when Daisy and Tallulah and Kelly told me about their crushes, and how I even admitted I have a little one on Ivan. Somehow, we're all still really smart, even with periods and crushes, and that's one fewer thing for me to worry about when it comes to growing up. I think about how Tallulah and I are spending a lot more time with our other friends recently, but that seems to be making the two of us even closer. I think about how our school has pad dispensers in every bathroom now because Eloise and her friends work fast. I think about how she told me her next project is inspired by me. She and her friends are going to volunteer with a charity that fights period poverty worldwide, and she said I can join them when I get back. I think about my mom's briefcase. I think about Gladys's book.

"Maybe the world will keep getting better," I say.

I breathe in the lilacs and hold on tighter.

ACKNOWLEDGMENTS

It takes a village to transform an idea into a book.

Karen Chaplin, you are a brilliant editor. Thank you once again for believing in my kooky ideas and giving me the freedom to take risks and make mistakes, and then, again once again, thank you for helping me to shape this story into what it was supposed to be.

Kate McKean, thank you as always for the endless cheerleading, for your belief in my writing and my characters, and for answering even the silliest questions that still pop up somehow, even over a decade into this thing we're doing together.

Thank you to everyone at Harper who contributed in any way to creating and distributing Piper's story. Thank you to Andrea Vandergrift for the cover design and to Julie McLaughlin for the breathtaking cover illustration. If this cover were a dress, I'd wear it every day.

Endless thanks to my amazing network of friends and family for your continued unwavering support, especially Mom, Dad, Elijah, and Maebh. You guys are my North Star.

And Greg . . . *Thanks* never covers it. I'm a writer without words.

In God's Great Way

by Jennie Davis
illustrated by
Pat Karch

Published by The Dandelion House
A Division of The Child's World

Distributed by Scripture Press Publications, Wheaton, Illinois 60187.

Library of Congress Cataloging in Publication Data

Davis, Jennie.
  In God's great way.

   Summary: Lonely in her new home, a little girl prays
to God for a friend.
   [1. Friendship—Fiction.   2. Moving, Household—
Fiction.   3. Christian life—Fiction]   I. Endres, Helen,
ill.   II. Title.
PZ7.M739In   [E]   82-7446
ISBN 0-89693-201-X   AACR2

Published by The Dandelion House, A Division of The Child's World, Inc.
© 1982 SP Publications, Inc. All rights reserved. Printed in U.S.A.

1 2 3 4 5 6 7 8 9 10 11 12 R 89 88 87 86 85 84 83 82

In God's Great Way

"I call on you, O God,
for you will answer me . . ."
—Psalm 17:6 (NIV).

Julie sat surrounded by boxes. She did
not like her new room at all. She missed her
old room where everything had a place.
She missed her other house that smelled
and felt like home. And most of all, Julie
missed her friends.

"Why did we have to move anyway?"
she said.

Nobody answered.

"Nobody hears me," Julie said. She went
to find her mother.

"I want to move back home," said Julie.

"Julie, this is your home now," said Mom.

"But I don't have any friends here."

"I know," said Mom. "But you will. It just takes time. And by the way, Julie, right now I need a friend. How about helping me fix lunch?"

After lunch, Julie went outside and sat on the steps. Some boys rode by on bikes. But they didn't wave. They didn't say "hi." They didn't even look up.

9

Julie sighed and went back inside. She began to unpack her little red case—just for something to do. She took out *Frog and Toad, Curious George,* and *The Cat in the Hat.* On the bottom was her Bible storybook.

That helped Julie to remember. God can hear me, she thought. I'll talk to Him. So Julie told God about how lonesome she felt. And then she prayed, "Please God, help me find a friend."

The next day, Julie sat on the steps
again. After a while, she saw a puppy on a
leash, pulling a girl down the street. The girl
looked up at Julie. But then the puppy
jerked hard, and the girl went stumbling
after him.

Julie watched them go. She felt like
crying.

Julie ran inside. "A girl just went by. But she didn't even wave or say 'hi'."

"Did you wave?" asked Mom. "Did you say 'hi'?"

Julie shook her head.

The rest of the day Julie and Mom put lots of things away and stacked lots of empty boxes on the back porch.

"Tomorrow," said Mom, "you can play in those boxes."

But I don't have anybody to play with, thought Julie.

The next day Julie woke up thinking about the boxes on the back porch. After breakfast, she pulled the biggest empty boxes into the front yard. She stacked one here and one there. She kept on stacking boxes until she had a box house. In she climbed.

A little while later, she heard someone
on skates coming down the sidewalk. Julie
peeked out. A girl skated by. But the girl
didn't wave or say "hi."

This time, Julie began to cry.

Pretty soon, Julie's mother came out to the box house.

"Julie?" she asked. "Are you all right?"

"Mom, no one will be my friend. And I even asked God to send me a friend!"

19

Mom crawled into the box house.

"Julie, sometimes when things don't go our way, we think God doesn't care," said Mom. "Especially when we've asked Him for something—and don't get it. But He does always answer—in His own great way."

"Then, will He send me a friend?"

"I'm sure He'll answer your prayer. But maybe you need to do something yourself."

"Like what?"

"Like being friendly," said Mom smiling. "Maybe besides praying for a friend, you could ask God to help you be a friend. How about that?"

That night, Julie prayed again for a friend. And this time she added, "Help me be a friend to somebody, too. Amen."

Julie's mother gave her a big hug.

In the morning, Julie ran out to her box house and wrote "WELCOME" on the front of it.

Then Julie heard the roller skates again.
Down the sidewalk came the same girl.

But before Julie could wave or say "hi,"
she saw the girl on skates fall hard on the
cement.

Julie ran to help. "Are you okay?" she
asked.

"Yes," said the girl, getting up. "I fall a lot. These are my new skates."

"That's my new house," said Julie. "Would you like to see it?"

The new girl took off her skates and climbed inside the box house with Julie.

Julie and Beth played in the box house all morning. They had several guests—the boys on bikes and even the girl with the puppy.

27

At dinner, Mom said, "I hope the trash collectors take all those boxes away tomorrow."

"Oh, no!" said Julie. "We still need those boxes! Tomorrow my friends are going to help me build a fort!"

"Friends?" said Mom. "Julie, God did answer your prayers—in His own great way!"

"Yes," said Julie.

That night, when Julie went to bed, she thanked God five times—one time for each new friend, and once for the puppy.